Hotter Than Wildfire

Books by Lisa Marie Rice

Hotter Than Wildfire

A Protectors Novel: Delta Force

Lisa Marie Rice

An Imprint of HarperCollins*Publishers*

HarperCollins books may be purchased for educational, business, or sales promotional use. For information please write: Special Markets Department, HarperCollins Publishers, 10 East 53rd Street, New York, NY 10022.

FIRST EDITION

Designed by Diahann Sturge

Library of Congress Cataloging-in-Publication Data is available upon request.

ISBN 978-0-06-180827-2

11 12 13 14 15 OV/RRD 10 9 8 7 6 5 4 3 2 1

To my darling Festivalettes.
You know who you are.

Acknowledgments

This book is fondly dedicated to May Chen, Amanda Bergeron, and Ethan Ellenberg—fabulous editors, fabulous agent.

Hotter Than Wildfire

Prologue

San Diego
Christmas Day

It was Christmas, but not for Harry Bolt.

The whole city was gripped by Christmas fever. You couldn't walk anywhere in the city center without being blasted by carols and hit up by old farts in fake white beards and red suits asking for money for the poor. Poor Africans, poor earthquake victims, poor illegal aliens.

Of course, no one really thought of the poor on their own doorstep. Those nice folks in church basements, the men in white beards and red suits, the school kids caroling, would run screaming if they had to see where Harry Bolt lived with his mom, her methhead fuckhead boyfriend of the month, and his baby sister, Christine.

There weren't any Christmas lights on their street down in the Barrio and there wasn't a Christmas tree set up in the basement rooms they lived in. No Christmas tree, no decorations, no presents. Hell, no food or milk, either.

Well, at least Crissy would eat today. He'd scrounged in the dumpsters behind three restaurants on restaurant row and, shaking his head at what people threw away, found fried chicken, mashed potatoes, turkey breast, and about five slices of cake.

On a roll, he'd walked into a toy shop and stolen a Barbie. The door alarm had gone off, but Harry was fast. He was always fast and he'd never been caught.

He smiled, thinking of giving Crissy the Barbie. She'd have to keep her squeals of joy down, not bother Mom and Fuckhead. Though when Mom was high, which seemed to be all the time lately, she didn't give a shit.

The last fuckhead had given a shit, oh yeah—he liked little girls. Harry had seen him get a hard-on when Crissy's panties showed once. But a knife held to Fuckhead's ribs, and a very clear warning—*touch my sister in any way and I will cut you up for dog meat*—kept him away. The next day, Harry stole six pairs of little-girl trousers for Crissy and she never wore a skirt again.

That fuckhead left and the current one—Rod—took his place. This one didn't like little girls, not in any way, but he did like beating up on people.

It was dark by the time Harry made it home on foot. He didn't have any money for the bus, so he had to hoof it everywhere.

He walked down the moldy stairs and pushed open the

cracked wooden door. There was complete, utter silence in the house. That was bad news. It meant either that Mom and Fuckhead had left a five-year-old alone in a house with broken locks in the worst neighborhood in the world, or they were high. Again.

They were high, he saw, as he closed the rickety front door behind him.

His mom was sitting on the broken couch, head lolling to one side, stare vacant. Shit. Where'd she get the money to score?

All the lights were out. The only light visible was from under the door of the room he shared with Crissy.

A shuffle in the corner where the table was. Rod, drinking a beer. He didn't even turn his head when Harry walked in.

The door to his bedroom opened. There was a low-wattage bulb in their room, and the light spilled into the living room.

"Hawwy!" Crissy's excited voice rang out. She ran to him and clutched his legs, grinning up at him. "You're back! Mewwy Chwistmas!" She was small for a five-year-old, hair a lighter blond than his, eyes the same light brown as his.

Her little arms reached up, their usual game. "Cawwy, Hawwy!"

He picked her up, holding her in one arm, keeping his bags tightly by his side with the other. Crissy weighed nothing.

Harry'd put on a spurt of growth recently and was developing muscles. Fuckhead watched his step around him now.

"Harry," came the deep voice in the corner. "Whatcha got in them there bags, boy?"

Harry's heart plunged. Fuckhead's voice was slurred, eyes narrowed and unfocused. He was higher than a kite.

This was bad. His mom just drifted off to sleep when she got high. Fuckhead turned viciously mean.

Harry swung the bags behind him, dropped them quietly to the ground. Fuckhead had a short attention span. If he didn't see them, he'd probably forget about them. "Nothing," he said. "Just some junk I found."

Fuckhead turned his head more fully and Harry's heart started pounding. Fuckhead's eyes were cold, inhuman, like the eyes of the feral dogs that ran in packs through their part of town. When he had that expression, trouble came fast.

Fuckhead's big, meaty fists opened and closed on the table, over and over again. Another bad sign. He was just waiting for an excuse to blow up, become violent. And though Harry was young and strong and fast, Fuckhead weighed almost 300 pounds and when he was high he didn't—probably couldn't—feel pain. He was like a violent robot.

Not to mention the fact that Harry couldn't run fast while carrying Crissy, and he'd never leave Crissy behind.

Something bad was coming. It was in the air. The dank, cold basement stank of the brewing violence about to be unleashed.

Harry did the only possible thing he could do, the same thing he did with the feral dogs. He couldn't fight a pack of dogs and he couldn't fight Fuckhead while he was high, particularly with Crissy to look after.

So he stared at the ground in submission, and kept quiet. The one thing Fuckhead hated was what he called a "mouthy" kid.

Crissy was utterly silent. Usually, you couldn't shut her up, but in her short life, she'd learned who was dangerous. She always took her cue from Harry. When Harry was quiet, so was she. In her five years on earth, she'd seen a lot of really nasty shit from this fuckhead, the fuckhead before him and the fuckhead before that.

Harry's hand covered Crissy's back. Though she was silent, turning her head into his shoulder for comfort, he could feel her little heart racing, fluttering with panic. She was terrified.

She was only five years old and she was fucking terrified.

Still staring at the ground, quietly picking up the bags, Harry backed away slowly, again exactly as if he were facing a pack of wild dogs. It worked. He quietly stepped into their room and closed the door.

He waited, listening.

Quiet, on the other side.

Crissy's head was buried in his shoulder. "Hawwy?" she whispered. "Okay now?"

"It's okay, sweetie." Harry pasted a smile on his face and patted his little sister's shoulder, wishing for the billionth time that Crissy had been born into another family. A family that would love her for the sweet kid she was instead of bringing her up in this shithole, where only Harry stood between her and being beaten to death.

Or worse.

He listened for a long time, but his mom and Fuckhead were quiet. For the moment. Mostly they were either fighting or fucking, sometimes both at once.

He had a stash of plastic plates and plastic forks he'd retrieved from a dumpster that he kept hidden in the closet. He brought them out and put them on the bed. Crissy watched him, wide-eyed, thumb in mouth.

Harry had once tried to break her of the habit, but it finally dawned on him that Crissy needed to suck her thumb for comfort. God knows there wasn't much of that in her life. He tried to shield her as much as possible, but he couldn't stop it all.

Well, even he and Crissy deserved something that would pass for Christmas.

He cut up pieces of turkey breast on her plate, spooned some mashed potatoes and slid it over to her. She was hungry, he knew she was hungry, because no one would have thought to feed her all day, but she waited until his own plate was full and he had a fork in his hand.

"Eat, Crissy," he said and she did. But only after he started eating.

It was funny. His mom had ignored Crissy all her life. She'd have aborted Crissy except she found out way too late that she was knocked up, and no doctor would perform the abortion.

It had fallen to Harry to bring Crissy up, though he knew fuck-all about bringing up a little girl and he was half wild himself. So though he'd done his damnedest to keep her fed and warm and at least moderately clean, he sure hadn't done anything to drill manners in her.

And yet it was as if Crissy had been born in some fucking palace in some far-off kingdom. No one had ever taught her how to eat. She'd picked it up herself, watching Harry. But where Harry ate like a wolf, she ate daintily, never making a mess.

She was a little princess stuck among the trolls.

She put her fork down neatly and smiled at him.

Harry reached out an arm and rummaged around in the

bag, pulling out the box. Of course it wasn't gift wrapped, but Crissy sure wouldn't mind.

"Here, squirt," he said, holding it out to her. "Merry Christmas."

Crissy's face lit up. Her only other doll was some raggedy thing that was missing an arm, but she loved it and fussed over that doll for hours.

A brand-new Barbie—Crissy was in doll heaven.

"Oh, Hawwy! A Bawbie!" she squealed. He tried to shush her, but it was too late.

The door to their room slammed open, bouncing off the wall and Fuckhead stood there, head almost touching the top of the door frame.

He swayed, shot out a hand to steady himself. His head wobbled as he tried to focus, and Harry thought, *Oh man, this is going to be bad. This is going to be real bad.*

Rod finally focused on Harry, who'd put Crissy behind him. She was clutching the back of his legs, completely quiet now. She never made a sound when Rod was in this mood. Rod was breathing heavily, already somehow in a rage.

"What's that brat hiding?" Rod's head thrust forward, like a bull ready to rush. "Hmm? What the fuck's she got in her hand?"

Rod lumbered forward and Harry stepped in front of him. He could feel Crissy following him, holding on to his jeans.

"Nothing. She doesn't have anything. Leave her alone."

Rod lifted his eyes, more a creature of the night than a human. Harry was only twelve years old, but he knew he was looking evil right in the face.

Rod leaned down and Harry tried not to flinch at the smell

of his breath. This close, he could also smell the sweat and the grease and the craziness. It was a terrifying smell.

"*So what the fuck's she hiding?*" Rod screamed, punching Harry in the chest. Harry stepped back, didn't fall.

A movement to his right. Harry looked down. A small hand held out the doll. Harry's heart twisted. Crissy was sacrificing her Barbie to the monster, to save her brother.

Harry tried to push her little hand back but it was too late. Rod's eyes lit up with a wild light. He snatched the doll. It looked ridiculously small and frilly in his huge paw.

He looked at it the way a monkey would, holding it this way and that. Harry could almost see the steam rising in Rod's crazy brain as he worked himself up into a rage.

He shook the doll in Harry's face. "So where the fuck did you find the money to buy this? You been holding out on me?" His voice rose with each word until he was nearly howling. It raised the hairs on Harry's neck.

The monster stepped back, dangling the doll from his hand. He lurched, rocked unsteadily, then found his balance again.

"You got money in here! I know it!" Fuckhead bellowed and ripped the head off the Barbie, then the two arms and legs. He tried to poke a huge finger into the holes, couldn't do it, tossed the trunk of the doll away. He looked around, eyes narrowing when he saw Harry's baseball bat. He picked it up, gave it a few experimental slaps against his left hand.

Harry backed slowly away, heart hammering.

Fuckhead stepped forward, giving a swing through the air with the bat. The whoosh of displaced air sounded loud in the room.

"What else you hiding from me, you little shit? I'll bet you got lots of stuff—you're not as stupid as you look. I'll bet you got just shitloads of stuff that *you're hiding from me!*" the last said in a bellow, as he turned and brought the bat down heavily on the rectangle of particle board resting on two trestles that served as Harry's desk.

The rectangle pulverized in an instant, dust rising in the room.

Fuckhead poked around the ruins for a moment with the tip of the bat.

"Nothing here," he growled, and swung the bat into the crates where Harry and Crissy kept their meager belongings. The crates exploded, tossing up jeans and hoodies and tiny T-shirts and shoes.

He turned to look Harry in the face. His eyes went down to Crissy then back up. He smiled into Harry's eyes.

"I know what'll make you talk. Take a bat to that little brat and you're talking, oh yeah." He swung it suddenly, viciously, against the wall, gouging a hole in the crumbly cement.

"Like that, punk?" he yelled. "What's the little bitch's head gonna look like, huh? Like a fucking watermelon that's dropped on the ground, that's what. You tell me where you've got your fucking stuff *now*! *Now! Now! Now!*"

He was screaming, slashing the bat viciously through the air, walking slowly forward. Harry stepped back, almost tripping over Crissy, who was clinging to his legs. He could feel her wild trembling. He didn't dare pick her up, didn't dare even acknowledge her existence. Fuckhead seemed to have forgotten about Crissy for the moment and Harry wanted to keep it that way.

"What you hiding, boy?" *Thwack!* Another huge hole gouged

into the wall. "You tell me *now*!" Another swing, barely missing Harry.

"Rod?" Harry's mom stood in the doorway, unsteady. Her eyes were glassy. "What's all the commotion?"

Harry had never been able to figure it out. His mom lived like a junkie—*was* a junkie, though it hurt his heart to admit it, because despite everything he loved her—but she spoke like a real lady.

The monster stopped, turned slowly around, thought processes almost painfully clear.

He smiled, baring his rotted teeth. "Your shitty son. He's hiding stuff from me, and I want it. He's got some money hidden somewhere, just for himself. What the fuck does he care about us? About our needs? All he cares about is the little brat."

Harry's mom was trying to process this through the fog in her head. "Harry?" she said slowly. She looked around the bare room. "Hiding something? What? Where?"

The monster seemed to swell with rage as he advanced on Harry's mom.

"You bitch, I'll bet you're in cahoots with him. All three of you, it's a conspiracy, you're robbing me and keeping me from what's *mine*!" His voice rose to a raw cry. "You three think you're so much better than me! Snooty bastards, I'll show you!"

Harry's mom frowned. "Hey, Rod, there's no need to—"

"And you're the worst of all, you cunt!" he roared, and swung the bat straight at her head.

The crack was loud in the room as Harry's mom crumpled to the floor, bright red staining her long blond hair. She lay still, a pool of red gathering around her head.

"You bastard!" Harry's head filled with rage. "You killed her! You killed my mom!"

Rod stood for a moment, mouth open, the rotted teeth of a methhead like dark tree stumps. Harry jumped him, fists flying. He'd been fighting since he was five, and though he had no training, he knew what he was doing. The first blows took Rod by surprise, then he shook his head and bellowed with rage.

With one backhanded blow, he slammed Harry against the wall, knocking him off his feet. Harry blacked out for just a second and came to just as Rod, screaming, brought the bat down hard on his legs. Harry cried out as his bones crunched.

Pain shot through Harry, so intense he nearly passed out again. He fought to remain conscious with everything in him, ignoring the ferocity of the pain, because Rod had straightened, knowing Harry was out of commission, and now was advancing on Crissy, step by step, screaming words Harry couldn't understand.

Crissy pressed against the wall, shaking, as she watched him approach with huge, terrified eyes.

Harry shook with rage. Rod had killed his mom. Fuckhead wasn't going to get Crissy, too. No way.

Harry tried to stand, but he collapsed in fiery agony. There was no way—both legs were broken, jeans already soaked with blood. A shard of bone had broken through the skin and stuck out from his left thigh, piercing his jeans. His hand scrabbled for his only hope as Crissy darted away from Rod's big, hairy paws swinging that bat.

Under the mattress was Fuckhead's cell, which he used to make his deals. Harry had stolen it from him a couple of days ago. Some instinct had told him he'd be needing a way to call for help.

Rod was screaming now, completely out of control, lunging for Crissy, who kept slithering out of his grasp. Hands trembling, fumbling in fear, Harry punched 9-1-1 and quickly gave the address. Rod's bellows could be heard in the background.

"Hurry," he whispered.

He was about to black out from the pain and had to grit his teeth to remain conscious.

Rod's huge hand caught Crissy by the arm and Harry nearly threw up when he heard the sharp crack of her small bone breaking.

"Harry!" Crissy screamed, terrified eyes meeting his, and he pulled himself over to her by his arms, moving as fast as he could.

But it wasn't fast enough.

Rod picked Crissy up as if she were the Barbie he'd held a few moments ago and slammed her against the wall. Blood spattered as Crissy's tiny body crumpled to the ground.

"*You son of a bitch!*" Harry screamed as his hand found the bat Rod had dropped. He swung it with all his strength against Fuckhead's kneecap and heard the sharp crack of his knee exploding.

Rod went down like a felled bull and Harry was all over him, swinging the bat against his head again and again until Rod's face was a mask of mushy red tissue that bore no resemblance to a human face.

Panting, Harry threw the bat away and pulled himself with his arms over to Crissy, ignoring the fiery pain as he scraped his way across the floor. He gathered up her limp little body, holding her against him, smoothing out her soft golden hair. He wept, the sound raw in the room.

In the distance sirens sounded, the last thing he heard before the blackness took him.

Chapter 1

Prineville, Georgia
Twenty years later
April 2

Gerald Montez paced his study as he listened to the track on the CD. The song was beautiful, though Gerald didn't give a shit about that. Beethoven, the Beatles—it was all the same to him.

But this song . . . oh yes. It was important to him.

"Turning a Blind Eye," by Eve. No last name. Just Eve. Like Madonna or Cher.

He'd read some online reviews of the track. There were lots of them. This Eve woman took up an inordinate amount of Internet time and space, because no one could figure out who she was.

Her vocals are warm and smooth, perfectly balanced by the acoustic instruments—guitar and muted trumpet. She folds in the notes, one by one, at times forging a melancholy exoticism with extensive quotes from fourteenth-century Mediterranean music and an overlay of Monk. Brilliant.

Gerald had no idea what the fuck that was about. All he knew was who sang it.

Eve. Mystery woman.

Only not so much.

Because though the jacket blurb said the mystery singer Eve had written the song, he had heard another woman humming it a year ago.

She hadn't even known he was there. She'd been humming some tune Gerald hadn't recognized but did realize was pretty. Humming and singing as she worked at the computer in her office. She hummed the body of the song, and the refrain was *turning a blind eye.*

Gerald remembered the scene very clearly because that's what he did. He noticed things and remembered things. He'd built a fucking empire because he noticed things and remembered things.

So he'd been guaranteed to remember that song. Not only that, but he'd been absolutely blown away by the fact that it had been *Ellen* humming and singing. Who knew?

Ellen. Uptight, straitlaced, buttoned-down, dependable Ellen, who kept her looks under wraps and was a fabulous accountant. Bookkeeper. Oh yeah, she had a degree in accounting, but basically she kept his books, so she was his bookkeeper. She kept them very well. Too well.

Staid, earnest, demure Ellen had these throaty, sexy sounds coming out of her mouth. Sounds he couldn't even begin to imagine her making. Sounds that made him look twice at her as a woman. And that's when he discovered she'd been hiding her light under a bushel.

Most women worked on themselves like crazy. Inch-thick makeup, plastic bags of silicone pumping up their boobs, high heels, short skirts, hair out to here . . . half the time when Gerald woke up next to a woman he'd fucked he realized that she wasn't a looker at all, she just knew how to apply paint.

Man, taking a second or third look at Ellen—serious, workaholic Ellen, whose clothes usually covered her neck to toe—he could see that she was a fucking *looker*—the real deal. If she bothered, she'd be turning heads. Obviously, she didn't want to turn heads, she wanted to keep books.

When he realized that she was starting to dig in to how he first made his money, he knew he'd have to fire her or kill her. Or . . . marry her.

That thought had shocked him.

It was her voice that did it. Gerald liked his women savvy and sexy and not too bright. He liked his sex rough. Even after realizing how beautiful Ellen really was, he hadn't wanted to fuck her.

But that woman singing . . . oh yeah. She was fuckable. There was a sexiness, a swing there, that just said *I'm fabulous in the sack*. So un-Ellen-like he'd actually checked her desktop to see if she had an iPod with speakers on. But no, that fuckable chick was Ellen.

Ellen, in bed. She might actually be teachable. What she was in the sack wasn't that important, though, because the world was full of women who loved rich men, and he was very, very rich.

What was important was having a presentable wife when he went to Washington to negotiate contracts. All those assholes who counted in Washington were big on "family values" even though they themselves had hotties of both sexes on the side.

Yeah—demure CPA wife with a soft voice. Perfect.

So he'd started his campaign to get her into his bed, something that usually took about five minutes. Maybe half an hour, tops.

He'd been absolutely astounded when he realized it wasn't working. She just wasn't interested.

What the fuck?

He was rich, good-looking, powerful. He had women crawling up his pants. Was she a lesbo? But he had two men follow her around and she didn't have women lovers, didn't have male lovers, didn't have anything. She worked, went home, watched some TV, read, went to bed early, got up early and started all over again.

Jesus, marrying her would be like marrying a nun. Still, who cared? All he had to do was throw her a fuck now and again; it wouldn't have to interfere with his sex life. Have her pop a few kids. Then they wouldn't be able to say anything at the fucking Pentagon about where they were spending their money.

He'd been starting to work it all out in his head when the cunt up and disappeared after talking at a company party with one of his men, who'd been shitfaced. Arlen Miller, who'd talked too much about Iraq and had paid the price.

And then Ellen was in the wind. Gone for a whole fucking year in which he sweated that she was spilling her guts to the FBI.

You don't cross Montez. That was a rule. Because if you do, Montez will hit back so hard they'll be finding pieces of you for the next ten years.

Now he had her. Ellen—bland, pretty Ellen Palmer, who didn't even wear lipstick, for Christ's sake—was Eve, whose voice was sex on a stick.

Eve's identity was this big mystery everyone got off on. Who knew who she was, yada yada. No personal info on the CDs, no website—the recordings were in the name of a company that had shell after shell around it. Something Ellen would know how to do in her sleep.

People didn't know how to think laterally.

Eve had an agent, and this agent had a name: Roddy Fisher. Lived in Seattle. Roddy Fisher was going to be very, very sorry he'd ever taken on Eve as a client.

Montez clicked on the intercom and ordered his personal jet to be ready, with a flight plan filed for Seattle.

Coronado Shores
San Diego

He relived it over and over again in his nightmares. Crissy always ended up a smashed little body and he always awoke drenched in sweat, heart pounding. Even when he came back himself from Afghanistan with a smashed body courtesy of an Afghani RPG, he dreamed of his little sister, dead at five. Murdered by a monster.

Harry rose, naked, and went out onto the small, deep balcony that gave out onto the Pacific. Some nights he went down in the dark and took an hour-long swim.

In the beginning, when he was still halfway dead, barely able to walk and not at all sure if he'd ever be anything more than a pathetic cripple—well, on those nights, he'd been tempted to gimp his way down to the beach and simply swim out to his limit, out past where he could never come back, and just sink beneath the waves.

It was frightening as hell that the thought was so fucking appealing.

And that was when he discovered that his brothers, who lived in the same building on Coronado Shores, took turns staying awake to make sure he didn't do just that.

For the first months, they took away his weapons, too. He'd screamed insults at them, but both Sam and Mike were strong-willed and had rocks for heads. He'd been given his guns back when they were sure he was out of the suicide zone.

That was when he'd taken up drinking, getting quietly blitzed night after night. They let him. It takes a lot of time and effort to drink yourself to death, and Harry simply couldn't do it. He hated waking up hungover, dry-mouthed, head pounding, staggering to the bathroom to vomit a thin gruel of beer and whiskey, unanchored by any food because he had no appetite at all.

He'd disgusted even himself.

Finally, he decided that if he was going to have to live—

because his fucking brothers wouldn't fucking let him die—he might as well become strong again. So Sam and Mike had recruited Bjorn, the Norwegian Nazi, and had helped him set up a fully equipped gym in his spare room, and for months he exercised at night until his muscles ached, until he'd sweated out every drop of moisture in his body, until he was so exhausted he couldn't think.

Sleep didn't come, but at least there were no images in his head.

But now he was back in shape. Simple weights or the treadmill couldn't take him out of himself, so he'd found another crutch.

He went back into his living room and sank on the couch. His living room—his entire home—was like his life: high tech and empty. He had state-of-the-art gym equipment, work station and entertainment center. The rest was emptiness. A bed and a desk and a couch.

His stereo set was top-of-the-line Bose, and he slipped his new drug into the slot, put on his headset and stretched out on the couch. The first strains of a beautiful voice arrived and it was like that first shot of heroin must be for a junkie.

Ahhh . . .

Eve. She'd become super-famous these past three months, but Harry had been hooked from the first song he'd ever heard her sing, when she was still unknown, a jazzy cover of "Stand by Me."

Her voice was utter magic. After the first notes, Harry was taken right out of himself, taken away to somewhere else, a better place. A place where men didn't kill little girls. Where men who'd whip a woman to death if they could hear the sounds of her shoes on the floor didn't try to blow you up with RPGs. Where you didn't long for the peace of death.

Eve had a smoky, velvety voice, clear as a bell, perfectly attuned to each song. She could do it all: rousing rock, smoldering jazz, tender ballads. There was nothing she couldn't do so perfectly that you couldn't ever imagine the song being sung any other way, even when you'd heard it a thousand times before by a thousand other singers.

Half her songs were covers, for which she recorded the definitive version—no other singer need apply. The other half, he'd been astonished to read on the jacket blurb, were composed by her. And though it wasn't stated anywhere, he also had the feeling that she played keyboard for some of the simple ballads.

It was all very mysterious. Maybe even a marketing ploy. If it was, it was brilliant, because the Net was alive with a thousand iterations of *who is she?* while fans flocked to buy her CDs. She got tens of millions of hits on YouTube, though the only images were sunsets, the sea, trees swaying in the wind.

Because no one knew who she was.

There were no photographs, she'd never been interviewed, had never given a concert. Identity top secret.

The online tabloids went wild.

They said she was black, white, beautiful, ugly beyond words, old, young . . . Harry didn't give a fuck. She could have been a three-hundred-pound hippopotamus with seven chins for all he cared. All he knew was that when he put on one of her CDs and his headset, the world—and him with it—simply went away.

WHO IS EVE? was a tabloid staple. Entire sections of *People* and *US Weekly* were devoted to smoking out her identity. According to the *National Enquirer* she was Bill Clinton's secret love child. Or George Clooney's. Or the Pope's. Depending on the week. Harry was just waiting for Eve to be a space alien.

What the hell did he care?

Harry lay back, closed his eyes and let her carry him away until the sky outside his living room windows went from black to pewter to pearl.

At seven, he reluctantly slipped his headphones off and headed for the shower.

Time to face another day.

Seattle

Roddy Fisher was thrown into the storage room by two of his men, McKenzie and Trey.

Gerald Montez was sitting in a comfortable chair because he thought it might take a long time to beat some information out of the guy. But looking at the worm, he thought, *Maybe not.* Maybe they could get this done fast.

Roddy Fisher, talent agent, was small and round and was already whimpering, though he hadn't even been roughed up yet. All that was still to come.

Montez was used to soldiers, men who'd been trained and trained hard to be tough, to resist. This guy was a soft target, the softest. Trendy clothes, manicured hands, no muscle definition at all. Gerald didn't know what Fisher looked like yet, because his men had brought him in with a hood over his head. Interrogation 101—keep them disoriented. And scared.

The guy was scared all right. He'd even pissed his pants. Fucking wuss.

Montez signaled with his hand and a bright spotlight was switched on, leaving the rest of the storage room in darkness. One of his men whipped the hood off and Fisher screwed his eyes up against the thousand-watt light.

Montez knew Fisher couldn't see him, couldn't see anything, actually, but still he kept his face blank, though he felt disgust. Fisher's eyes were swollen shut from tears and snot ran down his face, making the duct tape over his mouth glisten. Nobody'd touched him, beyond bundling him into a car and putting a hood over his head, and just look at him. Already in meltdown.

He hadn't even seen Montez's men behind him, standing ready beside a tray full of instruments that looked designed for carpentry work. Carpentry work on humans, to cut and pull and carve. And Fisher hadn't noticed the tarpaulin under his chair to catch sweat, blood, DNA.

Trey reached around and ripped the duct tape off Fisher's mouth. Jesus, Fisher winced as the tape was torn away. What a freaking girl.

"Oh God," Fisher sniveled. His voice was high and whiny, warbling with bodily fluids. "Where am I? What do you want?" His eyebrows furrowed. "Money! That's what you want! Take it, in my pants pocket." In his excitement he forgot his hands were in restraints. He scrabbled for his pockets. Finally, he lifted one hip. "In here. I've got three credit cards, you're welcome to all of them. I won't report them as stolen. And I've got two thousand dollars in cash. Take it. Take everything." His hopeful face lifted up into the light.

Montez waited until it became clear even to the idiot on the chair that he didn't want money. Fisher slumped, defeated.

After another long silence, Montez finally spoke.

"Where's Ellen Palmer?" he asked quietly. Be great if they could do this the easy way. Get the intel, ice the guy and go. Montez had a lot to do before this mess was over, and time spent away from business was money lost.

"Who?" Fisher's forehead scrunched up in confusion, utterly, completely clueless. He couldn't possibly be that good an actor. Not with the stress he was under. Not a soft civilian.

"Eve."

Fisher's features cleared. "Oh, *Eve*. I'm sorry, that information is highly confident—"

All the breath went out of him at the punch Trey gave him. It wasn't even a real punch, just a shut-up-and-pay-attention punch. Still, this Fisher asshole started wailing like a siren. Jesus. Montez waited until the noise died down and Fisher was sniveling.

"Eve," Montez said again.

Fisher shook his head. "Can't, man. My contract says—"

Another whack upside the head, not even hard enough to rattle teeth, and the wailing began again.

"Okay, okay! I'll talk!"

Christ. If he hadn't had a deep personal interest in the outcome, Montez would have left this to his men. What a waste of his time, interrogating this moron.

Montez moved his chair forward so Fisher could see him,

opened a file he held on his lap and pulled out a number of photos. He held up the first photo, the formal portrait that had been on the Bearclaw website, turning it so Fisher could see it clearly.

Montez tapped the photo. "Is that Ellen Palmer?"

Fisher's eyes widened. "No," he said, then held up his restrained hands in defense when Trey's hand moved back. "Don't hit me! I know her as Irene Ball. She uses the name Eve for her singing. I've never heard of an Ellen Palmer."

Trey looked at him and Montez nodded slightly. Trey's hand went down and the dickhead's breath whooshed out in relief.

"So." Montez leaned forward a little. "How did you meet her and where?"

Fisher was moving into familiar territory, Montez could tell. He even relaxed a little, which just went to prove that civilians are terminally stupid.

"I'm a talent agent, working out of Seattle. You ever hear of Broken Monkeys, or Pursuit, or Isabel?" Fuckhead actually looked hopefully at Montez, trying to impress him. Montez simply stared at him until his eyes dropped to his knees. "Well . . ." he drew in a deep breath. "I make the rounds of clubs and bars, because the Seattle music scene is great and throws up a lot of talent. One night I was in this club, the Blue Moon. I was there to talk to a guy, not talent scout. Blue Moon's had this pathetic singer for like, forever—got no voice and his keyboard playing sucks, but what the fuck? Beer's good and the chairs are comfortable. I'm thinking, talk to my guy and get out. Only turns out the singer was dead and this chick is singing. And man . . . halfway into her cover of "Every Breath You Take" I knew she was gold, pure gold. Asked the owner who she was and he shrugged. Said she was one of the waitresses, girl just showed up one day. Didn't have papers or nothing, but the owner—he's not particular. Half his staff is off the books. Five minutes after she started singing, there wasn't a sound in the club, and when she finished, she got a standing ovation. Never seen anything like it. So I go over to her, thinking she's unknown, she's hungry—she's a fucking *waitress* for Christ's sake!—I'll sign her up and she'll be grateful, know what I mean?"

Fisher looked around, searching for a little male solidarity. Montez shook his head. It was going to be a pleasure ridding the world of this shithead.

"Go on," he said quietly. "You signed her up, correct?"

"Yeah, but *man* did that bitch drive a hard bargain." A grating whining note crept into his voice. "Most musicians, they don't know dick about the music business. They learn as they go along. Some of them never learn. But Irene—Eve—shit, it was like she was born to it. She negotiated the toughest contract I've ever seen, right down the line. Boy, does that bitch know her numbers."

Yes, indeed, Montez thought sourly. *The bitch knows her numbers. And mine.*

"And that was the easy part. Because when I started talking gigs and recordings, man, she just went wild. Laid down the law. No concerts, only recordings. Recording studio had to be emptied out, musicians and sound engineer in another room with a separate entrance. And no interviews, no photos, no website, no nothing. That was her iron-clad bottom line, and

I tell you, I nearly walked away, because who needs this shit. But then, hell . . ." The idiot smiled reminiscently, forgetting where he was. "That first album went gold, the second platinum. It was a smart marketing ploy."

This was getting tedious. Montez wanted to wrap it up.

"So where does this Irene, or Eve, live?"

Fisher shook his head. "No fucking idea."

Trey's blow drew blood this time. When the idiot stopped screaming, Montez tried again.

"Where does she live?"

"I don't fucking *know*!" he shouted. "She wouldn't tell me! The address on the contract is a P.O. box in Seattle. No one knows where she lives."

Fisher was too much of a coward to lie. Shit.

"What's her cell phone number?"

Fisher's eyes lit with hope. He rattled off a number with a Seattle prefix, and Montez realized that was about all he was going to get out of this fuckhead.

"Okay, we're done here." Montez stood, and Fisher's eyes followed him eagerly. Idiot thought the whole thing was over. Montez glanced at Trey. "Take care of this," he said quietly, and exited the room.

He could barely hear the shot out in the corridor. Trey used a suppressor, just like he'd been told.

San Diego

Ellen Palmer checked the address on the small brass plaque outside an elegant, super-modern building in downtown San

Diego against the scrawled words torn off a napkin and verified that they were the same.

She didn't need to do that. She had a near-photographic memory, and if a number was involved, she never forgot it, ever.

Morrison Building, 1147 Birch Street.

Yes, that was it.

Ellen recognized what she was doing. She was stalling, which was unlike her. She was alive because she'd been able to take decisions fast and act on them immediately. She'd have been six feet under if she hadn't acted fast. Stalling was unlike her.

But she was so damned *tired.* Tired of running, tired of lying, tired of keeping her head down, in the most literal sense of the term. Security cameras were everywhere these days and her enemy had a powerful face recognition program. For the past year, she'd rarely presented her naked face in public in daylight.

Even now, when she was betting her life on the fact that she was moving toward safety, she had on huge sunglasses and her now-long hair was drawn forward around her face. She needed to buy a big straw hat.

There were two security cameras on the lintel of the twelve-foot street door of the Morrison Building, but Ellen kept her head down as she entered, walked across the huge glass and marble lobby and rode up in the elevator to the ninth floor. Remaining anonymous in the elevator was hard. The four walls were polished bronze that reflected as well as mirrors to the small security camera in the corner.

The door to RBK Security was guarded by two security

cameras, and you were either buzzed in or you dealt with a topflight security panel located on the right-hand side, because the door had no doorknob.

She lowered her head even more as a whirring sound came from above her head. Good God, their cameras were motorized!

Well, it *was* a security company, and she'd been assured they were really good.

They'd better be, because otherwise she was dead.

She rang the bell. There was a click and the door slid silently open. Ellen walked in gingerly, heart starting to pound.

Was this a good idea? Because if it wasn't, if she was putting herself into the wrong hands, there was no turning back, and she'd pay the ultimate price.

The lobby was wonderful—luxurious yet comfortable, with huge, thriving plants, soft classical music in the background, the faint smell of lemon polish, deep, plush armchairs. A secretary sat behind a U-shaped counter. She smiled in welcome.

"Are you Ms. Charles? Mr. Reston will be in shortly. Please have a seat."

For a second, Ellen didn't respond, thinking the receptionist was talking to someone else. But there wasn't anyone else around.

She closed her eyes in dismay. Of course.

She'd booked the appointment under the name Nora Charles, which was stupid. Any film buff would recognize it as a fake name, but she'd been so desperate when she'd called and she'd just sat through a triple feature of *The Thin Man, After the Thin Man* and *Shadow of the Thin Man* last night in San Francisco, waiting for the first bus to San Diego. An all-nighter at the cinema was the only thing she could think of to stay off the streets.

She'd started the journey the day before yesterday in Seattle and hadn't slept more than an hour or two in three days.

But exhaustion was no excuse.

Forgetting her cover name was terrifyingly dangerous. She was alive because she was always alert, always. Forgetting her cover name for just a second was inviting death. And if there was one thing the past year had taught her, it was that she didn't want to die. She wanted—desperately—to live.

Nora Charles was her fifth cover name in twelve months. *Forget all the others and concentrate on this one,* she told herself.

She was mentally putting together a little fake bio for Nora, just to give Nora a little heft in her head, when the receptionist suddenly said, "Yessir, I will."

Ellen really was exhausted, because she couldn't figure out who the receptionist was talking to. There was no one else in the lobby and she wasn't talking into a phone. Then she saw the very neat, very small and very expensive headset attached to one ear and understood.

Wow. She should have noticed it.

This was truly dangerous. Her exhaustion was catching up with her. She felt stupid with fatigue. Stupid people died, very badly. Particularly ones with Gerald Montez and his army after them.

"Ms. Charles?"

Ellen looked up. "Yes?"

"Mr. Reston has been delayed. But Mr. Bolt is free. They are both partners in the company."

"How—how long will Mr. Reston be delayed?"

"He doesn't know." The receptionist had a kindly look, unusual in such upscale surroundings. Usually an employee in such a swank, obviously successful company was snooty and remote. This woman looked gentle. As if she somehow understood. "It might be a long time. Mr. Bolt is very good, too."

Oh, God. Kerry, the woman who'd told her about RBK Security, had dealt with Sam Reston, who'd saved her life. She had no idea what this Mr. Bolt was like. Maybe Sam Reston worked on the down low to rescue women in danger and this Bolt didn't know anything about it. What then?

Ellen closed her eyes for just a second, wishing she could either rewind her life to a year ago or fast forward to a year in the future, when either she'd be settled in a new life or she'd be dead. Because if she didn't do something, *now,* she was surely headed toward a slow and painful death.

Gerald Montez didn't forgive.

But she kept having to make these split-second decisions, with no training for them, no way to judge whether she was making the right choice or throwing her life away.

The lion or the lady, every time, every day.

And now toss exhaustion and sleeplessness into the mix. How to choose?

She looked the receptionist in the eyes. Ellen was a good judge of character, and now she had to trust her instincts. The receptionist looked back at her calmly, seemingly undisturbed that the lunatic lady, who looked as if she hadn't slept in three days because she hadn't, was staring her in the face, taking minutes for a decision that shouldn't take a second.

Except—like all her decisions this past year—her life hung in the balance.

The receptionist stayed calm, eyes kind. Maybe she was used to desperate people. Maybe the desperate were tossed up on this doorstep daily.

"Okay," Ellen finally said, clutching her hands. *Please let this be the right choice.* She sent the prayer up to whoever was up there, who'd been noticeably absent lately. "I'll see Mr. Bolt. Thank you."

The receptionist nodded. "The second door to your right. Mr. Bolt's name is on the door. He's waiting for you."

Ellen nodded and slowly made her way to the big corridor on the right. As she passed in front of the desk, the receptionist looked up and Ellen saw understanding in her eyes.

"It will be okay," the receptionist said softly. "Don't worry. Mr. Bolt will make it okay."

No, it wouldn't be okay. It would never be okay again.

Harry sat at his desk, trying to clear his mind of his last client, London Harriman, heiress to a real estate empire. She wanted him to stop publication of a sex tape by a tabloid website.

She didn't mind that the sex tape was going to be put online, mind you. Oh no. She'd recorded it specifically in order to release it and she'd assured him that it had been shot "professionally." No, what had got her panties—or lack of panties—in a twist was that she wouldn't be in control of the timing or the release venue.

She wanted him to stop the gossip website from putting it up. She'd handed him a copy with a coy smile, saying she wanted him to watch it. So he'd understand.

London had come on to him, real heavy, but then Harry

imagined that London came on to anything with a penis, particularly if that man could even marginally help her in her goal of becoming the Socialite Sex Goddess of the World.

She was beautiful and buffed to a shine, wearing what he imagined at a rough guess—Sam's wife, Nicole, would probably know the amount down to the dollar—to be about a hundred and fifty thousand dollars' worth of . . . stuff, from the designer purse, designer shoes, designer shades, to the big flashy designer jewels.

She'd carefully and slowly crossed her legs, showing a pantyless crotch that had been shaved except for a little landing strip in the middle, so she had a designer twat, too.

Harry *hated* this shit, but he had been designated by Sam and Mike as the go-to guy for the asshole clients, and he owed his two brothers so much he accepted the Asshole Detail without complaint.

Plus, they both knew that he was constitutionally incapable of being rude or discourteous to a woman.

His curse.

After quoting double their usual fee, Harry got the details, the copy of the tape of the delectable London fucking the man du jour, and the name and website of the so-called journalist who was going to post the tape tomorrow.

Five minutes after the door had closed behind London, Harry had found the file on the online tabloid's servers, degraded it, left some spyware and a very clear message that any attempt to post the file would cause the entire archives of the site to be degraded beyond repair, effectively putting them out of business. He toyed with the idea of signing the message

"The Twat's Avenger" but decided not to. It was touch and go there for a moment, though.

Have to get your jollies where you can.

Five minutes, fifty thousand dollars. Not bad. And twenty-five thousand of that fifty was going into their Lost Ones Fund, their own personal Underground Railroad.

Twenty-five thousand dollars from London's trust fund would not be used to buy a fur or a week at a fancy spa or luxury rehab or a couple of Rolexes. That money would be spent on some abused woman who was running for her life. Most of the women who came to them left home under cover of darkness with nothing but the clothes on their backs, sometimes—tragically—with their kids. They did that because if they stayed they'd be beaten to death.

Harry and his brothers gave them a new life and enough money to start that life.

Great, great feeling. Maybe he should have charged London triple their usual fee. Buy some safety for a lot of little kids, that would.

He was frowning over that when Marisa announced the next client, a Ms. Nora Charles.

She'd had an appointment with Sam, but Sam had called to say that Nicole was having bad morning sickness and he'd come in when she was better.

Harry knew his brother Sam. Not even the threat of nuclear war would keep Sam from Nicole's side when she wasn't feeling well. Sam would stay by her side until she felt better. That was the bottom line.

Harry respected that. He liked Nicole, a lot. And he liked

it that she made Sam so happy. Well, happy . . . Sam seemed really happy with her when he wasn't panicking about some imaginary danger to Nicole around every corner. And now that there was a kid on the way, whoa.

Sam was going to have to dial down his crazy overprotectiveness, though Harry doubted he could. Sam Reston, big, huge, tough guy, good with a rifle, good with his fists, was a total wuss when it came to his wife. And the little girl on the way? Sam would probably keep her under armed guard throughout her childhood and let her date when she turned thirty. Maybe.

Mike was out on a recon for a jeweler who had received death threats.

So today Harry was it.

Nora Charles, huh? Did she think no one could remember the Thin Man movies? He sent up a little prayer. *Please, God, not another heiress under a fake name.* Harry had had his heiress quotient for the year with London even though it was still April.

He was bracing himself for more nonsense as his door slid open.

And then Marisa clicked twice on the intercom—their code—and he thought, *Oh shit.* Nora Charles had called on their special hotline, the underground railroad.

And then the most beautiful woman he'd ever seen walked in to his office.

Women were rarely clients of RBK Security, the mainstream, overground part of it, anyway. Mostly the clientele was corporate—something was leaking money and they wanted it stopped. Or they wanted their security system upgraded. He and Sam and Mike mostly dealt with their opposite corporate numbers, heads of security, or with the Big Guy himself—the CEO. Mostly men. And, of course, the odd heiress.

But the woman walking in to his office was definitely not an heiress. Not with those plain, nondescript clothes that were so rumpled they looked as if she'd slept in them. Not with those nails bitten down to the quick. Not with that glorious red hair tumbling wildly around her shoulders. Not with those dark circles under beautiful green eyes that were revealed when she pulled off her big sunglasses.

No, Harry thought sadly as he rose to greet her. She wasn't a pampered heiress. She was one of the Lost Ones.

Chapter 2

Ellen walked in to the office warily. Her friend Kerry had had dealings with the R of RBK, Sam Reston. So this was the B. Harry Bolt.

Kerry had talked about Sam Reston and hadn't said anything at all about the other two partners. Maybe Ellen was making a big mistake. Maybe this Bolt would turn her in to Gerald. Maybe she was signing her death warrant right now, she thought, as the door behind her slid silently closed, presenting a smooth expanse. She turned for a second, alarmed that the door had no doorknob and no hinges.

No way to get out.

It took her almost a full minute to realize that the button on the right-hand wall was probably the door release mechanism.

Heart pounding, Ellen turned back just as this Harry Bolt stood up. And up. And up.

He was amazingly tall. Amazingly . . . big. Huge, strong, unsmiling.

A lot of Gerald's operators had that look. Intent, focused, dangerous. Trained to hurt.

Ellen started to step back, but stopped herself. If there was one thing she'd learned in this past year, it was not to show fear. Her palms were sweating but she had no intention of shaking hands, so he didn't have to know.

"Ms. Charles? Please come in. Make yourself comfortable." Harry Bolt had a deep, calm voice. He watched her carefully, unmoving. Perhaps he realized that his size was unsettling and he did the only thing he could do to reassure her: stay still.

Heart thudding, Ellen walked carefully across the large office and sat down in one of two chairs facing his desk. Client chairs, clearly. If this was for real, if what Kerry had told her was true, and if this Harry Bolt did what Sam Reston did, then a lot of terrified women had sat in this very chair.

Were they all still alive? Had they been betrayed? Were they now rotting in some ditch or at the bottom of some lake, beaten to death?

Only one way to find out.

And yet she was so scared, it was hard to find enough oxygen to speak. She had to wait until she was certain that her voice would be strong and not shake.

This Harry Bolt didn't seem to have any problems with waiting. He'd taken his seat after her and just sat there, watching her.

His eyes were an extraordinary color. A light brown that looked almost golden, like an eagle's eyes. Ellen mentally shook herself. *Come on, you've got more important things to think about than the color of this guy's eyes. Like your life.*

She breathed in and out a few times, gathering her courage. Harry Bolt simply sat and waited, showing no signs of impatience.

Start obliquely, she thought. It would be a little test. If he had no idea what she was talking about, she'd go back outside and wait for Sam Reston, even if it took days.

Though she probably didn't have days. She might not live to see the sun set.

Deep breath. "The first thing I want to say is that Dove says hello. She says she's doing fine and she wants to thank you."

There. See what he made of that.

Harry Bolt watched her face intently, then nodded his head. "I'm glad," he said quietly, somberly. "Sam told me she's a good kid."

Right answer. Okay.

"Dove" was Kerry Robinson, and she *was* a good kid, but she'd had the bad luck to be married to a violent drunk who nearly killed her. Kerry Robinson wasn't her real name, and she'd known Ellen as Irene Ball. It didn't matter that their names weren't genuine because the danger to them was.

A year ago, Ellen had entered a world where women changed their names because there were monsters out looking for them. Somehow, Ellen had also entered some kind of sisterhood where not much had to be said to understand.

Some time back, Kerry had quietly told her that a man had been asking for her. It turned out he was only looking for a date, but Kerry had seen how scared Ellen was. And knew. So she'd given Ellen the special card with the special number on it that led to RBK.

"Are you in the same kind of trouble?" Harry Bolt asked quietly.

"Yes," she whispered.

"You're going to need to disappear?"

Among other things. "Yes."

He leaned forward slightly, resting his torso on muscled forearms. Ellen watched his hands carefully. They were large, scarred, powerful. He noted her glance and kept his hands very still.

She raised her eyes to his.

"I'm not the enemy," he said quietly.

Maybe. Maybe not.

She couldn't allow her vigilance to drop, not for one second. This man looked just as dangerous as any of Gerald's minions. More dangerous, even. He was perfectly able to repress those macho mess-with-me-and-you're-dead-meat vibes all of Gerald's men had, including Gerald himself.

This man was just as big and strong as the biggest and baddest of Gerald's men. And he'd been a Special Forces soldier. Ellen had read the thumbnail bios of all three partners in RBK at an Internet café, waiting for her appointment. She was going to place her life in the company's hands and she wanted to know what she was dealing with. So this Harry Bolt had been a Special Forces soldier and was way on top of the toughness scale, but his vibe was . . . calm. Serene.

Her intense anxiety went down half a notch.

They looked at each other, dead silence in the room.

Ellen was running possible openings through her mind when he said, voice still calm, "But you do have an enemy."

She nodded her head jerkily.

Oh God, this was so *hard*.

"Why don't you start at the beginning?" he suggested.

She drew in a deep breath. Beginning. Okay.

"I, um. I'm an accountant. A CPA." She thought about it, about the smoking ruins of her existence. "Or was. In another life."

Chapter 3

She's scared shitless, Harry thought. Words wouldn't reassure her, so he did the only thing he could do—stay still and let her open up to him. Exactly as you'd do with a frightened, wounded animal.

Was she wounded? Harry made sure not to move his eyes below her neck, but he had exceptionally good sight and peripheral vision. No broken bones visible, no casts, no bandages. No black eyes, but rather red-rimmed ones.

It was a good thing Harry couldn't see any visible damage, because he didn't know if he could have kept so still if she'd been covered in bruises.

It never failed to drive him crazy, how some men could hurt women and children. He had no idea how they could do it, but they did. He'd seen it all—snapped arms, dislocated jaws, black, swollen eyes, pulped spleens . . .

It was always horrific, but on this woman . . . bile rose in his throat at the thought of violence to her. She was slender, delicate, with the fair, creamy skin of a redhead that should never carry any kind of bruise, let alone one caused by violence.

She didn't have any internal injuries, because she'd moved gracefully and swiftly as she entered the room, as if forcing herself into it. Not allowing herself to back away.

If she'd been punched where it wouldn't show, she'd be moving slowly, carefully. Some women had to breathe very shallowly because someone had cracked or broken a rib. He'd seen a lot of that.

"How can we help you?" he asked, though he knew the answer. By taking her away from the bad guys.

She finally pulled in a deep breath. "Like I said, I was an accountant, a CPA, and a good one."

A note of pride entered her voice and inside Harry rejoiced. She hadn't been beaten down to the ground. Not yet. And now that she was here, not ever again. He'd personally see to that.

"I'm sure you were, Ms. Charles," he answered softly.

Her eyes flickered, because that clearly wasn't her name. Man, she was a lousy liar. Personally, Harry could lie like a pro. He could say to anyone that his name was Rumpelstiltskin and never bat an eyelid.

"Yes, um." She clutched her backpack with white-knuckled intensity. "I found a really good job just out of college, with a—a large company headquartered about thirty miles from Savannah. A company that had dealings abroad. It was challenging, but exciting."

She stopped, watching him. Harry simply breathed, kept his face neutral. She was going to tell this in her own good time.

She looked to the side and winced. "I was actually put in *charge* of the accounts department. Immediately. Which was a really big deal for someone just out of college with a brand-new degree and the ink barely dry on her license. I thought—I thought maybe the owner of the company had checked my grades, which were straight A's, and decided to give me a chance even though I didn't have any experience."

"And?" Harry prodded when she shut up.

"It wasn't my grades." She looked down at her lap then back up again, mouth firm. "My inexperience was a big plus in his eyes. The accounts were a real mess. He hadn't been paying all his taxes, either. It took me two years to start putting some order into his affairs. I'm surprised the IRS didn't come down on the company, though it was working mainly for the U.S. government, so he might have had . . . well, friends in high places."

By not a flicker of an eye did Harry let on that he felt a slight prickle of unease. The only kinds of companies that worked for the U.S. government and also worked abroad were defense contractors or security companies. And he knew just about every security company in the United States.

"In the meantime, although I was really happy to have the job and to run an office of five and manage the accounts of a multimillion-dollar company, something—something else started happening." She swallowed convulsively. "The owner started sniffing around me. And he wasn't taking no for an answer, you know?"

Oh Christ, Harry thought. *Here it comes.* He consciously schooled his face to blandness. His default expression was a ferocious scowl he'd been told was terrifying, and he didn't want to frighten her.

"Yes," he said quietly. "I know."

Her eyes met his. She made no bones about staring at him, assessing him, and he let her.

It wasn't a hardship. She had the most beautiful eyes he'd ever seen, even more beautiful than those of Sam's wife, Nicole. But where Nicole was a stunning, in-your-face beauty, a head-turner, this woman had a quieter appeal. You had to look twice to see how pretty she was, but once you did . . . wow.

Keep your head in the game, Harry told himself sternly. The woman was in trouble, maybe a day away from getting seriously hurt, or worse, killed. Reflecting on her expressive sea-green eyes and creamy skin and heart-shaped face wasn't going to help her.

She nodded, suddenly. He had apparently passed some kind of test. Luckily, the lady didn't appear to be a mind reader, otherwise his little spurt off the reservation mooning about her eyes would have scared her off. She was definitely not in the market for a man, that was clear. She wasn't dressed to seduce—in fact, her clothes were cheap and rumpled. None of her movements had those unconscious come-hither overtones so many attractive women developed.

He wouldn't blame her if she were to try a little seduction. She was obviously here seeking protection and he was a man willing to offer it. Throw a little sex into the mix, get him on board, bind him. Made sense.

But the vibes that were coming from her were anxiety and fear and a sort of dogged determination, not *Protect me and I'll make it worth your while.*

She breathed deeply. "He, um, stopped by my office a lot, put his arm around me—" Her face tightened at the memory.

"Pretty soon the whole company had the impression I was his—his lover, and nothing I could say could convince anyone otherwise. I'd just get these sly smiles and heavy hints that I had been hired for something other than my grades. And I sort of had to watch my words, because he was, you know, the *boss*."

"I'll bet it got worse," Harry said.

She blinked in surprise. "You're right." As if he was this amazing wizard with a crystal ball. He wasn't. He just knew his assholes. If Asshology were a course, he'd have a PhD in it.

"It was bad enough having people think we were lovers, but pretty soon word got round that we were *engaged*." She shuddered. "I heard he was shopping around for a ring. A *big* ring, because everything he does, he does big. That more or less did it. Much as I hated to leave the job, I started looking around for another one, but in this economy . . ."

Harry nodded. RBK was doing just fine, but it was the kind of company that thrived in times of trouble. It was thriving now.

"The situation became impossible. He was acting as if we were engaged, and we'd never even kissed! He's such a powerful personality, though, that the whole company just took it for granted that we were a couple. Then, a year ago, there was this party, this huge corporate do, celebrating a big government contract. The company rented the ballroom of the Hyatt Regency in Savannah and it was catered by this all-star chef." Her mouth quirked. "There was free booze, and more or less everyone got plastered, except for me. My body can't handle much alcohol. So I was, unfortunately, sober when one of the employees came up to me and bragged about how smart the boss was. He'd stolen twenty million dollars from the U.S. government and wasn't I lucky I was going to marry him?"

Harry's eyes widened and she nodded. "Yes, indeed. And frankly, it made a terrible kind of sense, because a lot of the accounts from the early days of the company just didn't add up. There was more incoming than could be accounted for. I think the boss knew I was sort of digging around, but I didn't know what I was looking for."

Harry frowned. "Did you ask for details from this guy? What was his name?"

She hesitated and he understood she was still weighing how much to tell him. "Frankly, the guy was so drunk he could barely articulate. But—he was actually boasting! When I said I didn't believe him, he pulled out a cell phone and showed me a snapshot of him, the boss, and two other guys. Soldiers, in Iraq. Standing next to what looked like hundreds of pallets stacked high with dollars wrapped up into bricks. The guy was falling down drunk but the photos were clear. Then he said—all that money was gone the next day, and no one ever noticed."

"What happened next?" Harry asked quietly.

He had a sense of where this was going. But he was also having trouble focusing on her story. It was riveting, but the quality of her voice was even more riveting. Soft and clear with the faintest tinge of Southern spice in there. It was mesmerizing, and tantalizingly familiar. Which was, of course, crazy, since Harry had never seen her before in his life. He was hallucinating, which was not good.

He needed to sleep at least as much as he trained. A good military rule.

"While he was telling me the story, so drunk he was nearly passing out, my boss noticed us across the room. He looked at me and at this drunk guy, and I've never seen a more menacing expression on a human face before." She shivered at the memory. "It certainly sobered up Drunk Guy. He went ash white, said to forget he'd said anything and disappeared so fast you'd swear you could see the dust. I was spooked. The boss started coming over and I hid behind a pillar and slid away. I needed to think about it, because the whole story rang really true. And explained all the anomalies I found in the accounts."

Harry was watching her, trying to concentrate on her words instead of the timbre of her voice, feeling slightly light in the head. Maybe this woman was like one of those sirens in Greek mythology, whose voices alone were so enchanting they made sailors crash into rocks. Jesus, he wouldn't be surprised. "And then?"

She huffed out a breath and got a closer clutch onto her backpack, nervous system tightening up. "The next day they found that guy's body. The drunk one who'd talked. I heard it on the early morning news. It was made to look like a mugging, but I don't think he was the type of man to be caught by surprise like that. They found his body by the side of the road with a bullet through his head and all his money and credit cards gone."

"What was the caliber of the bullet?"

Her eyes opened wide. "I beg your pardon?"

A lot could be told by the caliber, but she wouldn't know that. "Never mind," Harry said. "Go on."

"It was just too much. I—I guess I freaked. I didn't go to work that day, didn't even call in sick. I just—didn't show up.

Which was stupid, because anyone who knew me knew that was unusual for me."

"Hard worker," Harry murmured and her head came up with an expression of pride.

"Yes, I am. I've never taken a day off sick and I've been working since I was twelve." She shook herself. "Anyway, I thought all night about going to the police, but the thing is, the local police chief is a really good friend of my boss's, and a lot of the cops practice free shooting on his shooting ranges. My boss makes a point of contributing very generously to the Family Survivor's Fund. They would never believe me, not in a million years, not without proof, and I didn't have that. When the news came on about Drunk Guy being killed, I realized right then and there that I was going to have to go to the police or I'd be next. And then I happened to look out the window at a van parked across the street from my condo entrance, and men started pouring out. They were armed and they were Ge—my boss's men."

Harry froze. "What did you do?"

"I ran," she said simply.

Ellen could clearly remember the bright, blinding panic flaring in her head when she saw the men spilling out of that van.

Pure instinct took over. She didn't even stop to think about what she was doing. She didn't pack a suitcase, didn't do anything but grab her car keys and the thousand dollars she always kept in cash in an ancient copy of *Pride and Prejudice* and run down the back stairs to the laundry room, which led to an underground corridor exiting onto the back parking lot, where she kept her car.

She drove to the most eastern ATM she could think of, withdrew as much money as the system would allow, then turned west and began the long, long trek to the farthest point she could think of: Seattle.

"You ran," Harry Bolt repeated thoughtfully. His deep voice was quiet and calm.

She nodded. "I knew I had to keep off the grid, because my boss—my former boss—is good at finding things out. That's one of the things he does. And I knew he wasn't ever going to just forget about it. I think . . ." Ellen lifted her eyes to Harry Bolt's and searched his face, looking for something elusive. Some sense that he would understand completely and totally what she was saying. She found it. She drew a deep breath. "I think he's the kind of man who will keep looking for me until I'm dead. Can you believe that?"

"Absolutely," was the quiet answer.

Okay. Okay. Maybe this was going to work.

"I drove at night and slept in motels during the day. Sometimes I stopped for a week or two and waitressed in places where they don't ask for documents. Finally I made it to . . . a city in the north. I rented a room in a rough part of town. I paid cash, no questions asked. The landlady wasn't about to report my rent to the IRS. After a couple of days, I found a job as a waitress in this dive. I gave the boss a false name and I didn't show him any papers. The owner was—was good to me. I think—I think he understood."

Mario Russo, one of life's good guys. Big and rough looking, with only inches of visible skin not covered by tribal tattoos. He ran a funky bar frequented by an astonishing variety of humanity, but he didn't water his drinks, he didn't ask questions and if you behaved, you could stay forever in his place on one beer. Particularly on cold days.

Though he didn't have to, Mario paid her a little over minimum wage, which with tips was enough to pay for her room and her keep. He never asked questions, paid every Friday night, and was always somehow there if a customer got a little rowdy with her.

"About a week after I ran, I found out that—" Her throat constricted and she swallowed heavily. As always when she thought about it, her stomach seemed to slide greasily up her windpipe.

Ellen watched Harry Bolt watching her. Again, he showed no signs of impatience as he waited for her to continue her story. Not a muscle in his body moved. She suddenly had a flash of insight—he'd wait for her to tell her story in her own way, no matter how much time it took.

Up until now Ellen's focus had simply been, *Is this man my enemy? Am I going to get myself killed coming out in the open with him?*

But now she relaxed just a little and noticed other things about the man. He was so very tall, for one thing. Even sitting down, he towered above his desk. He was well built, too—dense, lean, tightly packed muscle with no fat anywhere. Amazingly broad shoulders, maybe the widest she'd ever seen.

Astonishing as his physique was, though, it wasn't the first thing you noticed about him. No, what drew your attention like iron filings to a supermagnet were his eyes. That brown so light it could almost be called golden. Intense, intelligent eyes that seemed to see more than most.

"You found something out a week after you ran," he prodded gently.

She drew in a deep breath. "Yes. I paid no attention to the news at first. I just fell into bed exhausted every evening. But finally one evening I decided to check up on what was going on back home." Her fingers tightened on the canvas of her backpack as she tried to keep her hands from trembling. "My boss reported to his friend the chief of police that I'd embezzled almost a million dollars from the company."

She watched his face, as she sat tense and miserable, reliving the shock of the accusation. She hadn't slept for two days afterward.

He blinked those narrow golden eyes. "That's ridiculous," he said, and she let out her breath in a long, relieved sigh.

"Yes. Yes, it is, but he obviously made it sound convincing. There was an interview with him on the local news and he was all, *We don't know what made her do this terrible thing—though she's been drinking heavily lately.*"

Ellen looked into his eyes and felt that hot stab of indignation all over again. "I don't know how he could say that without a bolt of lightning striking him dead. I rarely drink and I would *never* embezzle. But it gets worse."

"He accused you of being the dead guy's lover and insinuated you killed him." Harry Bolt said it calmly, that deep voice sure and steady, no problem, as if saying the sun rose in the east.

Ellen's jaw nearly dropped. "*Yes*. How did you know?"

"Guy sounds like an operator. He had various elements to deal with, and stringing them together that way took the heat off him, put it onto you, made sure you stayed in hiding and that no one would believe a word you said. Like killing four birds with one stone."

It burned that it had been so *easy* for Gerald. Part of it was her own fault. She'd led such an isolated life in Prineville. He could spin any story he wanted about her.

She sighed. "So I knew I had to stay under everyone's radar, and I did. For a year. It wasn't much of a life, but at least I stayed alive. Then, three days ago, something happened."

"Someone else die?"

"No. Not that I know of. But it scared the hell out of me. Coming home from work I happened to notice a man loitering in front of a shop window on my street. He was dressed like a homeless person, but by sheer chance, I recognized one of my boss's new hires from a year ago. If I hadn't recognized him, I'd probably be dead by now. So far I've managed to stay alive by sheer, dumb luck, but I can't count on it lasting forever. I'd made friends with the woman you know as Dove. I never told her anything, but I think she knew. And I think she was in the same situation. She gave me this and said that if I needed help, to call. And ask for Sam Reston."

Ellen opened her backpack and slid a small cardboard visiting card across the table. Her hands were trembling. He saw that. Those fierce eagle eyes saw her shaking hands and she curled them back in her lap.

Harry Bolt barely glanced at the card, but of course he'd know what it was. Not a normal business card.

The top of the card had a beautifully rendered bird in flight, the very epitome of freedom in few brush strokes, and a telephone number printed in the center of the card. Nothing else. No words. No name, no address. Just the symbol of freedom and a number.

The number didn't correspond to any of the official numbers

of RBK Security, either. There was no other information on the card. Just the stylized bird and a toll-free number. Which she'd called. One of the company's secretaries had given Ellen the city and address when she called.

It was a special phone line. Obviously the line for desperate women on the run.

Bolt watched her carefully. "Do you have any idea how these men might have tracked you down?"

Here it comes, she thought. "Yes, yes I do, unfortunately. You remember I told you I worked in this bar? More of a dive, really?"

He nodded his head gravely.

"Well, the place featured live music every Tuesday and Thursday evening. The music was provided by this ancient jazz singer who wasn't actually . . . um . . . very good. His voice was shot to hell by years of smoking and drinking and he had arthritis in his hands, but he'd been playing there for twenty years, the customers were used to him and, knowing the boss, he'd stay for another twenty. One night he didn't show up. We found out later that his heart simply gave out."

Honorius Lime. He'd been one of the good guys who'd found life simply too hard to face without the help of the bottle. He'd once had talent, but he'd flushed that, and his life, down the toilet.

Ellen had grown up with people like that. Talented but weak, living life on wishful thinking until there was nothing left but charity and then the grave.

She'd studied and worked so hard all her life to get out of that hole, and now look at her.

It was a sign of her exhaustion that she even let these

thoughts inside her head, because they were wasted energy and she couldn't in any way afford that.

She drew in a deep breath. "So my boss was left without live entertainment. I, um, I offered to step in."

For the first time, she saw lightness in his face. It wasn't a smile, but something amused him. "Do you have any talent?"

Well, that was the problem. "Some. More than poor old Honorius, anyway. So I started singing every Tuesday and Thursday and the place filled up. The boss gave me Wednesday and Friday off. He said I was bringing in so many new customers, he wanted me fresh. And then one evening, about six months ago, after I'd been singing there for a couple of weeks, an agent was in the audience. We talked after the gig and he asked me to record some songs and we did. He knew this great studio and we did it all in one day, in one take. Enough for two CDs. One just voice and keyboard and bass and sax and drums. Covers, mostly. I also had some songs that I'd, um, composed myself. Just for . . . something to do."

The solace of music. How grateful she'd been over this past year of terror and flight that she could find solace in music.

"I didn't think too much about it. I thought maybe he'd use the recordings for some private purpose or something. Play them at parties. But he didn't. He put out two CDs under a pseudonym and . . ." she shrugged, almost embarrassed, "one went gold and the other went platinum. We never thought—"

The words died in her throat as Harry Bolt jolted, looking as if he'd been stuck with a cattle prod. His face was tight and harsh. He placed his big hands on the desk and leaned forward on powerful arms.

"Christ," he breathed. "You're *Eve*."

* * *

Harry thought he was impervious to surprise. More or less everything that could happen to him already had. At least twice. He'd been a Delta operator and had been trained and trained hard not to show surprise.

Had there been any capacity for surprise left in him when he signed up, Delta had beaten it right out of him.

But right now, he felt as if someone had whacked him upside the head with a two-by-four.

Eve. Fuck him, he had Eve sitting right across from him, with that soft Southern-tinged voice he piped most evenings straight into his head.

And she wasn't a seven-chinned hippopotamus, either. She was a real beauty. Run down and scared, sure, but still gorgeous. While listening to her, it had been really hard to pay attention. He was ashamed of himself, but there it was.

Harry wasn't Mike, the man-slut. Harry'd been celibate for almost two years now, the whole year in Afghanistan, where to bed a woman meant her death by stoning, and the year after, when he'd come back in pieces and had had to put himself painfully back together.

It was as if sex had fled his life, and fuck him if it didn't decide to come roaring back into his life right this instant. He had a scared beauty in front of him and she wasn't thinking about sex, she was thinking about survival, so he should be ashamed of himself.

And he was, sort of. Except the hard-on took precedence over the shame.

Yep. Harry Bolt, Mr. Self Control himself, was getting a hard-on even though he was sweating to keep it down. Everything about this woman turned him on. That pale, porcelain skin that contrasted so delightfully with the rich, shiny, dark-red hair, the fatigue-bruised, beautiful eyes, the delicate lines of her cheekbones and jawline.

Even exhausted, rumpled, with deep purple smudges under her eyes, so tense she was practically thrumming, she turned him on more powerfully than any other woman he'd ever met.

And then . . . and then it turned out she was fucking *Eve*.

Harry was still getting over the shock of that when a soft knock sounded at the door separating his office from Sam's, and Sam stuck his head in.

"There was someone to see me?" Sam had a few lines in his face he hadn't had yesterday, so Nicole's morning sickness must have been bad. But if he was here, that meant she was feeling better and she'd come in to work. He wouldn't be here otherwise.

Sam looked at Nora Charles—or whatever the hell her real name was, though Harry could think of her now only as Eve—and at Harry, sensing the electricity in the air, and walked into Harry's office.

Sam's presence rearranged the molecules in the room and gave Harry a little space to get his head out of his ass and try to get his dick to go down a little.

Nora—*Eve*—was looking as if she'd been run over by a truck. She hadn't wanted him to figure out who she was. Even though her story had been carefully edited to keep all details out, Harry could figure them out now. The city in the north was Seattle. The agent was Roddy Fisher, who'd discovered Broken Monkeys and Isabel.

Sam was looking at him, at Eve, and back at him.

Eve was sitting at the very edge of the chair, clutching her no-name canvas backpack with white knuckles.

Terrified.

And Harry was a dickhead. Hard-headed, tough-as-nails Harry had morphed right into a fanboy and had scared this woman who, it turned out, was not just gorgeous, but who had a once-in-a-generation musical talent and was terrified.

If she was here, her life was on the line, and he had to get a grip on himself.

Harry turned to Sam, keeping his movements slow and unthreatening. "Come on in, Sam. Meet Eve."

Sam was pretty unsurpriseable, too. So maybe it was sleep deprivation, or the stress of watching his wife throw up her stomach lining, that had him opening his eyes in shock.

"*The* Eve? The singer?"

"That's highly confidential information," Ellen said sharply. Information that could get her killed.

So this was Sam Reston.

Ellen looked at him carefully. Though he didn't look like Harry Bolt at all—Reston was dark-haired with rough features; Bolt was dark blond with fine, angular features—they shared a look. Tall, impossibly strong, self-possessed.

And they both looked really dangerous. Not for the first time, she wondered whether she'd made a mistake in coming here. If she was wrong, if Kerry had somehow steered her to the wrong place, she could have sacrificed her life for nothing.

These men spirited away endangered women. You'd think that there would be softness and kindness in their gaze. That they'd be sort of like social workers, only taller.

These two men looked worlds away from being social workers. If she were told they were crime lords or killers, she'd believe every word.

No softness, no kindness, no discernible mercy.

What had she done?

There was silence in the room for a minute, two. Ellen's throat was too tight and dry for her to even think of speaking.

"Well?" Harry Bolt fixed her with an unblinking stare, light-brown eyes fixed as in an eagle's gaze, and just as impersonal. "You are Eve, aren't you?"

Yes. And I have just given you enough personal information to track me down. If you're not going to help me, I'm done for.

No. Of course not. What a ridiculous notion. And excuse me, I need to be somewhere else right now.

Yes. No. Yes. No.

"Yes," she blurted out, as if some seal across her lips had just been shattered. Except for her agent, no one else knew. Well, maybe her boss, Mario, because beneath his laid-back tattooed exterior he was really smart. Still, he'd never asked and she'd never told. "Yes. And I'm afraid that might be the way my former boss found me, though everyone on the production side signed a confidentiality agreement."

She'd made Roddy swear to secrecy and they'd drawn up the confidentiality clause together. She knew enough legal lingo to make it airtight and to make anyone think twice about selling out to the tabloids. The musicians had played in a separate room, with a separate entrance and had never even seen her, only heard her. She'd insisted on that.

Roddy hadn't really taken her seriously, but he had seen the marketing potential. At a time in which anyone in the media ran a website, blogged, friended on Facebook, Twittered, had RSS feeds and was linked in, a mystery identity was a sure-fire publicity gimmick.

Harry Bolt addressed Sam Reston without taking his eyes off her. "So, Sam, this is Nora Charles, aka Eve. She got our number from Dove. Eve, this is Sam Reston, the man who helped your friend."

She was vibrating with nerves, sweat trickling down her back and between her breasts. She knew her pale skin would be ice white with stress.

Sam Reston didn't even try to shake hands with her; he must have seen that she was on the knife's edge. He simply nodded soberly, said, "Ma'am" in a low voice and sat down next to his partner.

He addressed his partner without taking his eyes off her. "Harry? Sitrep."

Now both of them were looking at her intently. Most stares come off as aggressive, but theirs didn't. Just . . . intense. Like they were listening carefully to what she said, but other information was coming their way from her eyes, her hands, her feet. Maybe even her gut.

"Ms. Charles is an accountant. She worked for a company . . . in the South?" He raised his eyebrows slightly.

Ellen nodded shakily. She'd spent a lifetime getting rid of her cracker accent but there was still a Southern tilt to her voice, particularly under stress.

Harry Bolt continued. "At a party, a company employee told her that the owner of the company stole a big sum of money from the U.S. government in Iraq. Twenty million dollars."

Now it was Sam Reston's turn to raise his eyebrows.

"That employee died the next day. His forehead met a bullet. Men came for her and she ran. Her boss told the police and the media she'd embezzled a million dollars, maybe killed the guy who talked."

Her heart ached a little every time she heard that. She'd worked so *hard* to create a respectable life for herself and it was in shattered shards around her feet.

"I didn't," she said quietly.

Sam Reston frowned. "Of course not."

There was silence in the room.

"Can we know the name of who's after you?" Reston finally asked. "To help you, we need to know the nature of the threat."

Could they know the name? Ellen sat, heart thudding. Every cell in her body screamed, *No!* She'd spent the past year never mentioning that name to anyone.

On the other hand, it was entirely possible she was the last person on earth to know that Gerald Montez had stolen twenty million dollars from the U.S. government and had killed at least one person to keep that secret.

If she died, someone had to have this information.

Ellen didn't know these two men. But she did know that at least one of them had helped a friend survive violence and build a new life. She wasn't endangering them. Both of them looked perfectly capable of taking care of themselves.

And . . . and she'd kept this lonely secret so *long*. It had shattered her life. Something in her longed to let it out, as if telling them could somehow lift this dark cloud of evil hanging over her, blighting her life.

She pulled in a deep breath and told them a secret she'd nearly died to keep.

"The company's name is Bearclaw. My former boss's name is Gerald Montez."

The air in the room changed, like an electrical charge had been run through it. The two men looked at each other.

It was just a glance, the merest flicker of the eyes, but it touched off a wildfire of panic inside her.

She was used to masking her feelings, so they probably wouldn't realize that inside she'd just gone into red alert, panic pulsing in her head like the deep siren in a submarine when a torpedo is heading its way.

Oh God!

They knew Gerald. They knew Bearclaw.

They were probably friends. They were certainly in the same business, probably did business together. Might even have an interest in covering up Gerald's crimes.

In a flash, Ellen realized that she'd been insane to seek protection from men who were exactly like Gerald. A year on the run, and she'd just placed herself in the enemy's hands.

She could barely breathe, as if a giant hand had squeezed her rib cage. She had to will herself to think straight.

Whether she lived or died depended on her actions in the next minute.

"Here," she said smoothly, opening her backpack. "I have photos on my cell phone, I can show you . . ." She stopped, frowning. *Not too much, don't overdo it, just look faintly puzzled.* "That's strange . . ."

Look up and to the left, trying to remember something. Cool, casual.

"My cell phone isn't here . . . Oh!" *Eyes wide, remembering. Stand up, moving slowly,* even though her body was screaming for escape. "Oh my gosh! It must have dropped out of my backpack downstairs when I checked the street number. I'll be right back."

Move briskly, don't run.

She didn't even give them a chance to react. In a second, she was out into the reception area. She beamed a dazzling smile at the receptionist. "Forgot something," she trilled. "Be right back!"

In the hallway, the elevator was just closing its doors. She'd kept herself in shape, doing calisthenics in her run-down apartment every day, and a good thing, too, because she ran and caught the door by a hair, punching the ground floor button so hard it was a miracle she didn't punch her way through the metal.

It took forever. Finally, the doors dinged and she flew out through the huge glass street doors, blinking in the bright sunlight. And again, the goddess of runaway women was with her, because a cab swerved to the curb and let out a passenger.

She must have looked like a wild woman. The taxi driver threw her a startled look when she flung herself into the backseat and panted out the address of the small hotel she'd booked for the night. "Double the fare if you can get me there in ten minutes!"

The taxi driver was young, and looked like a college student. "Yes, *ma'am*!" he grinned and stood on the accelerator. There was a squeal of tires and she was pressed against the back of the seat. Good. As long as the driver didn't get them killed on the way, the faster she got to her room, the better.

Could they track her down? She thought it over. She hadn't called the Bird in Flight number from her cell phone but from a pay phone at the Greyhound station. The hotel she'd found was just over a mile from there, though. Would they be able to track her down?

Probably. These guys would have enormous resources at their disposal, including manpower.

And she hadn't even had a chance to sleep yet. She'd just washed up a bit before going to RBK. So now she'd have to leave, fast, and go . . .

Her mind pulled a blank.

Go where?

She'd plan that when she got to the hotel. Right now her entire being was panic bolted on top of exhaustion.

God, she was tired. The whole weight of the past three days, of the past year, was settling on her shoulders like a concrete mantle. She was usually pretty good at making snap decisions, but none that made any sense to her were coming at the moment.

Run. Again. But to where?

Georgia, Seattle, San Diego . . . geographically speaking, her next stop should be in northern New England, even though she hated the cold. Hole up in Maine or Vermont.

And how the hell to get there? Undetected by Harry Bolt and Sam Reston, who scared her almost as much as Gerald Montez? Gerald swaggered around, and he was dangerous because he could be unstable and had a violent streak to him.

Harry Bolt in particular struck her as dangerous, because she could clearly see the intelligence in his eyes.

Having a violent man after her was scary; having a violent, intelligent man after her was terrifying.

Oh, God.

She closed her eyes, overwhelmed, shaking. What next?

She drew a complete blank. Well, check that her cell phone was off, for one. It was a cheap prepaid throwaway and she made a point of keeping it turned off, using it only when absolutely necessary. RBK Security wouldn't have it, but you could never be too cautious. Or paranoid.

Ellen scrabbled in her purse and her eyes widened when she realized that she'd told Harry Bolt and Sam Reston the sober truth.

She really *had* left her cell phone behind. Not outside the building but in the hotel. The hotel she was going to have to leave as fast as possible.

The streets got a little meaner, then meaner still and then the cab pulled up in front of her hotel. Ellen paid and rushed toward the entrance.

A big hand grabbed her and slammed her against the side of a car while someone ran toward her with a gun. Pain streaked through her and the world blackened at the edges.

Chapter 4

Harry met Sam's eyes and refrained from wincing. Sam's eyes were so bloodshot it was as if he had opened up his veins and drained them right into his eyes. Nicole's morning sickness had clearly been preceded by a whole lot of night sickness.

Well, Sam was married to a stunningly beautiful woman he was crazy about and who loved him right back. They were expecting a much-desired little girl. What were a few sleepless nights in comparison to that?

Nothing.

"Montez," Sam growled. "That son of a bitch." His red eyes blazed. "Going to bring that fucker down."

Bearclaw was hated all throughout the U.S. military, but especially by SpecOps soldiers. Montez's men were not encouraged to show restraint and had no rules of engagement at all, unless you count *getoutofmywaymotherfuckerorI'llshoot* as a rule of engagement.

Four very good men had died badly as a direct result of Bearclaw's brutality, and Harry knew of at least two instances in which Bearclaw men had brought down fire on soldiers' positions through sheer carelessness.

"Oh yeah." Just the thought of Gerald Montez going after Eve made Harry's stomach roil. Montez was a scumbag who made money off the backs of U.S. soldiers. Bringing him down was going to be a pleasure. No way was Montez going to touch Eve, he'd make sure of it.

Speaking of which . . .

Oh, fuck.

"*Goddammit!*" Harry stood up so suddenly his chair thudded against the floor.

Sam's red eyes turned his way. "What?"

"She's gone. She ran." It pulsed through Harry in one electric moment of understanding. Eve had run out. Something had spooked her—something they'd said, something they'd done—and she'd run. Eve was now in the wind, with Gerald fucking Montez after her.

Every hair on Harry's body stood up. He could feel the hairs on his forearms scraping against the stiff cotton of his dress shirt. Fear pinged in every cell of his body.

Harry wasn't used to fear. Anger and outrage, yeah, sure. But fear? He hadn't been afraid of anything since Methhead Rod had killed Crissy. The worst thing that could ever happen to him already had. His own death was nothing in comparison to seeing Rod slam his little sister's body against the wall and watching her crumple to the floor in a pool of blood.

Well . . . right now was close. Eve was a woman of rare, almost mystical talent, a vulnerable, haunting beauty.

Eve knew something that could hurt Gerald Montez, who was utterly merciless. Montez wouldn't think twice about wiping her off the face of the earth, but not before skinning her alive first, to find out what was in that beautiful head that could hurt him.

He'd already ruined her life. He'd planted evidence of her embezzlement and the murder of the man who'd ratted on him. With local law enforcement in his pocket, she didn't dare ever show her face.

Harry didn't even want to think about what Gerald could—and would—do to Eve if he caught her. Which he would. He'd tracked her to Seattle, and Montez was no dummy. She was probably running straight into a trap, right . . . fucking . . . *now.*

Sam's eyes widened as Harry turned to one of the three top-of-the-line computers on his desk. He punched two keys and a clear image of the street outside their building appeared, crisp and clean.

"Fuck," he breathed. "There she is."

The monitor showed Eve running toward a taxi that had stopped to let a passenger out in front of the entrance. A second later the taxi pulled away, tires squealing.

Harry punched a key and the frame froze. He zoomed in on the license plate, highlighted the frame, copied it and entered it directly into a database he kept current for just such an occasion as this, in which speed was vital.

The database was a roster of TPMS IDs. The Tire Pressure Monitoring System probably was helpful for car safety, but it was fabulous for tracking down vehicles. Tire pressure measurement devices transmitted pressure data constantly to the onboard computer, each car with its separate ID—a safety measure that as a by-product was a quick way to track any vehicle manufactured since 2007.

The cab was a 2008 model Prius.

A soft ping and the ID was on his second monitor, superimposed on a map of San Diego.

"Sam!" Harry ran to the weapons locker, fitting himself with a light Kevlar vest, a shoulder holster with a Kimber 1911 and three magazines hanging from his belt. Comms system in ear.

He took the gun from the right-hand side of the locker. All the guns there were cold. Unregistered, untraceable. If Montez's men were around, this was going to be a kill.

He slung a jacket on to cover the whole thing and raced to the door. "Have Henry bring my SUV up from the garage. I'll call you from the vehicle. Keep following that cab and patch it through to my SUV's GPS. And kill the security cameras where the cab stops."

It was Harry who should have been at the computer. He was better at it than Sam. Sam was good at strategy; Harry was good with computers. But he'd have to leave Sam to take care of the monitors, because no way was anyone going after Eve except himself.

Sam moved to the chair in front of the monitor. He knew he wasn't as good with computers as Harry was—few people were—but Harry trusted him to do this.

"On it." Sam set up the transfer of the image to the onboard computer in Harry's vehicle. "You just make sure she doesn't fall into Montez's hands."

"You got it," Harry growled, and raced out.

Henry, the garage manager, must have had his spidey senses working overtime, because he had Harry's Cherokee idling at the curb, driver's-side door open, when Harry burst out of the front doors. Harry peeled out, keeping an eye on the GPS screen.

"She's going down Lark," Sam's calm voice came over Harry's earpiece.

"Yeah, I can see it." Harry was driving as fast as the road and traffic would allow. The cab was four blocks ahead of him. The light was still yellow at the intersection ahead . . .

Harry braked suddenly and pounded his fist on the steering wheel in frustration. A big delivery van suddenly appeared on the cross street, moving slowly. Harry would have run the red light, but now he was forced to wait.

Though no sound penetrated the soundproofing in the car, he knew his tires were screeching as he took off the second the light changed. Heads turned as smoke rose in the rearview mirror.

He was treating the vehicle badly, but who the fuck cared. The important thing was getting to where Eve was going fast enough to stop Montez's thugs from grabbing her if they were waiting for her.

With every second that passed, Harry was more and more certain that she was walking into a trap.

He punched a number on the screen, the office. It took

about five seconds to get through. All of RBK Security communications went through a proprietary satellite, which was owned by a company based in the Bahamas and seemingly located in Canada, and their calls couldn't be snarfed out of the air like most Bluetooth-based comms.

"Sir?" It was Marisa, who looked after the Lost Ones. She'd been a lost one herself and she was ferociously protective. No man trying to track down one of "her" girls would ever find out from Marisa that his victim had been to RBK.

"Marisa!" Harry barked. "Did this Nora Charles call from a cell?"

Tapping sounds, then Marisa's calm voice. "No, sir. She called from a pay phone from . . ." More tapping sounds. "The Greyhound bus station on West Broadway."

A light turned yellow up ahead and Harry gunned the engine viciously, pounding his way through the intersection, wrenching the steering wheel to avoid a teenager driving a Mustang. The gap was down to two blocks.

"Thanks, Marisa." Harry felt a little spurt of relief. If Bearclaw got hold of Eve's cell phone, they'd trace the number she'd called to RBK. Still, good luck with that. That one number, never used for ordinary business, was also registered in the Bahamas but routed through Canada. They'd never trace her through the number. But they could trace her through the phone itself, if she'd kept it on.

He could only pray that she'd turned the cell off wherever it was.

She was staying at the Curtis Hotel, he discovered, as the small red dot that was the cab stopped. With a voice command, Harry immediately superimposed a map of businesses over that spot and saw the name. It was only a block away.

He pressed the pedal down as far as it could go, taking in the scene at the hotel at a glance. One hand on the wheel, the other pulling out his Kimber.

No sooner had the cab pulled away than two men emerged from the shadows. Big men, armed. Overkill to pick up one lone woman. The first one to reach her pulled her arm up behind her back and slammed her into the side of a van.

Eve turned white with shock and slumped, dazed.

The fuckhead slapped her hard, pulled her arm up even more, bending down to give her instructions. He started manhandling her toward an off-white Transit panel van that had pulled up to the curb. The other guy opened the van's back doors. The van's cargo bay was empty except for blankets on the floor. The guy opening the bay was holding a .45 auto down along his leg.

Eve dug her heels in, clearly understanding that if she got in the van, she'd never get out again. She pulled against the arm holding her, outmatched, but not giving in. Harry watched her struggle, watched Fucker 1 backhand her again while Fucker 2 watched.

Seeing that, seeing her hurt, Harry's blood boiled. He shook all over with rage, except for his hands. His hands were steady and knew precisely what to do.

In a second he'd braked, shouldered the door open and leaped out onto the street before the vehicle stopped rocking.

He raced toward the man holding Eve. The man slammed her against the Transit's side again and reached inside his jacket. His reactions showed he'd had training, but he didn't have enough training to stop Harry. There wasn't enough training in the world for that.

Every instinct as a soldier told Harry to go for the armed guy first. It was practically written in stone. When facing an armed man and an unarmed man reaching for the gun, go for the gun that's in sight.

But Harry couldn't stand to see Eve manhandled for even a second longer. He ran straight up to the guy holding Eve, moved sideways fast in a smooth leg sweep, catching him as he lost his balance, pressing against him hip to hip, then rolling his hip to hold the guy in front of him as a shield.

Armed Guy had started shooting, controlled bursts from his automatic, but he was hitting the man in front of Harry. Harry braced against the impact of the bullets hitting the body he held in front of him.

The armed man stopped shooting and turned his gun on Eve, but Harry's gun was up and firing. A double-tap to the head and he dropped like a stone, only a star of pink mist dissipating in the air marking where he'd stood.

The whole thing had taken no more than three seconds.

Eve was on the ground, unconscious, but there was one more guy to worry about before Harry could help her. The van door slammed shut on the other side—the driver's side. Harry dropped to the ground and put a round in each ankle, watching bone splinters pepper the ground. Ignoring the screams, he raced around the front of the van and placed a round in the screaming man's head without a second thought.

There was no doubt that these fuckers' orders had been to bring Eve in alive if possible—dead if not. All three were armed—flipping back the jacket of the man who'd manhandled Eve showed a well-used holster and a Glock 17 seated in it, undrawn. He'd trusted his big fists to subdue a lone woman.

Harry gave him a vicious kick in the side, sorry that the fucker was dead, because he wanted to kill him all over again. He told himself the kick was to see if he was still alive, but that was bullshit. Some primitive part of him wanted to cut the fucker's chest open, rip his heart out and feed it to the dogs. Touch Eve and you died.

He looked down and his heart stopped. Just stopped for a long, horrendous second.

No.

This couldn't be. He closed his eyes for a second, sure that when he opened them again, he'd see bare asphalt at his feet and three very dead men scattered around the vehicle and that was all.

Life couldn't be that cruel. In the nanosecond in which this thought flashed through his head, every cell in his body rejected it as false. Life could definitely be that cruel. The cruelty of the world was never-ending, fathomless. The fact that something would break your heart was almost a guarantee that it would happen.

He opened his eyes again, the scene unchanged.

Eve, lying on her back, utterly still, blood staining her white shirt, staining her arm, pooling around her back. As he watched, a rivulet of blood broke from the pool and followed a groove in the asphalt invisible to the naked eye down to the edge of the curb, where it started dripping into a grate.

Harry dropped to his knees, because his legs wouldn't hold him up any more.

No, no, no. The words were a heavy drumbeat in his heart. No.

He refused even the thought of it. He hadn't been able to save Crissy, but *by God* he was going to save Eve, whose voice had saved his own life.

He was supposed to *save* her! That was the way it was supposed to be. Not once in the wild ride here, or while fighting Montez's goons, had it occurred to him that he wouldn't be able to save her.

He *had* to save her. He had to save her to save his own soul, because it felt like his own life's blood dripping down onto the street and draining into the gutter, instead of hers.

He couldn't let the monsters win all the time. His life had to have some meaning, some ability to stop the monsters, at least once.

Kneeling, Harry bent over her, tears pricking his eyes. The last time he'd cried had been over Crissy's lifeless body. The sweetest little girl in the world, destroyed by a monster. He'd cried until he'd blacked out.

He hadn't cried at the grinding, unbearable pain he'd suffered for all the long months of his recovery. All the pain in the world, concentrated in his body, but it hadn't made him cry, not once.

Now tears simply spurted out of his eyes as he gathered up Eve's limp body, bowing over her bloodied torso.

Oh God, why couldn't he *stop* it, just once? What the fuck had he been born for, if not to save Eve? To save all the Eves?

If only he'd been a couple of seconds faster in getting out of the building, if only there hadn't been traffic on the road, if only he'd reacted instantly when she'd left the office instead of waiting like an asshole . . . the *if onlys* piled up, as high as the sky.

Eve felt nearly weightless as he held her in his arms, tears dripping down, watering the blood on her chest. He held her and felt like howling, railing against the sky, the world, fate.

The dim sound of sirens penetrated his head. He'd been in some timeless zone of grief, but the world rolled on. Someone had called in the shootings and the police were on their way.

Harry looked down at the woman in his arms. The police were coming. That meant they'd figure out who she was and her death would be all over the newspapers.

Montez would read it and rejoice.

No, no way would Harry let Montez know that he'd won. That once more, sheer evil had prevailed. Let Montez think she was alive and out there, an ongoing and never-ending threat to him. His men sure wouldn't talk. Harry'd take her away and . . .

He froze, frowning. Eve's eyes had moved behind her lids.

She was . . . she was *alive*!

Oh God, she was alive!

And she was fucking well going to stay that way, he promised himself and her as he rose easily with her in his arms.

The sirens were coming closer. He placed her carefully in the lowered passenger seat of his SUV, rounded the vehicle and fired it up.

He was two blocks away by the time the cop cars arrived. He watched through the rearview mirror as six cops emerged from three cars, guns drawn, checking the perimeter. One reached down and put two fingers against the neck of the fucker who'd held Eve.

Harry rounded the corner and lost them, driving at exactly the speed limit so he wouldn't be pulled over.

He glanced over. Eve was still as death, skin pale as ice except where blood flecks marred the smooth skin, her shoulder and side a deep red. Even grievously wounded and unconscious, she was beautiful. With a voice that was magic.

She wasn't going to die. Harry wouldn't let her.

He'd die himself first.

Chapter 5

Prineville, Georgia

They weren't checking in. Montez had sent three men—three men who'd been trained by the U.S. government at about a million apiece, then he'd taken that training and tweaked it for another million—and they weren't answering. Nothing. It was as if they'd dropped off the face of the earth.

Fuck!

Montez slammed the green silk brocade of the fancy arm of the fancy armchair he was sitting on. He hated being in the dark. Hated it.

The security cameras around the site where that bitch Ellen's cell phone had been geotagged had gone out at precisely 11:47, exactly when Trey had sent a text message.

Package arriving in taxi

And then the cameras blinked off.

At the time, Montez was certain that his men had blanked

the security cameras so as not to leave a trace of the abduction, particularly if they had to off the bitch.

His men had their orders, sure. Montez wanted her alive and he'd made that very clear, but shit sometimes happened.

He told himself he wanted her alive to find out what she knew and to find out if she had any proof she'd hidden somewhere. At some level that was true, but it was also crap.

He wanted her alive because she needed punishing. It was the first thing he thought of every morning and the last thing he thought of every night. Before falling into a shallow sleep and dreaming of her.

Fuck this.

All Ellen's fault. All of it. Goddammit.

The money. It all came down to the money.

When he'd appropriated the pallets of bills that were just fucking *lying* there on the ground without even a fucking security guard, he'd planned on that being the first step. He'd seen it all in one powerful flash. The way to turn his life around, the way to become a *player.*

And he'd done it, hadn't he? The money had bought him enough land to qualify as a fucking country, and enough manpower to form an army.

Security work was low-hanging fruit in the early years of the war. Contracts flowed in like a river rushing to the sea. And then . . . the waters slowed, reduced to a trickle.

A few incidents were reported back to the Pentagon. At first, he didn't take them seriously. So a few Iraqis got offed. Who gave a shit? No State Department or Pentagon official Bearclaw guarded got hurt. That was the bottom line.

But Montez had enemies, and they started a whispering

campaign and the contracts slowed down. There was a lawsuit. Which he won, but it cost him two fucking million dollars.

The shooting range was expensive to keep up, and he was shelling out half a million a month in salary. The company was leaking money and he'd managed to negotiate the last two government contracts by a hair.

If Ellen ever showed up and had anything resembling proof, he was a goner.

The full resources of Bearclaw were now concentrated on finding Ellen Palmer, known as Eve, and wiping her off the face of the earth.

Apartment 8D
La Torre
Coronado Shores

Ellen opened her eyes, then closed them immediately, trying to process the white nothingness covering her entire field of vision. Was she dead? Was this the afterlife? White, flat, featureless?

Forever?

She ached. Every muscle in her body ached, except her shoulder, which burned. Worse was the utter feeling of exhaustion, weakness, helplessness.

The only good news was that if she were dead, it wouldn't hurt so much. Unless of course this was hell.

There was no noise except for some rhythmic . . . rustling sound. Or whooshing sound. Like waves on a beach. But how could that be?

She was lying on her back on what felt like a bed. Her hands moved slightly, fingering rough cotton. Sheets. One hand couldn't move well. She twisted it slightly and something tugged. Tape, a needle. An IV line.

The sharp smell of alcohol, the soothing smell of clean linen. A faint hint of coffee in the air.

A hospital? Or did death smell like alcohol and clean sheets and coffee?

She opened her eyes again and again saw an expanse of something white. Nothing for the eyes to fix on, just a featureless plain.

"You're awake," a deep voice said. Panicked, Ellen turned her head. The world tilted crazily, then righted itself. Of course. That wide, empty expanse was the ceiling.

Right next to her was a man sitting in a chair, looking tired, jaws clenched.

Her gasp sounded loud in the quiet of the room.

The last time she'd seen this man, he'd been running toward her, gun in hand.

Oh God, oh God.

Harry Bolt. The man she'd so foolishly turned to for help. The man who'd betrayed her, the man in the pay of Gerald Montez.

This, then, was the end. She'd run, but not hard enough or fast enough or far enough.

A wheezing, keening sound escaped her lips. It would have been a high-pitched scream, but she simply didn't have enough breath in her lungs to bring it out. Just the whimpering tones of a wounded animal as she tried to run away, bare feet scrabbling for purchase against the slick sheets.

She tried to sit up, but only managed to thrash around helplessly. The IV line was ripped out of her hand and blood pooled out under the bandage.

"Jesus, stop."

The man, this Harry Bolt, stood up immediately and placed huge hands on her shoulders, pinning her down, looking down at her with a frown.

Even in her desperation, Ellen could see he looked ten years older than he had before, deep grooves creasing his cheeks, dark circles under his eyes, cheekbones more prominent.

She struggled against his hands, but it was like struggling against a concrete block. She couldn't move his hands, not even a little bit. They stayed strong and steady on her shoulders, holding her down.

It was the most horrible thing of this horrible situation. She had no chance, none at all. The times she'd escaped Gerald's men she'd done it by reacting quickly, making the smart decision, moving fast.

Everything that had helped her before—swift reflexes, strength, the will to survive—all of it was gone. Her mind was muddy, confused, slow. It had taken her a couple of seconds to even recognize Harry Bolt, as if her mind had to focus just as much as her eyes did.

Even her ineffectual attempts to shake off his hands exhausted her. There was nothing left in her. She'd reached the end of the line, muscles lax and unresponsive. And, deep down, at an animal level, she no longer had the will or the strength to fight.

It was over.

She made one last pathetic attempt to shake his hands off her and subsided, her spirit sinking into her, spiraling down. There was nothing left to her, nothing.

She closed her eyes and felt the cool tracks of her tears at her temples.

"God, don't cry. Please."

That deep voice again.

Hard, heavy hands lifted from her shoulders, took her hand in his. In a second, without pain, the needle was rethreaded into her vein, the bandage gently pressed again to the back of her hand.

Startled, Ellen opened her eyes again and met his. Where she'd been expecting victory and cruelty, all she saw was fatigue and . . . kindness?

What—?

They stared at each other, Ellen's heart thudding slowly. "Are you going to kill me?" she finally whispered.

A spasm crossed his face and his head reared back. "Fuck no! Sorry." He shook his head, looking baffled and worn out. He turned to the room behind him and bellowed, "Nicole!"

Ellen continued watching his face. No craziness, no cruelty. He held himself still, one finger pressed gently on the back of her hand, holding down the tape.

A swift tattoo of heels and a woman appeared in Ellen's line of sight, bending over her.

Ellen nearly gasped. She was the most beautiful woman Ellen had ever seen. Long, midnight-black hair belling down to her shoulders, intense cobalt-blue eyes, fine features, a soft expression on her face.

Was this Harry Bolt's woman? Was *she* the enforcer? Was she the one who would kill her?

It was like having spikes pounded into her brain. With the hand untethered by the IV line and Bolt's hand, Ellen held her head where it hurt, so badly she whimpered again.

Never show weakness. It was a rule she'd lived by all her life, but right now, she was so weak she was rendered down to her rawest state.

Nicole lifted her hand and put it on her uninjured shoulder, the touch light and gentle. "It'll be okay," she said softly. "Everything will be all right."

That was a lie. Nothing would ever be okay again.

Ellen turned her palm over, crooked her index finger in the universal *come here* gesture. Even that taxed her strength. Nicole bent down to her, holding her hair to one side. She smiled. "Yes?"

Ellen arched her neck, trying to get closer, lifting her head a little. It fell back. She had no strength in her neck muscles. Nicole bent closer.

Ellen looked at Harry Bolt, then up at this Nicole woman. She was taking a huge risk. Maybe Nicole had no idea Harry was a killer. Maybe she was his girlfriend and thought he was an ordinary guy.

"That man," she whispered as Nicole bent her head closer. "Be careful. He tried to kill me."

She closed her eyes, exhausted. There, she'd said it. At least someone would know the truth before she died.

Nicole straightened, startled. She looked at Bolt then back at her. Bolt was completely still, the only thing moving his broad chest as he breathed. His face was taut, remote, completely emotionless.

Nicole laughed and Ellen jolted a little.

The laugh was genuine and so out of place in this room of pain and sorrow that it took Ellen a second to recognize it and process it. Nicole sobered as she looked down at Ellen, beautiful face suddenly very serious. Her hand passed lightly over Ellen's hair.

"Harry didn't try to kill you, my dear. Trust me on this. He saved your life. You were walking right into an ambush when he showed up. What's the last thing you remember?"

Ellen's hand opened, scraping lightly along the sheet, index finger pointing toward Bolt. "Him," she whispered. "Running toward me with a gun."

Nicole frowned and looked at Bolt again. "You didn't see two—" Harry Bolt held up a big hand, three fingers up. "Three men?" Nicole finished.

Ellen closed her eyes, trying to remember. It was all a blur. Getting out of the taxi, being slammed, shouts . . . *shouts.*

"Several men there. Yes." Her voice came out a weak croak. What else? "A—a truck. Someone opening the back of a truck. Not a truck, a van." It was all such a blur. Voices, shapes . . .

She opened her eyes.

"Yeah." Harry Bolt's deep voice was hard, rough. "They were going to take you away in that van. I got a chance to look inside it and there were restraints in there. Meant for you."

Ellen's heart skipped a beat at the thought of being in the hands of Montez's men, in handcuffs.

"Did they follow you? Do they know where I am?" Ellen

pushed the words out through the tightness in her throat. Maybe this Harry Bolt wasn't after her, but Montez's men *were.*

Silence. Nicole looked away uneasily. Harry Bolt just stared at her with his fierce eagle gaze. Finally, he stirred. "They're dead," he said roughly. "No one's coming after you, not anymore. Not ever again."

Ellen tried to rise on her elbows but she couldn't. She couldn't hold herself up and felt panic rising at her inability to *move.* She was trapped in this house, with people she didn't know. Her voice rose in panic. "He's smart. He'll have followed you, somehow, they could be coming right now, they could—"

"No," Bolt rapped out sharply, scowling. "No one's coming. We left before the police came. I used a cold gun, untraceable. I blanked out all the security cameras beforehand. Even if by some chance one of the men saw my license plate and called it in, and there really wouldn't have been time—it belongs to a shell company it would take a team of forensic accountants a year to trace. You're safe now and you'll stay that way."

He stated it like a law of nature. Gravity pulls toward the center of the earth. The sun rises in the east. You'll be safe here.

She twisted slightly, and pain shot through her shoulder. A reminder that "safe" was a relative term.

He noticed and reached for a bottle of pills on a table nearby. He took a pill, poured a glass of water from a pitcher and slid his hand under her head.

"Painkiller," he said. "It'll take effect in about ten minutes." He lifted her easily, somehow not hurting her.

Ellen met his eyes as he gently eased her head back on the pillow. She was so weak it frightened her. Maybe she wasn't in any immediate danger, but if she were, she'd be utterly helpless to defend herself. She needed help to swallow a pill.

It had to be asked. "What . . . what happened to me?"

Bolt's mouth tightened into a grim line. "You were shot, but thank God it was only a ricochet. Gave me a hell of a scare there, for a moment. You lost some blood, but it wasn't life threatening. If it had been, I'd have had to take you to a hospital, and you can be sure Montez is monitoring all of them. And anyway, by law, hospitals have to report gunshot wounds. I've had extensive medic training and I had everything I need here. You won't have the most beautiful scar in the world, but you're going to be fine. Maybe later, you can have plastic surgery on the scar."

Ellen shook her head, her hair rasping on the pillow. That wasn't important.

"How—" She coughed, to loosen up her throat. "How long ago? How long have I been . . . out?"

Harry's mouth grew, if possible, even grimmer, long grooves appearing in his cheeks. "Three days," he said, the two words falling like stones out of his mouth.

He looked . . . something. There was some strong emotion there. Anger? At her? Had she been keeping him from something important? Was he mad because she might have put him in danger? She couldn't tell at all what he might be feeling, only that whatever it was, it was strong.

Nicole looked at Bolt then back at her. "He hasn't left your side for three days and two nights," she said softly. "He patched you up and stayed with you. We all offered to help but he refused."

"All?"

"Me, my husband, Sam—you met Sam at the office—our housekeeper, Manuela, and the third RBK partner, Mike. You haven't met him yet."

Nicole's voice was as calm and smooth as if they were at a tea party and she were describing the guest list.

"We all said we'd be willing to stay with you. You developed a high fever the first night. Very high. Luckily, antibiotics took care of that. You drifted in and out of consciousness. Harry stayed right here. Except for going to the bathroom"—Nicole pointed to a door in the corner—"he hasn't budged from that chair in three days."

There was no answer to that. Ellen was mulling that piece of information over in her dull, sluggish mind when Nicole's face changed.

It was remarkable. Where before she'd just been this beautiful woman—okay, the most beautiful woman Ellen had ever seen up close and not on a screen—all of a sudden she smiled brightly and became even more gorgeous. She simply glowed.

Ellen had a limited field of vision. But the reason for Nicole's blinding smile walked up to her, put a big arm around her waist and bent to kiss her.

For the first time, Ellen noticed something about the way Nicole moved, a heaviness around the belly. She was expecting. And by the way her husband kissed her, it was a happy occasion.

Ellen's mom had had a couple of pregnancy scares while Ellen was growing up and it had been anything but an occasion for rejoicing. Usually because the man in question was already across the state line, and Ellen's mom didn't know how to take care of herself and Ellen, let alone another kid.

But this guy looked like he was going to stay, and was really happy about the pregnancy.

Sam Reston. The man Kerry had trusted to get her away safely. The man who'd saved Kerry's life. The man she said Ellen could trust.

A tiny lingering tension left Ellen's body.

There was still a question mark against Harry Bolt, but Nicole and her husband Sam felt safe.

Reston's head lifted and his eyes met his wife's. He smiled, a secret smile just for the two of them. For an instant, they were encased in a cocoon of love, the outside world completely forgotten.

Oh, man. A pang of . . . what? Jealousy? Longing? Whatever the emotion, it hit Ellen squarely in the chest. She was really weak; that's why tears pricked her eyes.

But still. She'd never loved anyone like that and no one had ever loved her like that. She'd never even *seen* that kind of relationship. Her mom had specialized in deadbeat boyfriends who were mainly out for a temporary bedmate and often just a bed.

Must be nice to be loved like that, she thought.

Reston turned to her and smiled. It transformed his rough face and made it almost . . . handsome. She wondered if a smile would do that to Harry Bolt's face, even though he looked as if he'd never smiled. Not once in his life. As if his face would crack if he smiled.

"Hi." Reston bent over the bed so she could see him more clearly. "Welcome back. We were a little worried, even though Harry here is a really good medic. He took good care of you."

Her eyes slid over to Harry Bolt. Maybe. Was she expected to say thank you?

"So . . . we're okay here?" Ellen desperately tried to read Sam Reston's eyes. They were dark and featureless, except when he looked at his wife. Then they burned. "Nobody can find me here?"

"Yeah, you're safe," he said.

"She needs a little more reassurance than that." Nicole jabbed an elbow into her husband's side. He looked as thickly muscular as Harry Bolt. He probably could barely feel the jab. "My husband here tends to be . . . protective of me. I don't think he'd let me be here if he felt there was any danger."

"Damn straight," Reston growled. "There isn't anything that can lead Gerald Montez here and it's going to stay that way."

For how long? Was she just expected to stay here—wherever *here* was—forever?

It was too much. Her body didn't have any energy left, not for speculation, not for hope, not even for fear. There was simply nothing left.

She closed her eyes, murmured, "S'all right," and heard a rushing noise as the world went black.

Chapter 6

She was just so fucking beautiful.

Harry knew Nicole and Sam and Mike thought he was being heroic or something, not leaving her side, but it wasn't that. Bolt cutters and a crane couldn't make him move.

All he wanted to do was watch her, and rejoice that she wasn't dead.

Another minute—hell, probably another second—and she would have been dead meat. Harry had seen so many dead bodies. You'd think he'd have become inured, but he hadn't.

And a dead woman's body . . . man. That just fucked with his head.

And a dead *Eve.* He didn't know if he could have recovered from that one.

A second later, and *poof!* He wouldn't be sitting here, holding her slender hand. He'd be burying her in the cold, stony ground, not even knowing her real name.

Harry knew that once he was dead, it was over. He'd done some good; he'd tried to, anyway. If he died before Sam and

Mike and Nicole did, they'd remember him. And Nicole and Sam's little girl would too, because he intended to stick close and be a good uncle. But basically when he died, that would be it.

Not Eve.

She was magic. If civilization survived, a thousand years from now people would be listening to her voice, to her songs. Some poor fuck who was hurting in the dead of night would listen to her and get enough out of that magic voice to face another day. A little light of beauty shining in the cold, dark world.

Who knew how much more music she had in her? She'd basically saved his sanity if not his life, and she'd only recorded two CDs. If he could keep her alive there was lots more where that came from.

He really respected her talent and her courage.

So . . . why the three-day woodie?

Because, well, that was part of it too. He was ashamed of himself, but there it was. He'd sat for three days and three nights looking at her face, memorizing the shape of it, the swooping line of her eyebrows, the thick lashes a shade darker than her hair, still and lush along her cheeks, the delicate line of her jaw, curving around to that pointed little chin with a tiny little dent in it. The little hollow at the base of her neck where the collarbones met. The soft, shiny hair pooling around her head, forming a russet frame.

Actually, keeping that hair had not been a good idea. It was a magnet for the eye. She should have chopped it off and dyed it a dull brown.

It wouldn't have made her less beautiful—she'd need to

burrow in a gunny sack for that—but at least she wouldn't have a beacon around her head.

Every single line of her was gorgeous—and fragile. So fragile. The long, narrow hands with the long, slender fingers, which he just knew had coaxed that gorgeous music from some keyboard. Even just lying there, one mottled from the IV line, they were prettier than any hands he'd ever seen before.

In every way, this was a woman any healthy male would instinctively protect. *Want* to protect.

How could there be sick fucks in the world who wanted to hurt her, kill her? How could there be sick fucks who'd hurt any woman, any child?

It still baffled him. He was thirty-four years old and he'd been around the world more times than he could count and he still couldn't wrap his head around it. How could any man *do* that?

And *this* woman, with the once-in-a-lifetime voice . . . he couldn't even begin to imagine hurting her.

Fucking her . . . well, that was something else.

If he had to be painfully honest with himself, that was part of the reason he wouldn't leave her side.

He couldn't.

It was as if, even unconscious, she'd thrown out invisible tentacles and lashed his dick to her bedside. His very, very hard dick.

Oh man.

He'd spent the past three days with a perpetual hard-on and nothing would make it go down. He willed it down by sheer grit when Nicole or Sam or Mike came in to check on her. Wouldn't that be something? For them to come in and find him with a woodie for a wounded woman? Harry disgusted even himself.

But when they were gone, when there was no one but the silence and Eve and himself, whoa.

He'd tried everything. Tried not looking at her, but that was a no-go from the start. He was here to keep an eye on her, to make sure she didn't crash, to respond to any need instantly—or that was what he told himself. The truth was, he couldn't take his eyes off her. Telling himself every single second that he was an asshole didn't help at all. He just accepted the idea and sat in his chair as if glued there.

Harry wasn't used to hard-ons he didn't do anything about. True, he'd only just started having them again after a year in Afghanistan—a no-sex zone if ever there was one—and then another year-long hiatus after he'd died and then been pumped back to life again on a medevac helicopter on its way to Ramstein via Bagram. Four surgeries and intense physical therapy just to be able to stand upright had taken the wood right out of his pecker, it did.

He'd spent many months in a wasteland of pain, acutely aware of the siren pull of death, because not even with all that he knew of hell on earth did he believe there was a hell after death. There was nothing after death, and for a long, long time, the thought of that blissful nothingness was so tempting, he knew his brothers kept a close watch on him so he wouldn't fall into its siren embrace.

Because death sounded an awful lot like peace. At some deep level, he'd been angry at his brothers for keeping him from that peace.

And then—and then this woman and her voice came along and he'd found something outside himself that gave him the strength to go on. She hadn't given him peace, but she'd reminded him that the world held glories still, beautiful things, even if he wasn't seeing them. Her voice had brought him back from the dead.

The hard-on was a real, real surprise, because though her voice was soft and sensual, her music wasn't sexual to him.

The woman herself was, though. And how. Man, from the second he saw her he'd been stunned senseless. It was only the realization that she was in mortal danger that punched him back to reality.

When he wanted sex and there wasn't a woman around, well, his hand knew its way around his body. He could take care of himself.

Not this time, though. Nope. After a couple of hours of wood, disgusted with himself, he'd gone into the bathroom to take care of the problem, and that's when his little head blindsided his big head.

His fist wouldn't do it. Just wouldn't cut it. Little head didn't want the fist. Little head wanted *her.*

Another woman wouldn't do it, either. That was the real shocker. There wasn't one woman Harry could think of that he desired a billionth as much as he desired the wounded woman on the hospital cot in his study.

No fist.

No other women.

He was shit out of options.

So he kept the woodie while watching over her. It hurt, but

it would have hurt him more to leave her side. To think that she might need something and he wouldn't be there to get it for her, man, no way.

Eve moaned and he straightened, watching her face. Her head shook from side to side, eyes beating behind her lids, tracking back and forth like windshield wipers. Whatever she was seeing in her sleep was wildly troubling, scaring her. Fierce cries were throttled in her throat as if even in her sleep she was trying to be quiet. Her breathing speeded up, became ragged. Her legs thrashed.

A choked whimper rose up out of her throat, the cry an animal might make in the woods at the sight of a terrible predator. A minute before dying. Her heels scrabbled against the sheets as in her dream she tried to scramble away.

Tears leaked from the corners of her tightly shut eyes and the whimper became a keening sound that made the hairs on his forearms and his neck rise.

Nightmare city.

Harry knew all about that. Knew all about the terrors of the night, particularly when they echoed the terrors of the day.

Harry reached out a hand to shake her gently awake when her eyes suddenly opened, wild and terrified. She gasped, the sound loud in the dark room.

"It's okay," Harry said immediately. God, he wanted to wipe that terrified expression off her face. "It's just a nightmare. Don't worry. You're safe."

"Safe," she repeated in a whisper and shuddered. She said it as if it were an unfamiliar word, an unfamiliar concept.

Something in his chest tightened. Safe. He was going to keep her safe or die.

Harry reached out with his thumb to wipe the tear tracks on her cheeks. "Yeah," he said, his voice hoarse. "Safe."

Her eyes roamed around the dark room, though there weren't that many features for her eyes to fixate on. Harry belonged to the Minimalist School of Home Decoration.

The room wasn't giving her any clues, so her gaze roamed right back to his face.

Harry was used to masking his emotions, had done it all his life. The world was one huge knife just waiting to plunge into soft hearts. He kept a hard carapace around him at all times, surrounded by very strong *don't fuck with me* vibes.

That didn't work here. She needed reassurance and Harry didn't know how to do reassurance. So he did the only thing he could. He let down his defenses, for just a moment.

Everything down, shield, vibes, even his woodie, a little. Because the thought of this magical, beautiful woman wounded and terrified and encased in nightmares was a real downer.

He looked her straight in her huge, frightened eyes. They glowed green with an almost unearthly light in the gloom of the room, reflecting the lights in the living room. She stared at him, eyes wide, unblinking.

"You're *safe* here, absolutely," Harry said again. He'd raised his voice a little and it echoed in the room.

She blinked and breathed out. He realized she'd stopped breathing for a minute. A vein had been pounding in her neck when she opened her eyes, the nightmare so vivid her heart pumped blood to her extremities to face the danger, even though her muscles were too weak to use it. But now the pulses slowed.

Her right hand unfurled, like a flower blossoming. Gently,

Harry sandwiched her hand between his. Her hand was cold, soft, delicate. Her eyes dropped to her hand in his, then back up to his eyes.

The lashes drooped.

"Safe," she murmured and fell back asleep.

"*Is* she safe? Really?"

Nicole stepped out of the bathroom in one of Sam's favorite nightgowns. Of course, all of them were his favorites. He loved them all, though he loved stripping her out of them even better.

Billows of fragrant steam boiled out from the open bathroom door. Sam closed his eyes and inhaled. The steam wafted the smell of her fancy shampoo and conditioner and moisturizer and hand cream and foot cream and cuticle cream . . . He'd become an expert on how many creams and lotions a woman needed in the ten months of their marriage. Each smell was fabulous, but swirled together, and with Nicole's unique fragrance underlying it . . . Jesus.

"Hmm?" Sam enjoyed watching his wife walking around their bedroom. His bedroom had changed beyond recognition since their marriage. It was full of girly things now. The bed had *flounces* around the bottom, the sheets were floral prints, there were watercolors on the wall, scented candles everywhere and crystal bowls full of flower petals. Silk drapes. Feminine overkill.

But Sam was a tough guy. He could take it.

Shit, to be married to Nicole he'd walk over red-hot coals barefoot. Putting up with some froufrou nonsense was nothing.

He walked to her, to his miracle of a wife, put his arms around her, pulled her to him. The baby was just starting to show and he could feel the little bump against his own belly. He loved that bump.

Up until it started to show, the little girl Nicole was expecting was more an idea than a reality. They knew she was expecting and in the meantime everything was exactly the same.

And then the baby bump and the morning sickness brought it home to him every day. They could feel her moving around in Nicole's belly. He could feel *his child* in her.

Sam loved his wife, he loved his brothers, he would die for her and for them without question—but they weren't his blood. This child growing inside Nicole would be the only human being on the face of the earth who was his blood relative.

It gave him goose bumps every time he thought about it.

Sam bent down and kissed his wife, moving one hand up to cup the back of her head. He was lost, just like that, at the touch of his lips to hers. He took a deep, shaky breath, every hormone in his body pinging to painful life, and held her more closely, right hand moving over her back.

The satiny material felt real good but her naked flesh, he knew from experience, would feel even better.

He knew this nightgown. There was a zipper . . . oh, yeah. And when the two back panels separated, he slid his hand over her satiny skin, pulling her even more tightly against him.

Making love to a pregnant Nicole was mind-blowingly erotic. He was heavy, so missionary would soon be out. Still, there were plenty of other positions, and Sam knew every one.

Sam picked her up and lay her on the bed gently and stood

there for just a moment, looking at her. He had an almost painful hard-on, but just looking at her, knowing she was his, was his wife, carried his baby . . . shit, that was the best.

"Sam," she said softly. "Is she?"

Oh man. He could smell her excitement, a smell that was imprinted on the most primitive part of his brain. Granted, Nicole would probably say that all of his brain was primitive, but in the most basic, reptilian part of his brain, that smell, *her* smell, would remain with him till the end of time. Nicole's arousal.

How excited was she?

"Sam?"

Only one way to find out. Eyes fixed on the dark cloud of soft hair between her thighs, Sam cupped her, right there where he wanted to be. Waggling his hand made her open her thighs to him and his hand slid in to cover her completely. The lips of her sex felt puffy, slick . . .

"Sam!"

He inserted a long finger and yes—thank you God—she was wet. Excited. Not as excited as he was, but then that was impossible.

He shifted forward, inserting his thigh between hers, opening her up.

"Oh, for—" Nicole slapped his hand away and clamped her thighs shut. "Will you *listen* to me?"

Startled, Sam's head lifted and he saw with consternation that she was looking exasperated. At him. It wasn't the first time he'd seen that look on her gorgeous face. What had he done now?

"Yeah, honey?" He smiled down at his wife. "What is it?"

"For the third time, *are* we safe here? Is Eve safe?"

Sex was instantly booted out of Sam's mind. He smoothed back a lock of blue-black hair, tucking it behind her ear. He looked his wife straight in the eyes and spoke soberly.

"Oh, yeah. Mike cleared her room. He said that he left absolutely nothing of hers behind that could in any way identify her. You trust Mike, right?"

"Yes," Nicole said softly. "Absolutely."

His heart gave one of those hard little pumps it sometimes did when he realized all over again how lucky he was. He'd have married Nicole even if she didn't get on with his brothers, but the fact was, they loved her almost as much as he did. Lucky, lucky man.

"We've gone over this, Harry and Mike and I, and we can't find a way that Montez can connect her to us. So she can recover here and we can set her up in a new life when she's ready."

Nicole gave one of her mysterious smiles.

Sam frowned. "What?"

She shook her head, the scent of her shampoo whooshing out from her and messing with his head.

"Nothing. Absolutely nothing. So—it's okay, then?"

"Absolutely." Sam picked up her hand and brought it to his mouth, utterly sober and serious. "I would never—and trust me when I say never—let you be near any possible danger to you and our child. You have to believe me."

"Oh!" Nicole looked startled. "I believe you, of course I do."

"Good." Blood was rushing out of his head, down, down . . . Sam bent and ran his mouth along her neck, and gave her a little nip. She loved that. It turned her on. He knew that through long practice. Nicole shivered and at that moment he lifted her leg and gently slid his cock into her. "Now." He pulled slowly out, then pressed back in. "Where were we?"

Prineville, Georgia
Bearclaw Headquarters

"I'm sorry, sir," the snooty political aide said on the phone. "But Senator Manson is unavailable at the moment."

Montez gritted his teeth, pulled the handset away so the bitch wouldn't hear him blowing his breath out in one controlled flow. Control. He needed to keep control.

"All right," he said, when his voice was steady. "When will the senator be available for an appointment?"

Never, you moron.

The unsaid words hung there, quivering.

Montez remembered this assistant to the chairman of the Senate Armed Services Committee, a tall, bony creature with two PhDs, one in political science and one in physics. Ferociously ambitious, biding her time on a senator's staff before she joined some hotshot think tank for ten times the salary.

She'd disliked Montez on sight, and it had been mutual.

"I think I can safely speak for the senator here," she said finally. "There has been some . . . adverse publicity lately with regard to your personnel. This is not a good time for the senator to be linking his name to yours. At least until all the ambiguities have been cleared up. Good day."

A click.

She'd hung up on him. Montez stared at the dead handset. The bitch had hung up on *him*.

He knew exactly what she was referring to. The media storm surrounding the shooting deaths of three of his employees in San Diego had shaken the company to its foundations.

He had sent three of his best operatives to pick up one woman. One small woman. It hadn't even occurred to him that they should go in without ID because it hadn't occurred to him that they could fail.

But they had. Spectacularly. Three men shot dead on the streets of San Diego. Three men with Bearclaw ID on them. There had been nothing Montez could do about it because the police got there before he could wipe the identities clean.

Three good men, former soldiers, crack shots all of them—and a lone woman had defeated them. Which was insane, of course. Especially when that woman was Ellen.

Montez had offered countless times to teach her to shoot. Lots of women got off on guns and, even better, got off on men who were good with guns. Not Ellen. She'd rejected his offer to give her lessons with barely masked horror, as if he were offering to teach her to kiss cobras. And she wasn't turned on by gunmen, either. Otherwise she'd have been in his bed long ago and this whole fucking mess would never have happened.

So it sure wasn't Ellen who'd gotten the drop on his men. Men who'd been mission-ready, primed to grab her. No one could ever get the drop on his men, Montez would swear to that.

But the fact was, someone had. One person. Though the San Diego PD had been incredibly tight-lipped with him—

you'd have thought *he* was the suspect, they doled out so little intel—Montez had hacked into their system and discovered that the bullets that had killed his men had come from one untraceable gun and one gun registered to Bearclaw.

One gun. One man.

One man had taken down three of his men, men who'd been ready for trouble. And he'd done it so fast and neat he hadn't left any trace behind. It was almost unthinkable.

Bearclaw had had a lot of really bad publicity from that. It was dying down only because the police had zip—no leads, no gun, no shooter. The bodies had been autopsied—and yes, big surprise, cause of death was massive trauma from bullet wounds in all three cases—and handed back to Montez.

None of the men had families, so Montez had made a very big deal of giving them a hero's funeral on company grounds, and had given all his employees the day off to attend. And all the while inside he'd been seething, furious that they'd botched a job that should have been *easy,* a fucking cakewalk, and had instead become a huge albatross around Bearclaw's neck.

It might, in fact, cost him the company, if he wasn't careful, because he needed that Pentagon contract, real bad, and right now.

Ellen Palmer was now in the hands of a very slick operator who could take three of his men out in minutes and get away laughing.

She was now ten times more dangerous than before.

Montez needed outside help. He hated to admit it, but it was true. He needed someone outside his company, someone who was *better* than the men in his company. Someone who would never be connected back to the company.

He knew one man who would fit the bill.

He dialed a number he'd committed to memory.

Piet van der Boeke. Originally South African, now a stateless person. The last sighting of Piet had been way up the Congo River tracking down a rebel warlord.

He'd done it, too. Piet was legendary. He didn't have a company or a stable team of men. He recruited men for each job based on the job specs. He was plugged into the world and he found the best man or men for the job each time. But he worked best alone.

Montez didn't want an army. He wanted one man, Piet. He'd done Piet a favor in '02, a big enough one that Piet had given him his private number and told him to call if he needed help.

Piet was a fine soldier, one of the best. But there were fine soldiers everywhere. Montez employed more than three hundred of them himself. Men who knew how to handle themselves in a firefight, how to shoot, how to survive an op. They weren't a dime a dozen, but there were plenty of good soldiers around.

What Piet did, better than anyone in the world, was track.

His mother had died giving him birth. Piet's father ran a hardscrabble farm three hundred miles from Johannesburg and, more important, at least two hundred miles from another white woman. Piet had been wet-nursed by the wife of the chief of the local Nguni tribe. The chief had basically brought him up with his own son, who had been like a brother to Piet.

While year after year Piet's father sat morosely over his unpaid bills, drinking bottle after bottle of whiskey, Piet was out in the wild, learning to follow sign. He enrolled in the South African Army the day he turned seventeen and proved to be a natural soldier.

But what was extraordinary was that Piet could track in all kinds of wilds. The savannah, the uplands of the Hindu Kush, Grozny, Peshawar, Belgrade . . . you name the place, country or city where a man had gone to ground and Piet would find him.

When he went private, he had clients coming out of his ears.

He'd been a natural at following sign for big game and he was a natural at modern technology. It was said that the U.S. military didn't want Bin Laden to be found, otherwise they'd have contracted Piet van der Boeke—then Bin Laden would be either in the dock or six feet underground.

The cell rang. He had strong encryption and knew Piet did, too.

"Yeah?" A bass tone in a strong Afrikaans accent, so strong even the voice distortion program couldn't quite mask it. The *yeah* sounded like *yiah*. But the voiceprint would be completely altered. Even if NSA could pluck this conversation out of the air—and the odds of that were a billion to one—there would be no voiceprint match.

It occurred to Montez that since he had no idea where Piet was, he could be waking him up. If he was in West Africa, where he heard Piet had set up headquarters, it'd be midnight where he was. But the voice sounded strong and completely alert.

"No names. We met during Moondust. I headed the team. Do you remember me?"

Moondust had been a private black op just over the Pakistani border, technically illegal. Piet and four of his men had been guarding and leading a *New York Times* journalist on the hunt for al Qaeda's bioweapons expert. The journalist had gone on to win a Pulitzer. What the article didn't mention was that their GPS had died on them and they had gone four miles into no-no land, over the border into Pakistan, and had been shot up by a cove of Taliban.

Piet had wasted every single tango but he was left with two dead and two wounded, including the journo. If the ISI, the Pakistani secret service, had caught them, the journalist would have been thrown into jail till the end of time and Piet and his men would have been hanged, not without some pain first.

Montez had been following a lead that one of Bin Laden's comms guys had his headquarters in a mud hut. But the mud hut was just that—full of goat herders with their goats—and Montez was ready to pull back with his men when he got an SOS from Van der Boeker.

Technically, it wasn't Montez's business at all. In fact, technically, helping mercenaries was illegal. But hell, it was only a couple of miles out of his way, he had manpower up the wazoo and it was a chance to get an IOU out of Piet van der Boeke. Better than money in the bank.

His team cut communication with their FOB for a couple of hours and went out to rescue Piet, his wounded and the journalist. The journalist was sworn to silence about the rescue, wrote an article that was turned into a book that became a bestseller and didn't once mention Piet or Montez.

"Yiah. I remember you, mate. You need something?"

"Bad. I'll send a company jet for you. Are you near Lungi?"

The Freetown airport was the staging area for most of western and central Africa. Busy and corrupt, a place where one more corporate jet wasn't going to be noticed.

"Yiah."

"Can you be there by fourteen hundred hours local time tomorrow?"

"Yiah."

"Good. The corporate jet will be in the name of—"

"I know the name." And he hung up.

Montez stared at his screen for a moment, then powered down the laptop, knowing that he'd just done the only thing possible to correct a really bad situation.

Yiah.

Chapter 7

Prineville, Georgia

Piet van der Boeke hadn't aged in the past eight years, Montez thought. His face had been deeply tanned and weatherbeaten eight years ago and still was. He was still wiry and lithe, moving swiftly down the steps that had been rolled up to the Gulfstream at the private airfield as if he hadn't just spent the past ten hours sitting down in a pressurized compartment.

"Thanks for coming." Montez clasped his hand at the bottom of the stairs. Piet's grip was strong and dry.

"No problem."

A car and a driver were waiting. Two minutes after Piet stepped onto the tarmac, they were driving away. The flight had been registered as a cargo flight. No one knew Piet was in America.

They both understood that the chauffeured limo was no place for a briefing, so they didn't talk. Montez opened a small fridge and silently handed Piet a bottle of spring water. Unlike most mercs, Piet was a teetotaller.

Montez had the driver go straight into the detached six-car garage that was connected to the main house via an underground passageway. Piet made no comments, just observed everything with his sharp gaze.

For the first time, Montez wondered what someone would think of his home. It was more than thirty thousand square feet and as luxuriously appointed as the crazy fag decorator from Atlanta could make it. Piet was an observer. He carefully studied his prey, both in and out of their natural habitats. Montez wondered uncomfortably just what Piet made of his own habitat, what he thought it said about him.

He shook that thought off irritably. He was going to offer Piet over half a million bucks for this job—who cared what the fuck he thought?

Finally, they were in Montez's study. Montez had his study swept for bugs twice a day. The windows were specially treated to break up laser beams; there was a thirty-foot perimeter around the entire house with motion sensors. No one was going to thread in a snake camera and mike.

They were secure.

Montez indicated a big, comfortable leather armchair and watched as Piet sank into it. After pouring himself a generous portion of a twenty-year-old Talisker he sank down into another one.

Piet might be a teetotaller, but that was no reason for Montez to deprive himself.

He studied the South African for a moment. Piet sat quietly, accepting the scrutiny. "I'm offering half a million," Montez began, and Piet held up a big, callused hand.

Montez didn't even let an eyelash flicker, but inside he was groaning with dismay. Had Piet's prices gone way up? Half a million was a real stretch for him at this particular moment, with no government contracts in sight. Fuck, what would happen if Piet's price had gone up to a million? He didn't even know if he had that kind of spare cash.

"I don't want any money," Piet said, and Montez's mouth fell open before he was able to school his face back to blankness. "You saved my life and I owe you. I always pay my debts. But I do this one job for you and that's it. You never call me again. Is that agreed?"

The bank account in Montez's head went *ping!* He shifted the half mil back onto the assets side and tried not to nod too enthusiastically his agreement. "Fine by me. And thanks."

Piet waved that away. "So . . . who am I after?"

"A woman." Montez watched him carefully. For some reason, some mercs had problems with women and kids, which made no sense to him. A gig was a gig.

But Piet merely nodded. "Who is she?"

"Ellen Palmer." Just saying the name made Montez's blood speed up. "Used to be head accountant here."

Piet's eyes were the lightest blue Montez had ever seen. In direct sunlight they looked so pale they were almost white. "Tell me about her."

Montez gulped down the rest of his whiskey to calm himself down. Just thinking of the bitch . . . "What do you want to know?"

His voice was calm, thoughtful. "What kind of woman is she? Flashy, loud? Quiet, bookish? Any hobbies? Is she the friendly kind? What does she look like?"

Well, that was something Montez could answer easily. He slid across two photos, both taken at a company picnic a year and a half ago.

Piet studied them carefully, spending about five minutes on each photo. Montez fidgeted in his chair. Damn, he wanted to get *going*. Finally, Piet spoke. "So tell me, tell me everything."

Montez did, leaving out only the dollar amount of the missing pallets in the Green Zone in Baghdad and what happened to Arlen Miller.

"And then?" Piet's voice was so fucking calm.

"And then the bitch just . . . disappeared. Been gone for a whole fucking year. I had men fan out, I had her phone tapped, I got her mail, I checked her credit cards. Nothing. It was as if she had vanished off the face of the fucking earth."

"But then you ran her down again."

Montez squinted suspiciously. "How the fuck did you know that? No one knows that."

"It only stands to reason. You wouldn't have called me in now if you hadn't. You found her and then you lost her."

Put like that, it made Montez's blood pound heavily through his veins. She'd slipped right through the fingers of two of his guys in Seattle. And it was a good thing his three guys in San Diego were already dead because he wanted to kill them all over again for letting her get away. Again.

"Yeah. There's this singer who became real popular, only no one knows her real identity. She goes by the name of—"

"Eve," Piet said, and raised his eyebrows slightly at Montez's expression. "Music travels the world, Gerald. And there's only one singer in the world whose identity is a secret. Most of them are—how would you Americans put it? Very *out there*. How did you connect the two?"

"Sheer chance." Montez felt the bile rise up in his stomach and swallowed it back down. "There was a radio on in the background at a restaurant about ten days ago. I heard a voice, a song. I'd heard them before. Ellen was singing that song in her office one day. It turned out that the song was written by this Eve, and I recognized the voice and the song, so I put two and two together."

"I understand she's been pretty good up until now about keeping her identity a secret," Piet said thoughtfully. "I heard she recorded in a separate room from the musicians. And she'd have the money now to buy herself a lot of privacy."

"Uh huh. But she didn't think to protect herself against the one guy who knew her identity."

"The agent."

Montez nodded.

"Where's the agent now?"

"Bear bait in the Cascades. He *was* in Seattle. So was she. She'd been there nine months."

"What did you get out of him?"

Montez ground his teeth. "Not much. He didn't know her real name, he never found out where she lived. She'd tell him where to meet him—some café or park bench. She never gave him zip."

Piet narrowed his eyes. "Except, I'm guessing, her cell number."

Montez nodded. "Yeah. It was a prepaid job, but we got an

address from that. We were waiting outside her apartment. Bitch never showed and then the cell was turned off. The next ping we got was two days later, in San Diego, of all places. Had to really scramble to get men there. Luckily, three of my men were working in Tijuana, so they left that job and came up. The phone was in a hotel room. My men called and the front desk said she was out. So they laid out an ambush." He ground his teeth. "My men are *good*. They all know what they're doing. I wasn't anticipating any trouble. In fact, I'd flown back here from Seattle because they had orders to bring her here. I've got . . . business with the bitch and wanted to be ready for her. But something happened and three good men are dead and she's still in the fucking wind."

"She had protection," Piet said.

"Oh yeah." It still burned. "One guy. One gun, one guy." He met Piet's eyes and saw that he understood completely. "Wherever she is, she's got protection."

Piet went silent for a full ten minutes. Montez couldn't stand it. He poured himself another whiskey. He'd puzzled this long enough. Let someone else work it out, goddammit.

Piet suddenly stood up. "Let's go."

"Yeah? Where to? San Diego?"

"No, Seattle." He pronounced it *See-ehttel*. "Nose around. We'll dig up your bear bait, stake it out, rattle her, make her show herself." *Hehsilf*. "Then down to San Diego."

Montez got up slowly, a little dizzy. "If we're going to dig around for intel, you're going to have to do something about that accent of yours. Sticks out like a sore thumb."

"Dude. Can't believe you said that." Piet plastered a hand over his heart, looking pained. His baritone switched to that of a suburban dad who coached Little League, with just a touch of surfer in it. Indistinguishable from a million other American male voices. He shook his head sorrowfully. "Hurt my feelings, man. Don't do that again."

San Diego

The next time Ellen woke up, he was still by her side, looking just as solid, as irremovable as before, only with a few extra lines in his face.

It was morning, late morning of a sunny day, to judge from the buttery quality of the sunshine. The windows were open, light cotton curtains fluttering in the breeze. The wind carried in a soft, regular plashing sound. They were near the ocean.

She moved her head, her hands. No more IV line. Her hands were free. She twisted slightly, ease in her movements. Her shoulder was a little sore, but the fiery pain was gone.

Her gaze roamed quickly around the room then landed back on Harry Bolt's face. He looked older, grooves etching deeply in his cheeks, smudges of exhaustion under his eyes.

"Hi." The deep voice was quiet, one corner of his mouth lifting in a half smile.

"Hi." She felt breathless. It wasn't physical weakness. She felt better, as if someone during the night had lifted that boulder from her chest.

The day was bright and sunny. The sound of the ocean pulsing melded with the faint sounds of a jazz sax in another room. She could smell salt water, fresh cotton and . . . coffee?

She pulled in a deep breath. "Am I smelling what I think I'm smelling?"

A smile flickered on his somber face. "Absolutely. As much breakfast as you can eat." His hand covered hers. "Please tell me you feel hungry."

"Oh yeah," she breathed.

His hand over hers was hard and warm, so warm some heat trickled up her arm. His smile had warmed her, too.

Um, actually, to tell the truth, his smile hadn't just warmed her. His smile had sent a burst of heat running through her entire body, the most amazing sensation. The sensation of . . . of life.

Suddenly, she couldn't stay on her back like a half-dead creature for one second longer. She bent her legs, digging in her heels, lifted herself up on her forearms . . . and found herself sitting up, pillows at her back. He'd lifted her up with total ease, as if she were a child. Carefully and smoothly.

"There you go." He smiled into her eyes and for the very first time, Ellen realized how incredibly attractive this man was. The outsized body, the gorgeous golden coloring—even his stubble glinted gold over that square-jawed face—it all added up to one hugely attractive package. Her fear of him had masked it, but the fear was gone now and she felt it in full.

That, in itself, was amazing. Something about the time she'd spent on this bed, drifting in and out of consciousness, had drained the fear right out of her.

She had a sudden muscle memory of him holding her hand for hours. Days.

"What day is it?" she asked suddenly.

"Thursday."

Ellen blinked. "I've been out for *four days*?"

"You haven't been out all this time, no. You woke up a few times." His eyes narrowed. "You don't remember?"

Maybe. Awareness was seeping back into her consciousness, a friend that had been gone too long. "Where am I?"

"My place. This is my study."

Her eyes refocused on him. "I've been here four days," she repeated, just to get it straight.

"Yeah." His lips pressed together into a thin line. "I told you this before. I didn't take you to a hospital. You were shot and hospitals and doctors must report gunshot wounds to the police. I imagined you didn't want that. Those men meant business."

"You're right," she whispered with a shudder. "I didn't want that."

"And I didn't want it either, because you can be sure Gerald Montez is watching hospitals and monitoring police stations." He pulled his chair closer to the bedside, the chair's legs scraping along the hardwood floor. He tightened his hand over hers. "He has no idea where you are. And it's going to stay that way."

"Um, to tell you the truth, I don't know where I am, either."

"I told you. My place."

"Which is?"

"Coronado Shores." His eyes widened at her blank look. "You don't know San Diego, do you?"

Ellen shook her head, amazed that it didn't hurt. "No, I've never been here before. I'm assuming it's along the beach, because it sounds like the ocean out there. So, you patched me up." She moved her right shoulder, lifted her right arm, moving with ease. Above all, that horrible feeling of weakness was gone.

She looked down at herself. She had a vague memory of wearing a huge T-shirt, but now she had on a pale peach nightgown. Pure silk. Absolutely gorgeous. Possibly La Perla. "More than patched me up. You seem to be pretty prepared for caring for women who've been shot. You've got a hospital bed, an IV line, presumably surgical instruments." She brushed her hands along the soft peach material. "Silk nightgowns. Do you have a habit of rescuing women?"

It was the wrong thing to say. His face froze, something, some strong emotion—grief?—crossed his features.

Harry stood up suddenly. "No, I don't often rescue women. The hospital cot and IV line come from my partner's house. His wife, Nicole, cared for her father at their house until his death."

"I sort of remember a beautiful woman coming into the room. I thought she was a dream. Was that your partner's wife?"

"Yeah. They were going to throw the hospital stuff out after her father passed away but they ended up storing it. I have a medical kit for—for emergencies. Nicole lent you one of her gowns. There are several other clean ones in a drawer for you. So as you see, I was equipped to help you. Luckily, you weren't shot directly. The bullet was a ricochet and it wasn't even that deep. I dug it out, debrided the wound and closed it up again. You have eight stitches. I used self-absorbing thread—they'll be gone in a day or two. They're not perfect, you might need some plastic surgery later—"

Ellen never wanted to be near a needle again in her life. "No, I'm good."

"You were out of it for a long time, but from what I could tell it was more exhaustion than the effects of the wound. Am I right?"

She nodded. A year on the run, and then almost seventy-two hours straight without sleep. There'd been bone-deep fatigue. Ellen drew in a deep breath, sending out feelers to the far extremities of her body. She still felt a little weak, but completely rested. Another thing—

"You were there, weren't you?" Ellen pointed to the chair by the bed. "All the time."

He hesitated a moment before answering, eyes watching hers. To see how she'd react? "Yeah. Except for bathroom and shower breaks. Nicole brought me some food from time to time. But mostly, yeah, I was here."

Wow. Four days and four nights, on a chair. "I'm sorry. It wasn't necessary. I don't think that I was in danger of dying or anything. You didn't have to do that."

"I did." His eyes bored into hers, that fierce light brown reflecting the light from the windows. "At times you were . . . restless. You had nightmares. You'd wake up terrified, panting. I couldn't leave you alone to wake up in the dark in a place you didn't know."

Now, *now* she remembered. The dreams that turned so quickly into nightmares, waking up terrified in the dark, a strong steady hand holding hers.

Warmth and strength, in the night. Not alone, in the night.

It was the reason she was feeling . . . refreshed. When she'd slept, when the nightmares weren't chasing her, it had been deep.

She hadn't slept one night through to morning this whole past year. She put herself into a shallow sleep, alert in some part of her brain to the noises of the night. A barking dog, a car's exhaust, a fighting couple, a slamming door—they'd all been enough to wake her, gasping for breath, grasping for the knife she kept under her pillow. The knife that was still under her pillow in her miserable little studio apartment, which she'd never see again.

These past nights, there had been stretches of real sleep. At some deep level, the animal part of her had known she was safe.

For now, there was no danger to her at all, unless you counted starvation. She opened her mouth to ask for some food, but he beat her to it.

"Okay. I'm going to get you some breakfast now." One last, intense glance, as if to make sure that she was okay, and he stood, hand still on hers.

She remembered he'd had on a dress shirt in his office, and now he was wearing a black tee that hugged his huge chest, the sleeves almost too small for those bulging biceps. He had an unusual figure—absurdly broad through the shoulders with big arms, very lean and narrow through the waist.

He lifted his hand and she immediately felt the chill, which was ridiculous. Warm wind was blowing in through the open French doors.

Ellen watched him walk away, tall, enormously broad-shouldered, T-shirt and jeans rumpled, and she felt bereft. Which was crazy. Her body might be sending frantic *it's all okay, don't worry* signals, but she didn't know this man at all. Granted, he might not be Satan's spawn or a spy for Gerald, but he could be anything. Mean, violent, even crazy.

Though as she was telling herself this, even she didn't take herself seriously. A violent, crazy man didn't spend four days and four nights on a chair in case a woman he didn't know woke up alone and afraid.

There were clattering noises and more good smells. Of bread and cinnamon, the dark chocolaty notes of coffee underlying them.

Ellen looked down at herself. Her shoulder itched, but it didn't hurt at all. She lifted her arm and sniffed. Someone had given her a sponge bath. She smelled fresh, of soap. She shifted the nightgown and looked at the neat bandage on the upper right chest. The bandage looked freshly applied. Curious, she lifted the tape and saw a wound with small, neat black stitches. The scar wouldn't be that big.

The skin was clean and clear around the wound. No infection.

Underlying all of that there was something else. A—a lack of something. Fear. She wasn't afraid.

Fear had been her constant companion this past year, day and night, expecting at any moment the incursion of masked men, the punch of a bullet or the hot slice of a knife across her throat.

She'd been afraid and lonely every single second of the past year.

Right now, she wasn't afraid and she wasn't alone. For a small span of time, she was utterly safe. She didn't even question it, this switch inside her that had been thrown. The switch from *Harry Bolt is dangerous* to *Harry Bolt is safe.* As crisp as an electrical switch. Darkness to light.

She couldn't stay long, of course. His business, and the business of his partner, Sam Reston, the one married to the beautiful Nicole, and presumably of the other partner she'd never met, Mike, was to spirit her away. Set her up in a new life. So as soon as she was completely recovered, they'd put some new documents in her hands and point her on a new road.

Alone, of course. There was no question of that.

There was no doubt in Ellen's mind that as long as Montez was after her, she'd be alone. And that might possibly hold true for the rest of her life.

So the important thing now was to savor every second of this time, while she wasn't alone. While there was a man willing to sit by her bedside night after night and who was right now rattling pans in the kitchen.

Though the temptation was there to simply bask in this feeling, she knew she had to become well enough to get going soon. Every minute spent here was a luscious, golden temptation. She couldn't afford to get used to this—to having someone look after her. To having a dangerous man on her side.

Now that her head was clear, flashes of memory were coming back. She couldn't remember every detail of what had happened outside her hotel but the heart of it was that Harry Bolt had come running toward her and had killed three of Gerald's men to save her.

A man like that on your side would make anyone feel safe.

She couldn't afford that. Couldn't afford to get used to the feeling of safety.

Get well and get out.

Step number one was to stand on her own two feet.

Okay. She'd been walking her whole life. How hard could it be to get back on her feet?

Ellen threw back the blanket, slowly shifted until her legs hung over the bed, looked down and swallowed. Whoa. The floor was way, *way* down. She'd never been hospitalized before. Who knew hospital beds were so high?

How to do this? Maybe one leg at a time? Shifting her hips, she reached down with her right leg, stretching to find purchase on the shiny hardwood floor. Ah. One foot planted on the ground, now the other—

Harry appeared at the door. "What would you like—*hey!*"

Ellen placed her left foot on the ground and her knees buckled. She gasped, stretched out her hands to break her fall and found herself swung up against a hard chest.

Her startled eyes met his. How had he moved so fast? He'd been at the door then he was right beside her to catch her fall. She hadn't even seen him move.

A memory stirred. Harry racing at what seemed like the speed of light toward her, gun out, already shooting . . .

The man was fast.

He was scowling. "What do you think you're doing?"

"Um . . . getting out of bed? I'm not an invalid. And you yourself said the wound wasn't serious."

Harry's scowl smoothed out as he looked down at her in his arms, golden eyes glowing.

"You're scared," he said softly. "You're scared of being weak. You're scared he'll find you when you can't fight back."

Oh God, it was like he was looking right into her soul. "Or can't run away."

"You don't have to be scared about that," he replied, in a matter-of-fact tone. "He's not going to find you. No one's going to find you. No one's going to hurt you, ever again."

Ellen glanced down at the floor, so shiny and stable and safe. That safety was deceptive, just as everything else was. She couldn't even stand on her own two feet on that floor.

"I know how you feel." It was so odd, having this conversation while being held in his arms in his study that had been turned into a hospital room. Somewhere there was a light pinging sound, exactly the sound a toaster would make when the bread was ready.

"Hmm?" He'd said something while she was completely distracted by—well, by the most incredible male body she'd ever touched.

Gerald's company had been full of buff men, often with that bodybuilder's waddle that was so unattractive and ridiculous. They all cultivated a real tough don't-mess-with-me air, but it turned out it was all a bluff, because Harry Bolt had beat three of them, hands down.

She could *feel* why he had prevailed. Instinctively, one arm had gone around his shoulders, her other hand braced on his chest. She'd never felt flesh like this before, like skin over warm steel. He was built like a racing engine, muscles long and lean, wrapped around big bones.

"I said, I know how you feel. I know what it's like to feel weak, barely able to stand. It's horrible. I hated every second of it, and I didn't have someone after me. I can imagine how you feel."

Ellen's eyes met his in surprise. He was perfectly serious, sober even. Long grooves in his cheeks, full mouth closed to a thin line, eyes grave. It seemed impossible to her that the man holding her in his arms as easily as if she were a child had been—

"What do you mean? You were *weak*? Weak how?"

Even saying it sounded outlandish. The parts of him she could see and feel—strong neck, the broadest shoulders she'd ever seen, huge sinewy hands—could never have been called weak. He was simply too large a man.

His mouth turned down and he shrugged one massive shoulder. Ellen dipped and rose with the movement.

"Got shot up in Af—where I was deployed, about a year ago. Had four operations in as many weeks. Lost sixty pounds. Couldn't walk for months. Yeah, I was pretty banged up there for a while."

Ellen covered her mouth with her hand, eyes wide. "Oh my gosh! I'm so sorry. It must have been really serious. How did you get back in shape?"

One side of his mouth turned up. "I can't take any credit at all. It was my brothers who forced me to get back in shape. Sam and Mike. You've met Sam, and Nicole. You haven't met Mike, though he's been here quite a few times to check up on you while you were out of it. I wasn't just banged up. I was depressed, too. Probably would have sunk into a sea of self-pity if they hadn't hired the Nazi to whip me back in shape."

"The Nazi?"

"Yeah. He wasn't actually German, he was Norwegian. Bjorn. Man, he was pitiless. Two hundred and fifty pounds of pure mean. He came every day for six months and he reported back to Sam and Mike. When I resisted he said he was more scared of them than he was of me. They would have whupped his ass. Me? At the beginning I was lucky if I could stagger a couple of feet before falling straight on my a—er . . . face."

Ellen soaked up the tones of affection when he spoke of his brothers. She hadn't realized that Sam and Harry were brothers. They didn't look anything alike, except for both being tall and exceptionally well built. But wait. Sam was named Reston. And Harry's last name was Bolt.

"How are you brothers? Same mothers, different fathers?"

"Blood brothers, not real brothers. Long story. Tell you some other time. But they weren't the only ones who helped me. You were responsible, too. I'm here because of you."

She simply looked at him, too astounded for words. "*Me?* I never met you before. How could I have had a hand in your healing?"

"Your voice. I listened to your music endlessly in the night. I think, in a very real way, your music saved my life, Eve." His deep voice had turned low, his gaze so intense it was like being touched by hands. "I wanted to stay in this world, in this life, to hear you sing. Hell of a thing to say, but it's God's truth."

"Ellen," she whispered.

"What?"

"Eve is my stage name. My agent chose it. Eve, first woman, woman of mystery, maybe—I don't know what his reasoning was. But my real name is just plain Ellen. Ellen—" At the last second, bells sounded in her head. She'd been about to tell him her last name, plunge off the precipice of trust, but she windmilled her arms in her head and stepped back. She trusted Harry, but right now telling him her last name made her feel . . . almost naked.

And she was, almost naked.

In his arms, she was suddenly, acutely aware of the fact that underneath a thin silk sheath, she was naked.

Harry, on the other hand, seemed to be fully aware of it. He wasn't fondling her, but he wasn't pretending she wasn't in his arms, either. His left hand—his very big and very warm left hand—enveloped her left breast, his right hand curved around her thigh.

It was the closest she'd ever been to a man in . . . in years. And to tell the truth, she'd never been this close to such a strong man, such a . . . a *male* man.

There'd been Ben, studying for his accountancy degree, like her. Nice guy, beanpole thin, much more interested in derivatives than sex.

And Joe, who had a Toyota dealership and was thirty pounds overweight and kept trying to stick what felt like a marshmallow in her.

Harry felt like another species. Bigger and stronger and tougher and faster.

He was looking down at her, gaze going from her eyes to her mouth and back. As if gauging whether . . .

Oh yeah. In answer to his unspoken question, Ellen tightened her arm around his neck and closed her eyes.

His mouth was as warm as his hands, only much softer. He tasted absolutely delicious—of coffee and cinnamon and butter. His twisted his mouth slightly, opening hers, and his tongue licked hers.

She pulled in a startled breath at the electric current that ran through her at the touch. Searing heat that took her breath away.

It was way too intense and she pulled back.

His mouth was slightly wet from hers and it was a huge temptation to run her finger over his lips, just to see again how soft they were, the only soft thing in a hard man.

He lifted his head, just slightly, so that his mouth was only an inch from hers.

Harry's eyes were golden flames, burning hotter than the sun.

"Where were you going just now?" He was so close his coffee-tinged breath washed over her face.

She had no breath to answer him.

Oh God. The kiss had electrified her. This was insane. It was just a *kiss*. It wasn't as if she had never been kissed before. But it was the most sensuous kiss she'd ever had, almost as intimate as sex itself. And, oh, it had been so *long* since she'd been held. Since she'd even touched another human being, even the most casual touch, let alone this assault on the senses.

She erected a small mental barrier against him, against the oh-so-tempting and oh-so-dangerous feelings of sensuality and safety he sparked in her, and stiffened a little in his arms.

"I, um, I need to get to the bathroom." *And I need to get out of your arms.*

Harry turned and carried her into the bathroom, gently putting her on her feet, holding on to her arms.

Ellen found that she could stand. The support of his hands felt good, too good, and she took a small step back, away from his grasp. "I hope you're not thinking of staying here while I use the bathroom."

She was painfully aware that she was in the presence of an amazingly attractive man, dressed only in a wrinkled gown, even if it was silk, with bed head and probably moss growing on her teeth.

Being on the run meant many things, including a loss of dignity.

Those golden eyes saw too much, understood too much.

"I won't stay if you don't need me." His golden gaze was keen, he searched her eyes, took a moment to answer. "But I'm going to be right outside. If you need my help, all you need to do is call. I'll hear you." He nodded to the sink. "There's an unused toothbrush and a travel-sized tube of toothpaste there. Soap and a towel are on the counter."

"No moisturizer?" she teased.

"Sorry. Whoa." He shook his head, surprised. "Not even a hint of moisturizer. But I'll buy some later. Nicole can tell me what to buy and where. Or better yet, I'll have her buy it." He stepped back out of the bathroom. "Remember, I'm right outside," he said, and closed the door.

Ellen used the toilet, then walked to the sink. The bathroom was very large and very spare. All the fixtures were white and the walls were tiled in white. There were white glass-fronted shelves on the left-hand side and a huge shower on the right.

There was no trace of a woman. Ellen told herself that it was absolutely no business of hers if a woman lived here or even if a battalion of women trooped through his bedroom and bathroom nightly, but she was whistling in the wind because the spurt of relief she felt at seeing his toiletry items—one comb, one brush, one toothbrush, one half-squeezed tube of toothpaste, an electric shaver—on the sink was unmistakeable.

The brand-new plastic-wrapped toothbrush and travel-sized tube of toothpaste had COMPLIMENTS OF THE HILTON HOTEL on them.

She eyed the shower, tested her knees, and thought, *What the hell.* A second later the nightgown was on the floor and she was in the shower.

Bliss.

She'd lived in such miserable hovels over this past year. They had reminded her of the places she'd lived in during her childhood and that she had worked so very, very hard to put behind her.

Hard work, intense study, focus like a laser beam to get her degree while holding down two jobs, all that hard work at her first big job, and yet this past year had brought her back full circle to what she'd fought so hard to escape.

The dirt-cheap motels as she made her way west, with the rust stains in the toilets and the pubic hairs in the shower. The rented rooms with a grudging trickle of hot water. She knew those kinds of places intimately.

She'd made a lot of money on Eve's records, but it had all gone to the company she'd set up to receive the monies. She hadn't figured a way to draw on the money without drawing attention to herself. Her money might as well have been on the moon.

So this shower was pure luxury.

Harry Bolt seemed to have a no-frills approach to décor, but that seemed to be more a reflection of his taste than his pocketbook. He sure hadn't stinted on the bathroom. The shower stall was ten times larger than her last shower in her rented studio apartment and had six shower heads. She stood under the pounding hot water and let herself go.

In one of her under-the-table waitressing jobs she took for a few days in a small town near Denver, another waitress had taken a shine to her. The waitress was flaky, a New Ager, but had been kind and warmhearted. She had a bunch of theories about water—that flowing water takes trouble and bad karma away.

Maybe. Maybe not. But she was sure feeling better.

Ellen hummed. She always sang in the shower. She sang when she was happy, to celebrate. When she was sad, to cheer herself up. When she was frightened, for bravery.

Such a mixed blessing her voice and music had been to her, all her life. Her mother had been a lost soul, living on the fringes of the music world, dreaming of making it big while drinking too much and smoking too much and failing to hold down jobs.

The irony was that her mom hadn't had much of a voice. There might have been something there when she was young, but by the time Ellen was ten, it had long gone. Cindy hadn't taken care of herself, in any way. What little voice she had had succumbed to the cigarettes and the liquor and the unhappiness. First her voice had gone and then her life, when Ellen was seventeen.

And her mother had been so *angry* that Ellen had been given all the talent in the family. When she was little, her mom dragged her around fairs and open-mike bars. Ellen could sing harmony with a wild boar. Her voice held her mother's voice up. But then, as she got older, the owners of the bars started wanting just Ellen. But by that time, Ellen had seen enough of the underside of the music world and had discovered math.

Cool, rational math. So perfect. So shiny and sublime.

Always dependable, always. Two plus two always made four. Everything else in her life was unstable, transient, unpredictable. Once she discovered math, there was no going back. She finished high school a year early and in college simply dove into her studies.

Music was no longer necessary to eat. It became her private joy. In the shower, driving, on walks. A private joy and solace.

Like now. Stressed and uncertain, scared and without a future, Ellen poured the music out of her like the water from the showerheads, and both cleansed her.

Out of the shower, it took her only a few minutes to be ready. She couldn't find a hair dryer, so she simply toweled her hair as hard as she could and combed it. No moisturizer, so once she was dry, she put the nightgown back on, and that was it.

She placed her hand on the door and hesitated. The shower and the singing had taken her out of herself for a little while, but behind that door was reality, waiting to take a big bite out of her.

A man who'd saved her life, a man she found almost insanely attractive, was waiting there. For the moment, he'd spread a mantle of protection over her, but she couldn't huddle there forever.

Apparently, what RBK did was place women under threat in a new life. Harry Bolt hadn't managed so far because she'd been wounded. But Ellen could only imagine that he was hoping she'd hurry up and get better so he could get back to his life.

In a day—two, three, maybe—she'd be on her way. Maybe he'd wait till the stitches were completely absorbed. So maybe she could have as much as a week, feeling the lack of fear like a gentle, warm wind on her face.

But sooner or later, she'd be out in the cold. Relocated to somewhere improbable, like North Dakota or Wyoming, though if they gave her a choice, she'd choose mild winters and sunshine over snow any time. But still. This, as in so many things over this past year, was out of her control.

So she'd find herself in some strange town, with a new identity and a new name to get used to. Scared of making friends, working low-level jobs. Keeping her head down. And now, never singing, ever again.

Her heart beat painfully at the thought.

This moment, this precise moment, she thought. Remember it. Feeling warm and unrushed, with a paladin behind the door, safe.

Remember, because it won't last.

She pushed the door open.

There she was!

Harry nearly dropped to his knees. The sounds coming from his bathroom had been so heavenly, he had to pinch himself to make sure they were real.

The music coming out of her mouth had been amazing. If a Martian had to find out what humans were like, all he had to do was listen to Eve. Ellen.

And on top of it, she was herself a beauty, a sort of extravagance of talent. You'd think that having that voice, that ability, would be enough, but no. Who could possibly imagine that a voice like that came out of the luscious mouth of a beauty like Eve? Ellen.

It was hard to think of her as Ellen. Though maybe not, now that he thought of it. If Eve was going to be a beauty, then you'd think she'd be this big, in-your-face beauty.

Instead, Ellen had a fresh, quiet loveliness. Unobtrusive and hidden. You had to look twice to see it, though after you did, you couldn't look away, ever again. Clear, pale, poreless skin; large, uptilted green eyes with heavy lashes; small, straight nose; slightly oversized mouth that made you think of music and, well, sex.

She was small, slender, with a narrow ribcage, which was strange because when she sang jazz, she could belt it out like a smokin' mamma.

She came out of the bathroom hesitantly, first sticking her head out, as if waiting to see if danger lurked, then pushing the door wide open. The movements of a woman who was still afraid, who'd been on the run for a year.

She was right to be afraid, because that fucker Montez was still after her and would be for the rest of her life unless Harry stopped him. Preferably, stopped him dead.

Her running days were over, though. Harry would stand for her.

Part of the hesitation was over him, he knew that. He'd done everything possible to reassure her, but it was clear that her last memory had been of him running toward her at breakneck speed with a gun, and then she'd woken up in a strange place with a bullet wound.

The human mind works on all sorts of levels. It is capable of fine sentiments and refined thinking, which is very good while drinking tea and discussing the politics of the day and the latest movies.

But what saves your life is the primitive part of your brain. The one that takes signals from the world as it is, not as you'd like it to be. The part of your head that pings and sends up smoke flares when dangerous men are around.

Harry was a dangerous man.

Harry looked at her through the eyes of a mercenary, a man trained to break people. She was sleek and fit, but slender. She moved with the grace of a dancer, not an athlete. She was extraordinary, with a once-in-a-generation talent, beautiful and graceful—and prey.

They'd break her in five minutes.

Her luck couldn't hold out forever.

It wouldn't be luck operating in her life from now on, it would be Harry, and he'd bend the fates his way. He'd bet on himself against any man, and he was highly motivated.

Not to mention he could always count on his brothers, Sam and Mike. The three of them were unbeatable. You didn't want to mess with Harry Bolt, especially when he was backed up by Sam Reston and Mike Keillor.

She was watching his face, trying to take her cues from him, looking a little lost and maybe even scared. His usual expression—or so his brothers told him—was grim. He knew how to scare and intimidate; he had that down pat. But now he needed to hearten.

A smile, that's what was needed. And he knew how to do it, too. Tighten muscles at corners of mouth, show teeth . . .

By God, it worked! Ellen's face lightened and she smiled a little in return.

Step number two, feed her.

He took her by the hand and turned toward the kitchen. For

the first time, he was glad he had a big apartment. When Sam had found it for him, he'd hated it. It was so big and empty, with room after room he didn't need and didn't want. It was still mostly empty space, because he'd never taken the time or the trouble to decorate.

But now he was glad that it took a while to get from the bathroom to the kitchen, because he could hold her hand. Her hand was small and soft in his and it felt . . . good. Damned good.

He nearly snorted, thinking of what Mike would say. Mike, Mr. Unromantic, Mr. Fuck-'em-and-leave-'em. Holding hands wasn't part of Mike's style. Harry wouldn't have thought it his style, either, though it had been a long, long time since he'd touched a woman in any way.

Maybe that was why he got off on this so much. He was just holding her freaking hand, something kids did on a playground, not that he'd ever held a girl's hand when he was a kid. As a kid, everyone had avoided him. His household had been bad news even in the slums they'd lived in.

Now he got it, totally. Got why there were all these gauzy ads on TV, youngsters holding hands in a park, oldsters holding hands in the old folks' home.

It was nice. It was more than nice. It was warmth and connection. She looked up at him as they crossed the huge, bare expanse of his living room and smiled. He smiled back, lost himself in her eyes, and barely missed smacking his shin on the coffee table.

He instinctively shortened his strides, slowed down to keep pace with her. She was still weak and moved slowly.

Fine with him. He'd walk holding hands with her till sundown if he could. He was still savoring the feeling of her palm against his, trying to figure out the last time he'd held hands with a woman, when they finally arrived in the kitchen.

Her eyes widened when she saw what was on the table. A French press full of steaming coffee, a big platter of bacon and eggs and toast, two stacks of silver dollar pancakes and a small pitcher of blueberry syrup.

And—because Nicole had insisted—a big bowl of peeled and diced fruit and a couple of jars of plain low-fat yogurt, which he thought tasted like cardboard. But you didn't say no to Nicole. That was the law.

Harry held out a chair and she slid in as if her knees wouldn't hold her any more. He frowned. She was still weak. She needed food and rest and exercise, in that order.

He slid into the chair at a right angle to hers. "I can't claim all the credit for this breakfast," he said, pouring her some coffee. He held up the milk pitcher and raised his eyebrows. She nodded and he turned her coffee a pale tan. "Nicole and Sam's housekeeper decided a couple of months ago that I needed fattening up, and she's just continued bringing down food by the bucketful ever since."

Her eyes widened. Harry knew what she was thinking. He was a solid two twenty. It was all muscle, but no one looking at him now could possibly know that he'd been reduced to bone and gristle a year ago.

She'd taken two silver dollar pancakes, poured four molecules of blueberry syrup over them and was eating daintily.

Everything about this was just so great. Eve, in his kitchen. Okay, Ellen. But she was also Eve. And—unexpected bonus—lusciously beautiful.

The hot water of the shower had put some rose under the ivory. Her colors were just incredible. The sun was shining in through the kitchen window and she lifted her face into it, closing her eyes.

Harry hungrily watched her face as the sunlight brought everything to life. The deep-auburn eyebrows, delicately arched, the long, lush eyelashes slightly lighter at the tips, the full mouth so deeply red it didn't need lipstick—unpainted, it was enough to bring a full-grown man to his knees. Not to mention the dark-red hair that revealed a thousand colors in the light, from dark brown to coppery red to streaks of blond. It was thick and glossy and starting to curl as it dried. A curling loop hung over her shoulder and he had to dig his fingernails in his palms to force himself not to pick it up and run it through his fingers.

They'd kissed, yeah, okay. But women had this invisible rule book men weren't allowed to read, and he didn't know if some time had to pass from kissing her to fondling her hair.

He'd have the right to touch her soon, though. And not just her hair. All over. Oh yeah, he would.

"This is delicious. Thank her and Nicole for me."

"You can thank them yourself," Harry said easily, as he transferred half the bacon and scrambled eggs to her plate. "We're invited to dinner at Sam's tonight."

For some reason that alarmed her. Her head rose and the coffee cup which she'd been holding to her mouth trembled. Harry reached out and cupped her hand with his.

"I don't want to be any trouble," she said. Her voice was tight and strained. "As soon as I'm better, I'll be on my way. With some help from you and Sam. So, really, there's no reason to include me in any dinner invitations."

Harry listened calmly, refraining from rolling his eyes. He didn't even dignify that ridiculous statement with an answer. She was here and she was staying.

Instead, he leaned forward and watched her eyes. It wasn't a hardship. In the morning light they looked like the finest green marble, with darker veins of color running through them. Back in his office, her eyes had been bloodshot with fatigue, dark purple smudges under them. Now the whites of her eyes were as clear as a child's, the skin underneath fair and unblemished.

"Why did you run?" he asked. She sucked in a little breath, the sound loud in the silence of the room. "You came to us for help, you were safe with us, but you ran away. Why?"

Ellen put the cup down carefully on the saucer, focusing on her hands, as if it were a difficult and delicate task. She looked up, finally.

"I thought—" she began, and stopped.

"You thought?" He gave in to temptation and picked up the deep-red lock that had fallen forward and smoothed it back. Fuck the rule book. "What did you think?"

She met his eyes and he nearly winced at the misery in them. Beautiful deep-green eyes full of pain and sorrow and a deep loneliness. She sighed. "You know I got your name through Kerry. Or the woman you know as Kerry because that's the name you provided her with."

Harry nodded. He wasn't the one who'd set Kerry—or Dove, or whatever the hell her name had been originally—up in her new life, Sam was.

But had the roles been reversed, had it been Sam who'd been wounded, Harry or Mike would have been the ones to help Kerry into her new life. Her story had been terrifying. A rich, powerful, brutal, alcoholic husband who'd put her into the hospital over and over again, and who sooner rather than later would put her into a grave.

"She shouldn't have talked," Harry said gently. If she hadn't talked, Ellen would probably be dead by now, but they drummed into the women's heads that no one—*no one*—was to know their story. It was their first line of defense. No one was to know, ever.

Shelters had their hotline, which was the way the women found their path to RBK. It was way too dangerous to have an informal network of women talking among themselves. The men after them were brutal, but they weren't necessarily stupid.

"Yeah." Ellen nibbled at a corner of a piece of toast, then put it down, pushed the plate away. "She knew that—believe me, she knew that. We became friends almost despite ourselves. We were both waitressing off the books. I could just tell from what Kerry was reading and the way she spoke that she was well educated, way overqualified for what she was doing. We just drifted together, I think, because we were both so . . . so *lonely*."

Harry nodded again. He knew. The women they spirited away had to keep their heads down for the rest of their lives, otherwise they were dead meat. But women are hardwired to make connections. They have to do real violence to themselves not to.

Unlike guys.

If Harry hadn't had Sam and Mike, he'd have spent the worst periods of his life—after Crissy's death and after Afghanistan—completely alone, never speaking to another human being. And while he'd been wounded, he hadn't even wanted company. Sam and Mike pushed themselves into his life, never taking no for an answer. Because Harry's instinctive response was to turn his face to the wall.

"So you became friends? Told each other your stories?"

She sighed. "Not really. Neither of us sat down to 'tell our story,' as you put it. It's more things that slipped out. I told you how this guy stopped by and asked about me. When she told me, she saw how panicked I was. She put that card in my hand, said that if I needed help to turn to Sam Reston in San Diego." Her mouth tightened. "But then last week, like I said, I was coming back to my room after the evening shift. It was dark. I rented a room in a bad part of town and was used to being careful, being aware of my surroundings. But more because it's an area of drunks and addicts than anything else. I thought Gerald would never find me. But there he was—one of Gerald's men, dressed as a bum."

"Must have freaked you out."

Ellen gave a shaky laugh. "Yeah. You could say that. I keep a little running-away kit in my purse at all times. Cash, a big, floppy hat, sunglasses. I ran. They'd be watching airports and stations, I knew that. The only thing I could think of was a bus. I just hopped on the first bus south, went to Portland, then San Francisco, spent the night in one of those seedy all-night cinemas that show classic movies. At least it wasn't showing porn—I don't think I could have stood it."

"You watched the Thin Man movies." Harry could see it—a terrified Ellen on the run, huddled in the dark in a movie theater. Alone and scared. "Nora Charles."

She huffed out her breath. "Yeah. I was so tired, so scared when I called, it was the first name I could think of."

"Here. Eat that." He pushed the plate back to her and put command into his voice. He didn't normally do that with women, but he made the exception with her. She needed to eat. More than that, Harry needed her to eat food he'd provided for her. "And after you've finished, you can tell me why you ran from us."

She slanted him an amused look, those brilliant, uptilted eyes narrowing. "Yes, *sir!*"

Damn straight, yessir.

She ate half of what was on her plate and pushed it away again. "Before you say anything, I'd love to finish everything on the plate, it's all delicious, but I simply can't. My stomach is cramping."

A hot flush of shame shot through Harry. In his zeal to see her eat, he'd completely forgotten how much Sam and Mike had had to coax him to eat when he'd first come back to San Diego a broken man. His stomach had rebelled at nearly everything. For a time there, he'd eaten with either Sam or Mike standing over him until he choked down every bite.

"Okay," he said gently. "Now talk. Why'd you run from us?"

"It was your faces," she said.

Harry's brows lifted. Granted, he and Sam weren't beauties by any stretch, but still . . . "Our faces?"

"When I mentioned Gerald and Bearclaw. You knew him and you knew the company, I could tell. And you looked at each other. It was quick, but I caught it. You run a security company, like Bearclaw. I thought I'd jumped straight into the frying pan."

"Yeah, we know Montez," Harry said grimly. "But trust me, RBK isn't anything like Bearclaw. That fuckhead Montez—pardon my French—cost Sam four of his men in country. Bearclaw and its men are a menace. We'd love to get back at them. That's what you picked up on."

She paled, a long, slender hand moving up to cover her mouth. Her voice was low, shaky. "Oh God, I'm so sorry. I ran for nothing. I put myself and you in danger for nothing."

Harry couldn't stand to see her upset. He pulled her hand away from her mouth and brought it to his own.

"You couldn't have known," he said softly. "It's not your fault. Being able to react fast has kept you alive so far. You couldn't have known that we're Bearclaw's enemies, not friends. But the big question is, how did they track you down? How could they be waiting for you at your hotel?"

"I used my cell phone as an excuse, but then I realized I really had left it at the hotel. It's still there."

"Actually—" Harry reached back to the counter and threw a plastic object onto the table. "Your cell is here."

Ellen reacted as if he'd thrown a snake onto the table. "Oh my God! He can track us! He can tell where I am!" She was fumbling for the controls when Harry put his hand over hers to still it.

"No, he can't track us. It's off, and Mike removed the battery and the SIM card in your room. While I was taking a bullet out of your shoulder, Mike was removing all traces of you from the hotel room. It was just your cell and a travel toothbrush, but they're gone. And he wiped down all surfaces with bleach. He checked the phone very briefly while in your room—Montez would know you were there anyway if he sent men to snatch you—and he saw that you'd only called one number."

"My agent's number. I bought a cheapie cell just to communicate with him. He didn't really understand why I wanted to remain anonymous, thought it was some kind of PR ploy, but he played along. It's a prepaid. No one should have been able to trace me through it unless . . ." Ellen's voice died as she lost what little color she'd had.

"Unless they got to him," Harry finished for her. He pulled out his own cell. "Let's call him."

"No!" She pushed his cell away, her voice rising in panic. "Oh my God, no! They'll trace it back here. They'll trace it to *you*! You'll be in danger, too."

Harry opened his cell again. God, she was worried about him. She was on the run for her life, and she didn't want to put *him* in danger. He didn't usually explain himself, but this time he made an effort.

"Don't worry," he said gently. He held his cell up. "It's a special phone. Or rather, a special software program. The call is routed through a couple of servers and, anyone tracing it will think the call originated from a cell about fifty miles from Calgary, Canada. The cell is billed to a company we've set up that has two dead men as owners. It's better than being an anonymous prepaid because it fu—er . . . messes with people's heads. Anyone trying to trace it just wastes a lot of time."

She just watched him, pale and trembling and the most beautiful thing he'd ever seen.

He'd memorized the number, punched it out, listened to the rings at the other end. Tried again. "Home number?" he asked quietly.

Ellen gave him the number. Another minute, listening to the phone ring and ring.

"Where else can we try?"

She was trying to hide her agitation. "I've never known him not to pick up his cell. He lives on that damn phone. Where's a computer?"

Harry led her into the living room, to his laptop. He switched it on, switching on the anonymizing program at the same time. No one was going to be able to trace anything back to this laptop, or the IP.

She was feverishly typing. "Oh no! He hasn't updated his Facebook entries in a week, and he hasn't tweeted in a week either." She lifted troubled eyes to his. "This is so unlike him. He's so proud of staying connected. What are we going to do?"

There wasn't much choice. Harry had a friend in Seattle, or rather he was a friend of Mike's—a former Marine turned SWAT member. "The only thing we can do," he said. "Call Seattle PD."

Chapter 8

San Diego

"Two silk shirts, three cotton sweaters, a cotton skirt, two pairs of jeans and a couple of sweat suits, one powder blue and the other hot pink. It'll look great with your coloring," Nicole said triumphantly, pulling clothes out of boxes. "And . . ." She stretched the word out, reaching behind the sofa and pulling out a beige-and-pink bag. "Voilà! La Perla," Nicole breathed, more or less like one would say, "Voilà! The *Mona Lisa*!"

Ellen peered inside and blinked. Silk and lace and satin, in sherbet colors. Wow. Better than the *Mona Lisa*, oh yeah.

She pulled out a pale-lilac silk bra and panty set with lace inlays and held them up reverently. They were pure works of art. She was just about to hold the bra up against herself when she heard a choked sound and looked over.

The three men of RBK were seated on a sofa, happy and replete. They'd just consumed an unholy amount of food, all of it exquisite. Sam Reston and Mike Keillor were looking amused and interested.

Harry looked as if a nuclear explosion had just occurred inside his head, behind his eyes.

Ellen peered down at herself and realized that in her excitement and pleasure, she'd been a hair's breadth from trying on underwear in front of three strange men.

Well . . . two strange men.

Harry didn't feel like a stranger anymore. Harry felt . . . wow. She didn't know what Harry felt like, she didn't have any personal experience with what he was making her feel, but "stranger" wasn't a part of it.

Maybe it was the fact that he'd spent days holding her hand. She didn't remember much, but there had been a definite feeling of something powerful watching over her as she'd slept. A dragon guarding her. A knight defending her.

Nice feeling.

Right now, though, as she let the incredibly sexy and appealing underwear—so unlike her usual very plain white cotton bras and briefs—slip through her nerveless fingers, what Harry was making her feel wasn't nice. It was hot.

Hot as in sex. Sex on a stick.

The three men sitting on the very long and very fashionable couch in Sam and Nicole's very large and very elegant living room were all fit and good looking, but Sam and Mike couldn't hold a candle to Harry.

Harry was like a god. A golden god. Sam was darkly sun-tanned and underneath that he was swarthy. Mike had the light-blue eyes, light skin and dark hair of the Irish. Harry had been painted by the hand of a greater god.

He was as tall as Sam Reston and as muscular, but where Sam was densely muscled, Harry's muscles were tighter, leaner, extremely broad shoulders tapering down to that ridiculously small waist and lean hips. His hair was golden, his skin was golden, his eyes were golden. He looked like an Incan god made flesh.

There was enough heat in his eyes right now to make them glow.

"I, ah . . ." Ellen didn't know what to do with her empty hands. They felt clumsy and tingly. She missed the silky feeling of the underwear that had flowed like multicolored water through her fingers, and it occurred to her in a rush of embarrassment that the only thing better than the feel of the silk and lace would be Harry's skin.

She traced the thick line of his ash-brown eyebrows, uptilted in the center as if he were perpetually skeptical, followed the line of his whiskers down to his neck, where ash-brown chest hairs peeked out from his open-necked shirt.

She had to distract herself, do something.

First, manners.

She smiled at Nicole. "I can't thank you enough for those clothes and for this." She swept her hand down at herself. Nicole had lent her a dark-green linen shift that came to midcalf. On Nicole, who was tall and willowy, it probably came to just below the knee. Ellen had nearly wept when Harry had shown up with the shift. The shift made her feel female again.

Womanly. Particularly when she saw Harry's eyes widen as she came out of the bathroom.

She hadn't had much to work with, but she always carried bobby pins in her purse and had put up her hair and put on some lipstick. You'd think from his look that she was ready for the red carpet at Oscar time. He'd actually held out his arm like some nineteenth-century romance hero and they'd walked into Sam and Nicole's huge apartment arm-in-arm.

The dinner had been fun, relaxed and relaxing. Sam and Nicole were a great couple, obviously deeply in love. Even though Nicole had an almost intimidating level of beauty, the kind that turned heads, she was so friendly that after five minutes Ellen almost forgot how gorgeous she was.

Her husband never did, though. His eyes were locked on to his wife and he rarely let go an opportunity to touch her, even if only to lay a big hand on her shoulder or a quick caress to her cheek. Nicole was just as much in love as he was and smiled at him often.

It was new to Ellen, this degree of marital devotion. Her mother had specialized in either pathetic drunks or manipulating womanizers. Sometimes both at once. She'd had dozens of lovers throughout Ellen's childhood, and not once had a man ever looked at her mother with love.

Mike was much shorter than the other two but looked almost twice as broad. He was fun and had coaxed her into eating more than she wanted. He behaved like a big brother—lighthearted and teasing.

Only Harry had sat throughout dinner silent and brooding, his eyes never leaving her.

All of them had made a huge effort for her.

She turned to Nicole, who was folding the underwear, placing the pretty, delicate items back into the thin wrapping paper and putting them back in the elegant bag.

"Thanks so much, Nicole. Of course I'll pay you back, just as soon as I can access my money."

Nicole waved an elegant hand. "Absolutely not, my dear. I can't tell you the fun I had this afternoon, shopping for you. I'm getting out of the habit of nice underwear, unfortunately." She smiled and rubbed her belly. "I'm getting as big as a whale. Pretty soon I'll just dress in sheets. Who knows if I'll remember what nice underwear is like after giving birth?"

Sam rolled his eyes. "You're not as big as a whale," he growled. "You're *pregnant*. There's a difference." He lay his big hand over her belly, nearly covering it entirely. "And you're more beautiful than ever." She smiled into his eyes and silence descended on the room. Ellen could tell that she'd disappeared for Sam and Nicole. They were wrapped up in their own world.

Mike broke the silence. "Whoa." He held his broad, callused hands up in a time out sign. "Major mush alert. Cut it out, you two. Come back to earth." He turned to Ellen. "Okay, Nicole doesn't want your money, but I know how you can pay her back."

Harry glared at him. "Mike . . ."

"Shut up." He smiled at Ellen. "Sing for us."

"What?"

"Sing for us. And you can play, right? There's a piano in the library. You're this big-shot singer, right? I don't know anything about music, but Harry here listened to you for about forty-eight hours a day, day in day out. So you've got to be good."

Ellen looked around at everyone except Harry. If she looked at him, she'd just drop right down into his golden gaze and never come up for air. "Nicole? Sam? Is that what you want?"

"Oh, yeah." Nicole smiled. "I didn't have the nerve to ask. It's a good thing that Mike doesn't know the meaning of the word *embarrassment*. But now that he's asked . . . yes. We have a piano in the library. It was my mother's, and we had it tuned a couple of months ago. I took lessons on that piano for ten painful years and all I have to show for it is the ability to play a truly awful 'Für Elise' on it. And I need a metronome to do it." She beamed at Ellen, her smile lighting up the room. "Please," she said softly, glancing at her husband, at Mike and at Harry. "We'd love it. Even Harry, who has forgotten how to talk." He switched his glare to her and she laughed.

You could cut a steak with Harry's jawline.

"She's been wounded," he said tightly. "She's just out of bed. I don't think it's fair to ask her—"

"I'd love to," Ellen interrupted. She rolled her shoulder. She couldn't even feel the stitches. "I'm a little stiff in the arm but my hands are okay. And presumably you guys are not going to throw me off the island for a missed note, right?"

These people had taken her in unquestioningly, Nicole had put herself out, shopped for her. Singing for them in return was nothing.

"Come on, then." Nicole led the way into another huge room, this one lined with bookshelves. One thing for sure, this baby was going to grow up with room to play in. Sam was right by his wife's side, followed by Mike. Harry walked in with her.

He bent down. "Are you up to this?" He sounded tense and worried. As if she'd been asked to plow the back forty without benefit of mule instead of playing and singing, which she loved.

She smiled up at him. "Yeah. Don't worry about it."

He walked her to the piano and sat her down with as much formality as if she were about to sing at Carnegie Hall.

To her surprise, the piano wasn't an old family upright but a real grand piano. A Steinway, no less, and beautifully in tune, she found, as she tried a scale from C with her right hand.

Unlike Nicole, she hadn't had formal piano lessons. The only lessons she'd had had come from Buzz Longley, an old honky-tonk guy who'd lived with them for about eight months when she'd been twelve. He'd been an alcoholic and a skirt chaser and a deadbeat, but he knew his music. He'd have been famous if he'd been able to show up on time and sober for gigs, but he was never able to master the art of reliability, or sobriety.

For some reason, he'd taken it upon himself to teach her how to "tickle the keys," as he put it. It hadn't felt like lessons, but they were, she realized now. He'd casually corrected her fingering, made her do scales she hadn't realized were scales because he kept her laughing telling bawdy stories of the Nashville circuit. But he'd taught. And she'd learned.

Buzz had been a man who traveled light: a duffel bag, his snakeskin boots and a keyboard. When he left in the middle of the night, she discovered he'd left her the keyboard.

So though she didn't have formal training, she certainly knew how to accompany herself.

Without really thinking about it, Ellen put together a little

RBK playlist. Songs that played well in a large room that didn't have great acoustics, songs that the three men and Nicole might be familiar with and enjoy.

But first, one of her favorites, one that few people knew.

A chord, another chord, a riff, and she segued into an old Celtic song, "Home of the Heart." Like most Celtic songs, it broke your heart, just ripped it in two. Ellen had always loved it because she suspected that the composer, like her, didn't have a home of the heart. It wasn't a remembrance of something lost but a dirge for something never known. Something eternally beyond your grasp.

When the last note had disappeared into the quiet room, she changed gears, plunging into the exuberant notes of "Sweet Caroline." It wasn't a song women sang often, so her soprano rendering took people by surprise. She'd always loved the song, loved its hopefulness and verve.

Without missing a beat, she moved into "Honky-Tonk Woman," then "Smoke Gets in Your Eyes," then a song she'd composed years ago in college, where she'd stayed in her dorm every weekend studying because she couldn't afford to let any grades drop, while her roommates were having fun outside. It was called "Listening at the Window." It was funny and bittersweet, with an undertone of regret. She followed that with "Bridge Over Troubled Water," "New York State of Mind," "The River of Dreams" and then, because she loved Billy Joel so much and couldn't get enough of his songs, "Piano Man."

While she sang, it happened. It didn't always happen, so she was thrilled when it did.

She lost herself completely in the music. Totally. The entire world fell away. She forgot her troubles, the danger she was in, the fact that she was on the run and had found only temporary refuge here, the loss of her old life, her loneliness and despair . . . all gone.

There was nothing in her head but the beautiful music, her hands playing completely on their own. She didn't have to think of the playing at all. Buzz had called her a natural, and maybe she was. It felt as if the music flowed from her fingers like water from a natural spring. It came from her heart, sure, but it came from the sun and the earth and the very air around her.

She had no idea where she was, who was listening. It didn't make any difference whether there was one person or a thousand or even no one. The music was hers, now and forever, and her soul took ease for the space of the songs.

She finished with her favorite song in all the world: "Stand by Me." It had always seemed like one of those phrases that said it all. Stand by me. All you needed in this life was someone to stand by you.

She sang it slow, like a ballad, a ballad for the lost ones, for all those who'd never had a loved one stand by them, and she sang it like a requiem, because it was a world in which so few stood by anyone. Because so few people were loved.

The last note echoed in the room. She often sang with her eyes closed, completely absorbed in the music. But eventually, as all good things must, the music finished and she came slowly back into the world.

A little sadly and a little reluctantly, because the music had been like spending time in a sun-dappled garden where nothing bad could ever happen. And now she had to return to the world, the real world, full of danger and cruelty.

Her hands fell from the keyboard and she opened her eyes and looked at her little audience, expecting polite smiles, maybe a little light applause.

Instead, Sam and Mike were looking stunned. Harry was looking hard, grim. Nicole wiped a tear from her face.

Ellen was alarmed, particularly at what she saw in the men's expressions. "What?" She looked at Nicole. "It was that bad?"

"God. No, not at all." Nicole gave a watery smile. It was a good thing Ellen liked her so much, otherwise she'd hate her for looking so great even when she was crying. "It was—it was just so moving, so beautiful. Your voice—I can't describe it. And that last song. I never really thought of it that way before. It made me think of my father. You're so talented, Ellen. No wonder Harry listened to you for hours on end."

Ellen looked at Harry, startled as he suddenly stood up and crossed to her. "Time to go home," he said, putting his huge hand under her elbow and lifting. She rose, because it was either that or leave her elbow behind.

Before she knew it, they were at the front door. Harry didn't appear to move fast, but she scrambled to keep up.

"Thanks for dinner!" Ellen managed to call out over her shoulder at three utterly surprised faces. She and Harry stepped over the threshold, the door whooshed shut behind them and they were alone in the hallway.

Chapter 9

San Diego

Harry stood in the elevator with Ellen, going down to his apartment, concentrating on the word *down* because his boner was about ready to punch a hole through his pants.

He stared straight ahead, willing Ellen to stare straight ahead, too, because if she looked down, she'd understand exactly what that abrupt exit from Sam's house really meant.

Harry was sorry for the way he acted. Or he'd be sorry tomorrow, just as soon as some blood returned to his head. Or he fucked her.

Whichever came first.

He didn't even recognize himself. He knew he could be as rude as he wanted to his two brothers; rudeness bounced right off their broad backs. But he'd behaved abominably to

Nicole, who'd arranged a nice relaxing evening for them, never expecting that it would be cut short by a maniac. Nicole deserved better.

And man, Ellen deserved better, too.

He thought his heart would explode listening to her, listening to *Eve,* in the flesh. Singing live, for him, something he'd never even thought of asking from whoever was up there, because it was too absurd to even contemplate.

And yet, there she'd been, in Nicole and Sam's beautiful library, weaving her spell. Listening to her music in the dark—that had saved his life. Listening to her playing live, not five feet from him—well, that had been magic.

And it turned out that this magical voice was attached to a gorgeous face and a stunning little body that had awakened his long-dormant libido.

Nicole was a beautiful woman, almost outrageously so. She had a head-turning, traffic-stopping kind of beauty. Ellen's beauty was quieter, more delicate. She didn't turn heads, or at least not right away. And yet, Harry had barely been able to look at Nicole when Ellen was in the room.

Everything about her fascinated him—her delicate manners, that soft, compelling voice with a smile in it, the clear, porcelain skin and uptilted green eyes. She was a little too thin, making her look incredibly fragile. But that was probably because she'd spent the past year in hiding with murderous thugs after her.

Harry's fists tightened and he saw Ellen look up at him, startled. That was another thing about her, besides looks and talent. She seemed to have an extra sense, another gear to her.

That was great, because it had probably saved her life, but it had also made her run from Sam and him. And now she was picking up on the violent emotions coursing through him at the thought of Gerald Montez after her.

He was emoting aggression and violence and she picked up on that. It wasn't directed against *her.* God, no. He'd rather shoot himself in the chest than hurt her in any way. But how could she know that?

Harry forced himself to relax, muscle by muscle. Wrenched the hatred of Gerald Montez out of his head, like ripping out a strong weed with deep roots. There would be a time to savor killing the sick fuck, but that time was not now.

Now was the time for sex, and he had to get the violence out of his system before he even thought of touching Eve. Ellen.

Killing and fucking were related. He didn't particularly like the thought, but there it was. Soldiers needed sex after a fight—hard, fast, rough sex. Preferably not with a wife or a girlfriend, because what they were getting out of their systems was not nice and not gentle.

Harry rarely trusted himself with a woman after extreme violence because the thought of hurting a woman, even a little, even if she *wanted* rough sex, even if she asked for it—man, no. Just couldn't do it. He steered clear of the ladies when the adrenaline of violence was still sloshing around his system. He either drank or ran or used his fist.

Unlike Sam and Mike, who were lions hitting the bars where women congregated like gazelles at the watering trough. Well, not Sam, not anymore. Harry didn't think Sam was even aware of other women now that he was married to Nicole.

Mike . . . well, Mike was a slut. He'd fuck anything female that held still long enough.

Harry had to eject every ounce of violence from his system right now. He wanted to take Ellen to his bed with a ferocity that scared him. He wanted her bad and he wanted her *now.*

He had to tie her to him with sex. Make her *his.*

Sweat trickled down his back, and it wasn't the sweat of sexual excitement. No, it was the greasy sweat of imagining this amazing woman with her fingernails pulled out one by one and then her fingers cut off with shears, knuckle by knuckle. Imagining her waterboarded, gang raped . . . the horror was coming off him in waves.

That wasn't going to happen. If he had to handcuff her to him, so be it. No one was going to touch her, ever again, unless it was him.

But to be absolutely certain that he could keep her safe, that nothing bad would happen to her, he had to bind her to him. Make sure she obeyed him instantly. No more bolting because he'd slanted a glance at Sam.

So she had to obey him, stay put where he put her, and not take matters into her own hands. A year ago, she'd stepped off earth and had landed on a vicious planet where all the inhabitants were predators. The usual rules didn't apply. The usual rules got you killed, and you died badly. Harry knew that planet intimately. It was where he had been born—his native land.

The best way to keep her safe, tie her to him, to make her do exactly as he said, when he said it, was sex. Hot, intense sex. And lots of it. So much she couldn't even begin to imagine being separate from him. So much so that in danger, she'd do what he said instantly, instinctively.

Because back at that hotel, it had been so close. If she'd zigged instead of zagged, if she'd arrived one minute earlier or he'd arrived one minute later, she'd be dead right now instead of messing with his head.

The elevator pinged, the doors opened onto his floor and like a switch being thrown, the sweat of fear turned into the sweat of lust.

Approaching Sea-Tac Airport

"The pilot's started his descent," Montez said, and Piet grunted.

Montez had slept, eaten two gourmet sandwiches chased with an excellent half-bottle of Shiraz, and watched a movie.

Piet had neither eaten nor drunk anything. He hadn't even used the crapper. He'd spent the entire three and a half hours tapping away at a computer, staring ferociously into the monitor. Out of curiosity, Montez had stopped to look on his way to the bathroom, but all he'd seen had been a grid and some numbers flickering on the screen.

He was sick of the silence, sick of Piet acting as if he didn't even exist, but he didn't dare complain. He just hoped Piet hadn't lost his touch. He had no idea what he'd been doing for the past eight years. Crocheting, for all he knew. Maybe Piet couldn't track any more, maybe—

"Got it," he said softly.

Montez shot up. "What? Got what?"

Piet slid the monitor around and Montez stared blankly at the screen. It looked like one of those kid games—connect the dots. There were about ten dots in a cluster and four outlying dots. All the dots were different sizes.

It made no sense to him. He lifted his eyebrows.

"She's a woman on the run," Piet said. "She'd keep a basic level of preparedness, and I imagine that would include keeping her hands free. So if she had a cell phone, I imagined she'd have Bluetooth technology. A hands-free headset and mike."

Montez shrugged. So?

"Bluetooth emits a radio signal, which can be tracked over time. It's called snarfing. What you're seeing is tracks of the Bluetooth signal, over time. So these are the places she's been over the past three months, which presumably is when she acquired the prepaid. The size of the dot indicates the number of times she was at a specific site and the time spent there. The larger the dot, the closer the connection to her."

Christ. Montez bent forward to look at the dots. Now if only—

As if in response to his silent request, Piet punched a button and the dots were overlaid over a map. A street map, Montez saw. Of Seattle!

All of a sudden he saw it. He was looking at a map of all the places Ellen had been over the past months. She had kept her life simple, in a tight spiral around Larsen Square.

Piet tapped the dots, starting with the largest one. "That's where she rented a room. That's a bar that plays jazz two nights a week, called the Blue Moon. She was there almost every night until recently. Probably working, until she started selling so big. That's a food market, that's a bookshop, that's an Internet café." He tapped a large dot. "And that's a boardinghouse with three rooms. Two men and one woman. One of the men is a traveling salesman who rents the room because it's cheap by the month, but he's only there six or seven nights a month. The other man is a sixty-year-old librarian. And the woman?" He pulled up a photo from the DMV. She was young, pretty, blond. "Name's Kerry Robinson, but the ID doesn't really hold up that well, so I think we can assume it's a fake. And she works at the Blue Moon. I think she's Ellen's friend."

Montez looked at Piet with new eyes. Fuck, the man was good.

"So I guess we're going straight to the woman."

"No." Piet shook his head. "First we resuscitate the agent, make sure he's found. Then we pay a visit to Kerry Robinson. First her agent, then her friend. We're going to rattle Ellen Palmer's cage and smoke her out."

San Diego

Ellen stepped into Harry's apartment warily. There was a completely different vibe here, now. Something had changed up at Sam and Nicole's place. The air had become somehow supercharged.

Harry placed a huge, warm hand to the small of her back and urged her gently forward, as if she were reluctant to enter. Well, maybe she was.

She was so tense it was a miracle her muscles weren't twanging. Her heart was pounding, but she couldn't tell why. Her limbs felt heavy; the air was thick and hot.

Harry moved slightly away from her into the room and she nearly fell forward, as if he had a huge force field around him that generated its own gravity. He was at a sideboard. "Do you want some whiskey?"

Did she? She wanted . . . something, that was for sure.

"Um, yeah." Her throat was tight. Her voice was scratchy. She cleared it. "Thanks."

The gurgle of whiskey was loud in the silence. Harry walked over holding two glasses and pressed one into her hand.

She looked up at him. How could he get more handsome by the hour? How was that possible? In the penumbra he was just magnificent, a golden god looking at her with heat in his golden eyes.

She brought her glass to her mouth and he his, then she hesitated when it was at her lips. They both hesitated. Finally, Harry put his glass down without tasting the whiskey.

"That's not what I want," he whispered.

Ellen set hers down too, blindly. "Me either."

They stepped forward, both of them, and in a second she was in his arms, which was easier for Harry than it was for her.

She wanted—oh so badly—to embrace him, but he was so tall and his shoulders so broad, it was impossible. And then it didn't matter that she couldn't fit her arms around him because he was kissing her and she blew up in flames.

He didn't have any problems, though. One arm was around her waist, one big hand cradling the back of her head, covering it. It was a good thing that hand was there, because her neck muscles went lax.

His mouth was eating her up, tongue stroking hers, and every time their tongues met, heat flashed through her and all the muscles in her lower belly clenched, hard.

Harry lifted his head, slanted his mouth, and it was like another kiss altogether, longer, hotter.

He tasted of the wine they'd had for dinner and the chocolate mousse for dessert and sex.

He slanted his head again, lightly bit her bottom lip, and she moaned.

It was as if she'd flipped a switch. Harry stiffened and tightened his arm around her and she could feel everything, his hard chest muscles, lean belly and huge, erect penis. Heat flashed everywhere in Ellen's body. She just lit up from the inside, this small nuclear detonation that melted her insides, made her legs weak. It was entirely possible that Harry's arm around her waist was the only thing holding her up.

So much power and heat, she instinctively wanted more of it, stepping even closer to him, feet between his, the heat becoming a furnace where their loins touched. Her tongue touched his in a silky stroke and she could feel his penis lengthen.

This time it was Harry who moaned. "Bed," he groaned, when he lifted his mouth from her for a second and she nodded enthusiastically and pulled his head back down to her.

There was some rusty sound coming from his chest and it took her a second to identify it. Laughter. Grim Harry Bolt was laughing.

She smiled beneath his mouth.

Still kissing her and kissing her and kissing her, Harry bent at the knees and lifted her up in his arms—the stuff movie scenes are made of. But Ellen didn't know of many men who could do it like Harry. He simply lifted her in his arms as if she were weightless and carried her away with no sense of strain at all. Not even his breathing changed.

No, wait. While moving in the darkness through the seemingly endless rooms, Ellen lifted herself up a little by tightening her arms around his neck and bit his mouth lightly, running her tongue over his lips, and oh, yeah, his breathing changed.

Lifting a full-grown woman in his arms didn't do it but bumping the sexuality up a level sure did.

It was a good thing his house was mainly empty because Harry wasn't looking where he was going, he was kissing her with his eyes closed as if to savor every aspect of her mouth.

They reached the bedroom and he gently put her on her feet, holding her shoulders in his big hands.

Ellen slowly opened her eyes, hands curled around his sides. Under her palms, she could feel the hard, lean planes of muscle moving as he breathed.

They looked at each other, the soft waves of the ocean coming through his open French windows like the sound of the world breathing.

Harry looked almost in pain, his face drawn, deep grooves bracketing his mouth. He huffed out a breath. His light eyes almost glowed in the penumbra as his hands tightened on her.

"Okay. I don't know how we're going to do this. If I'm not in you inside of five minutes, I'm going to die. My heart will simply explode, and it won't be pretty. But the thing is this—I haven't had sex in a couple of years, which creates two problems. One, I don't have any condoms. If I had any condoms in some drawer somewhere they'd be powder by now. And two, I can't promise to pull out because I'm going to come the second I'm in you. It won't mean anything because the way I feel right now, I will stay hard for the next ten years, but I don't have any control over anything right now." He huffed another breath. "What are we going to do?"

Ellen didn't answer right away. He had on a white shirt, which he'd put on to go upstairs to dinner at Sam and Nicole's. She had the impression a white shirt was about as formal as he ever got. She couldn't even begin to imagine him with a tie. Good, one less thing to worry about.

She reached around and ran her hands slowly up his chest, savoring the feel of him, hard and lean and perfect. He wasn't wearing an undershirt, and as her hands moved up, she could feel male nipples under her palms and she stroked one with a thumb.

Harry jumped. There was no other word for it. His breathing rate increased.

"Ellen?" The cords of his neck were standing out and his jaw muscles were tight. "Did you hear a word I said?"

"Hmm?" Up, up, until she came to the top button of his shirt. She undid it, then the next one and the next one and the next one. Until his shirt hung open, coming together only under his belt.

Oh. It was enough to make her slack jawed. There wasn't a pirate in any romance novel who could even hold a candle to

Harry with his shirt open. His chest hairs were a mat of curly, dark-blond hair that covered his pectorals, thinning down to his belly button. There had never been a chest like this in the history of the world. Even his scars were beautiful.

"Ellen?" He sounded strangled now.

She brushed one panel aside and saw a hard male nipple with a light copper aureole around it. Moving forward slowly, as if in a dream, she nuzzled it. When she licked him there, just to see what he tasted like, he jolted again.

"For Christ's sake, woman," he gritted.

Delicious. He tasted absolutely delicious. Salty and sweet, at the same time.

She smiled up at him. "If you're worried about disease, it's been much longer than two years for me. So I guess we're both disease free. If you're worried about performance, believe me, whatever you do, you'll be better than me. If you're worried about pregnancy, I had to go to a doctor a couple of months back. I had stopped having my period because of stress. I was prescribed a series of shots, one a month, to regulate them. As a side effect, they're contraceptive, too. My last shot was ten days ago, so—"

His eyes had widened as he listened.

"Christ," he breathed, eyes fixed on her face. "Bareback."

It took her a second to realize what he meant. "Oh, um, yeah."

He exploded into action, reaching behind her to take the pins out of her hair, hands moving down to unzip her dress, tugging her panties down before it had had time to pool at her feet, pulling her shoes off, lifting her out of the dress, placing her on the bed, ripping his own clothes off—the bottom buttons of his shirt pinged all over the empty hardwood floor—and coming down on top of her.

Ellen barely had time to register what was happening when he spread his knees, strong hairy thighs opening her legs, reaching down to open her up, and she felt the huge, hot, hard head of his penis and then his hips tightened and he moved hard inside her, shaking and sweating. He barely made it all the way inside when his penis swelled and he exploded inside her, every muscle tight as she felt the hard jets of semen in splashes of warmth inside her.

He was holding tightly to her head, kissing her hard, groaning into her mouth, hips rocking back and forth as he continued spurting inside her and it went on and on, until he finally collapsed on top of her, hot and huge and heavy and sweaty, breathing like a bull.

"God," he breathed then jolted. "Your shoulder!"

He lifted himself up on his elbows, looking appalled, and Ellen pressed down on his neck. "It's okay," she said softly. "It doesn't hurt."

With a deep sigh, he settled back on her, broad chest bellowing, as if he'd just run a marathon.

His breathing gradually slowed. His face was buried in the pillow next to her head.

"You should be singing 'Rocket Man' about now," he said into the pillow, his voice muffled.

Ellen smiled up into the ceiling. "Well, something tells me you're not done yet."

He was huge inside her. Climaxing hadn't made him soften

a bit. His orgasm had had a fabulous effect, though. He'd pumped so much moisture into her that she was able to accommodate him. That first entry had been painful. He was large and she hadn't made love in a long time.

Harry turned his head on the pillow and smiled at her. "Oh man," he breathed, the words a little slurred. "I'm not ever going to be done. Gonna stay right here the rest of my natural days."

She took in a deep breath, or tried to, anyway. The man weighed a ton. It didn't make any difference, though, because who cared about breathing when there were all these fantastic sensations flooding her system?

His back alone was a source of fascination. Huge, broad shoulders, lean, hard planes of muscle that she could follow with her fingertips, one by one. She cupped the ball of his shoulder, pressing hard with her fingers, unable to make any kind of impression. If he weren't so warm, she wouldn't believe she was touching human skin.

Power hummed just under the skin, the kind of power she'd never felt before from a human being. An otherworldly energy, a life force that thrummed up through her fingers, just by touching him.

And it was an incredible aesthetic experience, too, because the man was so ripped. She traced her fingertips and then her palms over his shoulders, his back, following the powerful lines of the muscles. Amazing, just amazing, that any man could be so strong. Over the shoulder blades—steely muscles over bone—along the deep indentation of his spine, the strong muscles wrapped around his ribs. She sighed in deep contentment when she reached his backside, digging in her fingernails, which here too failed to make any kind of dent, and raking them up over his butt.

That had a real effect, as she felt his penis ripple and swell inside her.

"You like that," she murmured against his shoulder.

"Mm." Harry smiled lazily and turned his head just enough to kiss her shoulder. One big hand ran slowly up her rib cage and cupped her breast, thumb circling her nipple. "I like everything."

His thumb made another slow circle and her vagina contracted, hard. "You like that, too."

Ellen barely had enough air to speak, because the rush of heat had incinerated her lungs. He wasn't even moving and it was the best sex she'd ever had.

"Yeah."

"What else?" he asked, nipping her earlobe, moving his mouth lower to scrape his teeth along her neck. Goose bumps broke out all over her body and she contracted again around him.

The neck! The neck was an erogenous zone! She ran the palms of her hands up and down the hollow of his lower back while he licked the area behind her ears and she contracted again. Behind the ears . . . who knew that was erogenous? When he breathed into her ear goose bumps traveled over her skin again, and when he raised himself up a little on his elbows, face suddenly serious, eyes narrowed until only a golden slit showed, and licked her ear, she contracted again. And again.

She could feel his breathing pick up against her ear and could feel against her hands the bunching of the muscles in the small of his back as he started rocking inside her. Small movements at first, each sparking off a wildfire of sensations, then one long, deep plunge, and another, and she stopped breathing, stopped moving, because in another second . . .

Her entire body contracted around him, arms and legs clinging, her sheath clenching tightly around him over and over again, the pleasure so intense it was electric, almost unbearable, his movements sharp now, his penis rubbing right against a concentration of nerve endings, each one going off like a little firecracker . . .

The bed was creaking, slamming against the wall, and they were both sweating, every molecule of their bodies conspiring to make them cling together, everything so intense she wanted to scream, but she couldn't because he was kissing her so hard, tongue deep in her mouth. Each breath she took she breathed in Harry, every move she made brought him closer to her, his chest rubbing against hers as he worked inside her, hard belly slapping against hers, so that it was as if his entire body were making love to her, from his mouth to his toes.

Closer, she wanted even closer, to all that power and strength and heat. She held him even more tightly, entwined her legs around his, and bit him on the jaw in her excitement.

It was as if she'd shifted a gear in him. His entire body gave a kick and his movements inside her grew faster, stronger, the friction burning her up. The large base of his penis ground against her, against the flesh that had become supersensitized, sensations so intense they hovered on the knife's edge of pain, and she could feel another orgasm coming, speeding toward her like a freight train. She stiffened, back arching, breath caught in her lungs, and hung there, shaking, on some kind of plateau, and then she simply exploded, contractions sharp and fast around him.

He exploded, too, movements hard and strong, erupting inside her until her entire body was marked by him, inside and out.

It was simply too much, sensory overload. Lungs bellowing, heat pulsing in every cell of her body, she saw stars behind her closed lids. The craziest cliché in the book and it was true.

Her muscles slowly settled, grew lax, her breathing slowly coming back to normal. They were plastered together by his sweat and hers and her entire groin area was wet with his semen and her excitement.

It had never really occurred to her how . . . how *earthy* sex was. How incredibly intimate. The sex she'd had up until now had been polite, even a little remote. Now she felt Harry's skin as her own, his breaths as her own.

They were as close as two human beings could possibly get. He was inside her, his body entirely covering hers. Mouth, chest, sex twined with his.

The cold and loneliness she'd felt this past year was simply banished. *Poof!* As if it had never existed. She was joined to this man every way there was, skin rubbing against skin. She was sure she smelled of him and tasted of him.

"Oh," she breathed, and couldn't say anything else. Words were blasted from her head. There really weren't any words for what she felt, only sensations. Warm, golden sensations.

"Oh yeah," Harry agreed in a rough whisper.

Silence descended. Not the awkward silence of two people

who didn't know what to say to one another, but the silence of something too big for words.

Harry was still hugely hot and hard inside her. Wasn't that unusual? Weren't men supposed to . . . to detumesce after sex? After two climaxes, surely he should have lost his erection.

But no.

Ellen's eyes closed and she felt as if she were floating in a warm ocean, floating, floating . . .

"I hope you're not thinking of sleeping," Harry whispered in her ear. "Because I haven't even begun."

Chapter 10

Seattle

"Christ, hurry up." Montez hopped from foot to foot, breath pluming in the frigid air. He wasn't dressed for an op and it was fucking *cold* up here on Cougar Mountain, ten miles from Seattle.

Driving up, they'd stopped at a hardware–fishing gear–grocery store in the sticks and bought two shovels, gloves and a big tarp.

He hadn't actually been there when his men had buried the body, but his men had sent him the GPS coordinates, precise to the inch.

Once they were over the spot, Montez had started to dig side by side with Piet, but Piet had simply held up his hand and motioned him to one side.

O-kay.

Truth be told, he didn't mind that he wasn't allowed to grub around in the peaty soil, unearthing a dead body. Piet wanted to work alone? Fine.

Piet must have done a lot of gravedigging in his life, because he worked as steadily and regularly as a machine. Within half an hour, there was a huge pile of dark, loamy earth piled up next to a coffin-shaped hole with clumpy dark sides.

With half an ear, Montez had been listening to the sounds Piet was making, like a sort of music, with the background a steady whistling noise through the pines. *Slide-hiss, clunk, patter. Slide-hiss, clunk, patter.* The iron of the shovel biting the earth, shoveling under a clump of earth, being tossed to the side.

The sounds changed and Montez walked to the side of the hole.

Piet was digging around something. Something that was appearing minute by minute as he dug, like an image coming out of a bath of photography chemicals. Soon, Piet had dug all around and a body was exposed. Montez looked down, shining his flashlight. Blond hair, now dark with clumps of soil, a fancy designer jacket, creased and filthy, brand-new boots, still shiny. He recognized those. He didn't recognize anything else.

Skin sloughing off from bones. Skin dark, features bloated beyond recognition. Montez frowned.

Piet glanced up briefly, without stopping his movements. "Looks different—been in the ground a week, yeah?" He spread the big tarp around the right side of the hole, letting some of the tarp dangle down over the side. "Help me," Piet grunted, and Montez jumped in with him into the hole. They muscled the dead weight of Roddy Fisher up onto the tarp, rolling him up in it. At the end of the exercise was a long, sausage-shaped plastic roll that Piet heaved up onto his shoulders as easily as hefting a shovel.

"Let's go," he said.

"Go where?" Montez had no idea why he needed the body.

Piet settled the body onto his shoulder. "To stake it out, as bait."

San Diego

Harry usually woke up abruptly, coming up out of sleep like a deep-sea diver cresting the surface at the last second with a gasp. He had nightmares often, and coming awake instantly was a self-defense mechanism.

Get me out of this fucking hellhole, fast.

But now he woke up in swoops, each stage with a little more sensory input, each stage better than the last.

First, eyes closed. A sensation of warmth. He usually woke up from his nightmares icy cold, no matter what the weather outside was like. Now, he felt warm all over. There was a soft, warm weight on his left side, spreading warmth throughout his body. He moved his hand, cupped around something soft and warm.

He felt . . . good. Fantastic, in fact. He rarely slept through the night and was usually tired when he woke up. It wasn't until he had his second or third hit of coffee that he felt ready to face the world. Now he woke up so refreshed he felt like a lion.

There was something soft and gently rounded attracting the palm of his hand like a magnet. He ran his hand up and down, encountering warm . . . woman.

His eyes popped open. He hadn't any sex since before Afghanistan. He'd been living in Nosexistan for two years.

The sex he'd had before was technically okay, but impersonal. He never wanted to stay the night and he never had women in his own house. Her place or a hotel room, he didn't care, as long as it wasn't his own space. And he always left after the sex, before falling asleep. Sleeping the night through with a woman made him vulnerable.

He never knew when he'd have one of his nightmares, waking up screaming in the night. No one could know how messed up he was, and he couldn't mask it asleep. In the night, he was exposed and open.

So the feel of a woman under his hand was surprising. Terrifying, actually, because it felt so damned good.

He looked down and smiled. A mass of shiny, red-brown hair was spilled over his chest. He saw a pale, perfect profile, lashes so long they cast a little shadow, skin like cream with a touch of rose underneath, so unlike the icy white color she'd had while he'd sat vigil beside her.

She was a quiet sleeper. Even with her head on his chest, he couldn't hear her breathing, but he could feel the slight rise and fall of her narrow ribcage. She was tickling a few chest hairs with her exhalations.

A slender arm crossed his chest, a narrow, long-fingered

hand curled around his ribcage, holding him even in her sleep. His skin tingled where it touched hers, all along his side. One bended leg was thrown across his, knee just under his crotch. If he hadn't had a massive hard-on, the knee would have been right over his dick.

He hadn't gone down even for a second since they'd kissed. Not even close. It was like he was plugged into this electrical socket called Ellen that made everything in him stand up.

Last night flashed through his mind in one pulsing, red-hot memory and his cock lengthened and thickened. He couldn't see his dick because sometime in the night he'd pulled the covers up over Ellen's shoulders, but by God he could feel it.

After being essentially dead meat, a hanging piece of flesh he forgot about for days at a time, useful only as a conduit for pissing, his cock now throbbed with feeling. It had had a taste of something it wanted more of. Much more. So much, he couldn't imagine ever being sated.

He obviously was pumping something into the air, because Ellen stirred, eyes moving back and forth behind her lids. Suddenly, her eyes opened wide and they found themselves staring at each other.

He watched her as she blinked, trying to put together the unfamiliar pieces: his face, the fact that they were both naked, that she was plastered against his side. She stirred, her leg glancing across his cock. His very hard cock.

She turned stoplight red. It was amazing to watch. One pulse and her color changed completely, down to her breasts. Or at least what he could see of her breasts. Harry would have happily checked to see whether the red ran down to her nipples, but she was suddenly clutching the blanket around her as if it were a lifeline.

He tried not to sigh. If it were up to him, he'd simply turn her a little, lift her leg with his hand and slide right in. Oh yeah. That first, fiery moment when he entered her . . . oh man. Nothing in his experience of fucking had come even close.

Was she sore? She had to be. She'd been so fucking *tight* that first time he entered. Good thing he'd come immediately and lubricated things a little. Harry had no idea how much time he'd spent in her—even the concept of time passing had fled his mind—but it had been a lot. She had to be sore.

And, come to think about it, most of last night had been about him, not her. The level of excitement he'd felt had simply fried his brain.

He was always in control while fucking, it was Harry's Law. He had always been big and strong, and . . . well . . . big all over. It was always possible to hurt a woman while fucking—squeeze too hard with his hands, hold her too tightly, plow her too hard.

The thought made him really sick, so from that very first time standing in a doorway, he made sure he was in control and not hurting her. That was Rule Number One.

And, alas, there was also Rule Number Two, which was, Don't let her get too close.

Fucking was great, a fabulous stress reliever. Mostly fun, always exciting.

Relationships, not so much. He'd never really had a relationship, actually. Being someone's partner meant . . . talking. Opening up. Letting her into his head.

Letting her see the demons.

No. Absolutely not. What was in his head was going to stay there. The only people he let see his vulnerabilities were his brothers. They knew and they weren't talking.

So fucking was great, and if the lady wanted more than that, here's the door, the world's full of men.

Last night had been an eye-opener. First, he hadn't been as much in control as he'd have liked. Actually, he hadn't been in control at all. Not once had he thought his moves through, parceling out the intimacy, this much and no further. There hadn't been any governing mechanism at all up in his head. It had all been in his body, and not just his cock.

There had been this enormous sense of . . . letting go. He hadn't held anything back, not emotionally and, unfortunately, not physically. He'd quit when Ellen had become practically comatose.

She hadn't complained, though. She'd smiled at him, stroked him gently, touched him in a way that . . . oh man. There weren't any words. The emotions roiling around in him felt good, but really unsettling and brand new.

Well, enough navel-gazing. He was ready for round two—or was it round five?—but she wouldn't be.

Still, that left a lot of room for other things.

Kissing her neck, nuzzling her collarbones, down to those small yet spectacular white breasts with the deep-pink nipples . . . he got sidetracked at the nipples because they tasted so fucking good. Like a cross between vanilla ice cream and the ocean.

Yeah.

Ellen's hands were on the back of his head, fingers deep in his hair, and that felt really good, too.

It all felt good. Incredibly good, in fact. Touching her pale skin, the taste of her, her hands on him . . .

He sent the hand not stroking a breast down over her side, following that incredible dip of her narrow waist, across that flat belly and ah . . . bliss. The lips of her little cunt were soft and swollen, moist. He touched her at the opening, his finger and his mouth on hers making lush sucking sounds in the morning silence, then tested her inside.

Warm, soft, wet. But there'd been just a little hesitation there, the tiniest of flinches, which she immediately stifled. Yeah, time for plan B.

Harry kissed his way over that lovely belly, down to where his unshaven chin caught a little in the soft cloud of dark-red hair between her thighs. And farther down.

He settled between her thighs and lifted her legs and opened them, content for the moment just to look.

Jesus, she was so fucking beautiful, even here. Soft and pink, small petals unfurled, tender flesh glistening. He looked up and met her eyes, those gorgeous green eyes. There was this moment of magnetic connection that frightened him, so he bent down, opened her with his fingers and kissed her, exactly as if he were kissing her mouth.

Her cunt tasted even more delicious than her breasts. Sweet and salty, utterly intoxicating.

And oh, man, he could *taste* her arousal. He tilted his head for a better, deeper fit and she clenched, a hot, warm pulse against his mouth, followed by the softest of sighs.

He urged her legs even farther apart with his hands and she was fully open to him now, completely his.

Every stroke of his tongue was met by a pulse, a sigh, then a moan. Deeper, deeper . . . her thighs started trembling and then suddenly she stiffened, gave a wild cry that echoed in the room, and started coming against his mouth, her entire body tightening under his mouth and hands, soft moans rising higher when he licked her clitoris.

Oh God, there was nothing better than this, nothing. He forgot everything, even his own body, completely immersed in hers as she came and trembled against him.

The trembling slowed, stopped and she gave a big sigh. Her arms flopped to her side, exhausted. He was pretty wiped out himself. He opened his eyes and looked at her, suppressing a grin as he crawled back up to her.

She had her head back, staring at the ceiling, one arm off the mattress, breathing heavily.

"You okay?"

"Huh." She wriggled fingers and toes. "Yeah. I think so. Everything seems to be working, though I think I either blacked out or had a religious experience there."

The grin broke out. He was feeling pretty good himself. He could climb a mountain and wrestle lions and tigers to the ground if he could just get his muscles to work.

"You know what?" she asked the ceiling.

"No, what?"

"I'm hungry. *Starving.*" She slanted a glance at him without moving her head. "I could eat a horse and spit out the bones."

"Uh huh." Harry wriggled his own toes, or tried to. Nothing much was moving. "As soon as I get some motor control back,

I'll take care of that for you. Could do with some grub myself."

God, it was true.

Harry couldn't remember the last time he'd been hungry. When he first came back from Ramstein, eating had seemed impossible. It was as if his stomach were filled with sand. The very idea of food had nauseated him. It was only because Sam and Mike insisted, to the point of buying takeout and standing over him until he choked down as much as he could without actually vomiting, that he had eaten at all. He'd almost forgotten what it felt like to be hungry.

Christ. Sex, hunger. All those forgotten things were roaring back, as if he'd been away for a long time and had just come back, stronger than before.

He was hungry and he wanted another round with Ellen as soon as she could manage it.

She turned her head, looked down. "Uh uh. Don't even think about it. Not until you feed me first. There are, like, rules."

"Oh yeah, I know." Of course there were rules. Not letting your lover go hungry was right up there. He smiled at her, his head hitting the pillow, the edges of his field of vision going gray, black.

"Get food right away," he mumbled. "Rest my eyes first."

Ellen made a little clucking sound of exasperation. "Big bad warrior, can't even stay awake. I think I'll do a little foraging in your kitchen, see what's there."

"Do that," he slurred sleepily. He tried to remember if there was any actual food in his kitchen, but couldn't get his head to work that much. He could feel his extremities. That was more or less it as far as a functioning brain was concerned.

He heard rattling noises from the kitchen, the smell of coffee reaching into the bedroom. The ping of the microwave. She'd obviously found something to work with.

Maybe he could wheedle her into bringing him breakfast in bed. Oh yeah. Feeding each other whatever she'd drummed up, sipping coffee. He had a small jar of honey somewhere; he could drizzle a little over her breasts and lick it off.

On that very happy thought, his mind drifted, went away.

Until he heard a sharp crash, the sound of glass breaking, and Ellen's scream.

He was out of bed in an instant, heart pounding as he scrabbled for his Glock. He ran into the living room, not knowing what to expect but ready for anything.

Ellen was sitting on a chair, laptop open, a shattered glass on the floor, shards glinting in the morning sunlight. Water was still spreading out over the floor.

A hand covered her mouth. She was that icy white color again.

She turned to him, desperation in every line of her face and burst into tears.

Seattle

"All over the news. She can't help but see it." Montez closed down the Yahoo News site and turned around. "That'll rattle her."

"Oh yeah." *Yiah*.

Piet looked into the rearview mirror of the rental SUV. It showed the rain-spattered street of secondhand-clothing shops, pawn shops, a palm reader, a Chinese laundry and the Blue Moon. Kerry Robinson was coming on duty at noon. Montez would have waited until she came off her shift. It would be dark then, less chances of anyone seeing them.

But Piet had argued that in tracking, time was of the essence. They had a bead on where Ellen had been—San Diego. And she was with someone. Every day that passed was a day in which she and her unknown protector could decide to move on, and they'd lose her again. Not to mention the fact that two big shocks in close succession were more likely to throw her off course than two big shocks that were separate.

Montez thought it was all bullshit. That Piet was just anxious to get the job done and get away. But what the hell could he do? And if he were truthful with himself, he wanted this over, too. Yesterday. The bitch had taken way too much time and attention, had taken him away from work at a really tough moment, when he needed to concentrate to keep his company afloat.

He hadn't argued with Piet and so here they were, at five to noon, on a rainy Seattle street.

Christ, Montez thought, looking out of rain-spattered windows, what lousy weather. How could anyone live here? It was all so gray and empty. Everyone looked like drones, even the kids. Even the losers who frequented the Blue Moon. Out-of-work day laborers, drunks, guys who looked like they hadn't shaved or washed in a week. They all trickled there into Loser Central.

The street was almost empty. A car went by every five minutes, moving slowly because of the rain accumulating in the gutters. And every single goddamned person crossing the street stopped at the red light, even if the street was empty and you could see into fucking Canada, standing in the pouring rain until the light turned green, and even then, they looked both ways before crossing.

Crazy.

He missed Georgia. He missed the warmth and the sunshine. He missed his men, who were properly deferential, not like Piet, who half the time pretended he wasn't there. Everyone treated Montez well back in Georgia. His men, local LEOs, who shot for free at his ranges, and women who knew he was rich.

A massive spurt of rage went through him at that thought. He never favored one woman over another. They tripped in and out of his bed and they all got a little something—a gold necklace, a pair of earrings—but no one got more than anyone else.

He'd been willing to make a big exception for Ellen. Hell, he'd been willing to *marry* the bitch, and look how she repaid him! He should have—

"There she is," Piet said quietly, and Montez wrenched his mind back from where it was seething. He put himself back into the op zone, where everything was cool and emotionless. Fast and efficient. Get the job done and get out.

"Let's go," Piet said, and shouldered the door open.

Chapter 11

San Diego

"Any more news?" Harry asked quietly.

Mike flipped his cell phone closed and shook his head. He'd been San Diego SWAT for a couple of years and though he was now a partner at RBK Security, he still had lots of buddies in law enforcement, men he'd trained with in SWAT training courses. He'd called the friend of his at Seattle PD they'd called earlier to check out the whereabouts of Roddy Fisher.

Before the cops even made it to Fisher's house, his dead body had showed up.

"No. The news agencies got it all. Except for the fact that apparently the guy'd been buried and dug up."

"Wh—what?" Ellen looked up at Mike. Her face had lost all color. Even her lips were white. She was shivering uncontrollably though the day was warm. Harry had put a blanket on her shoulders, but it didn't seem to help.

"Besides the—the signs on Fisher's body—" Mike took one look at Ellen and censored what he'd been about to say. The signs of torture. "Besides those, they found some clumps of dirt on his body. Not much. Forensics says the clumps of dirt are consistent with the chemical makeup of the mountains surrounding Seattle, one in particular. Cougar Mountain."

"That's not much help," Harry said sourly. "Only narrows the area to about a hundred square miles. Maybe more."

"Yeah." Mike checked a pad where he'd taken notes. "This isn't for public consumption yet, but the way they're figuring it, the guy was buried then disinterred. By the state of decomposition of the body, they're figuring he was killed seven days ago, maybe more. That's about all they've got. No leads, no clues. We might suspect who did it, but so far there's no evidence linking anyone, let alone Gerald Montez, to the murder." He closed his notepad. "But I'm going to send my pal an e-mail telling him to look into Gerald Montez's whereabouts, and why."

Ellen looked up, her face miserable. "Local law enforcement around Prineville is in Gerald's pocket. He cultivates officers. Offers them free shooting time, gives generously to police charities, hires some guys from the police department from time to time. He pays them very well. I don't think you'll get any help from them. Gerald could be standing over a dead body with a smoking gun in his hand and they'd look the other way."

"Well, you can be sure Seattle PD isn't in Montez's pocket," Mike said grimly. "And my guy there is a good guy. No one's going to buy him off. Ex Marine." He said it as if it clinched his argument. Mike was incredibly proud of having been a Marine and he kept in contact with former Marines all over the country. Marines were good guys. *Semper fraternis*. The second half of the motto. Always brothers

Harry was former Delta. Delta operators were sneaky and calculating. It was the nature of their job, a lot of which was undercover. It wasn't impossible to imagine a former operator sliding over to the dark side. Not a Marine, though.

Ellen looked like she was having trouble taking it all in.

Harry sat down next to her and put an arm around her shoulders, feeling the deep shudders going through her. She leaned into him gratefully, huddling against him as if for warmth.

His natural impulse was to pace the floor, a way of shaking the rage that pulsed through him. But Ellen needed his warmth and strength, so he had to tuck the rage away and concentrate on her.

And, of course, the fucker after her. The one who'd massacred her agent.

It was all over the news now. Partly because Roddy Fisher was a really big name on the Seattle music scene and partly because of the way he'd died. Tortured, shot in the head, then his long-dead, naked body handcuffed to a railing in Kerry Park.

The park's security cameras had been blanked at a quarter to four in the morning, when the body had apparently been displayed. At 3:45 the cameras had blanked; at 4:20 they came back on and Fisher's body had appeared.

It was really hard for Harry to even think with Ellen so

terrified and distraught next to him. It had taken the three men and Nicole half an hour to convince her that she wasn't responsible for Fisher's death.

That would be the fucker Montez.

"Here, sweetie, drink up." Nicole placed a cup of tea in Ellen's hand, which shook as it emerged from the blanket. Harry cupped his hand around hers so she wouldn't spill boiling tea all over herself and he nearly winced at how icy cold her hand felt. She was in shock.

He'd told Nicole to put a ton of honey and a finger of whiskey in the tea.

"Go ahead, honey. Drink," he said quietly, lifting his hand toward her mouth. She shuddered again and sipped.

"Thanks, Nicole." Ellen looked up, tried to smile for Sam's wife, and Harry's heart nearly broke. Her world had been shattered once again. Sam and Mike were standing, tense and angry, spoiling for a fight.

Harry was really, really glad they were on his side, because right now he was a wreck. He'd lost all his analytical powers and was tuned exclusively to the shivering, lost, beautiful woman by his side.

"I'm so sorry, Nicole," Ellen whispered for the hundredth time. She looked at Harry, Sam and Mike. "I'm so sorry to have involved you in all of this. I need to go, to—"

"*Bullshit!*" Harry exploded. He felt like his head was going to blow apart.

"Dude, can it." Mike's deep bass was steady. "You're not helping." He crouched down in front of Ellen and took her free hand, enclosing it in his two huge hands.

"This is not your fault. None of this is even remotely your

fault, Ellen. Montez is a bad guy and he has to be stopped. We'll do it because that's what we do. You don't worry about us."

Ellen swallowed convulsively, her long white throat working. Her mouth was trembling, tears at the corner of her eyes. "What if something happens to you? To Harry or Sam or you or . . . or *Nicole*? Because of me? I couldn't stand it. I'd rather be dead. This is my fight. I can't drag you guys into it."

"We're already in," Sam said grimly. "No turning back. So you need to go over everything again for us. Tell us everything you know. The more intel we have, the better we can find this fu—asshole and take care of him."

Ellen breathed shakily, in and out. Harry held her even more tightly against him. Another shudder ran through her.

She'd been on the run for a year. She'd been shot. They should get off her case. "It's okay, honey," he said gently. "Maybe some other time—"

"No!" Ellen threw her head back, eyes closed, clearly gathering her strength. When her eyes opened again, the shivering was gone. Hands and gaze steady. She stayed like that for a minute, two. Harry could actually see her resolve shaping. "I can do this. If you guys are taking him on, you need all the ammunition I can give you. I can't let you down."

Harry saw Mike and Sam exchange glances. *Good girl.* The words were in the room, though they didn't say them aloud. At that moment, Harry admired Ellen more than anyone he knew.

He and Sam and Mike had made sure that they were well equipped to deal with the monsters in the world. They were all super-proficient with weapons of every shape and size, and Mike—well, Mike was probably one of the best sharpshooters in the world. They were all big, strong men, trained in martial arts. They'd all been in firefights and had prevailed. They had all the tools in hand to track down and destroy someone like Montez.

But Ellen . . . shit, Ellen had nothing in her to fight him with. She was alive because she was smart and thought fast on her feet and because luck had been on her side. She was brave, but bravery without skills to back it up was really just another way to get yourself killed.

Ellen was beautiful, incredibly talented, and kindhearted. In another, better world, that would make her respected and admired. In this world, where men like Gerald Montez ruled, that made her roadkill.

Harry'd lost Crissy. He hadn't been able to protect his baby sister, no matter how hard he'd tried. The sweetest little girl in the world, and an ogre had snuffed her out like a candle.

This stopped, right here, right now.

Ellen was *not* going to fall in Montez's hands. Not now, not ever.

And he, Harry, was going to have to pull his head out of his ass, PDQ, because his blind fear for her wasn't any use to her at all. She needed him razor sharp and cool, not this trembling wreck of a man, terrified of losing her just as he'd lost his sister.

"Start at the beginning, honey." Everyone's head turned to him, which meant he'd been sounding like a lunatic before. Harry nodded his head—*don't worry, I'm back*—and Sam and Mike dipped their heads slightly—*glad to hear it*. "From when you ran. The reason you ran. You said you'd been working for Bearclaw for a couple of years, right?"

"Yes. More than two years." She was sitting upright, voice clear and steady, hands clenched tightly in her lap. "I kept coming up against inconsistencies, things that bordered on fraudulent accounting. He thought I wouldn't notice anything. He hired a CPA because the law required it, that was all, but he was fiddling the books. That was clear to me by the first week on the job."

Man, did you hire the wrong woman, Harry thought.

"So like I said, there was this big company party on the eighteenth of May, at the Hyatt Regency. One of Gerald's minions, Arlen Miller, comes up to me, puts his arm around my shoulders and starts telling me how lucky I am to have hooked up with a guy as smart as Gerald. He was so drunk you could have lit his breath. I didn't really listen at the beginning, and I'm sorry now that I didn't. But all I wanted was his heavy arm off my shoulders and to get home. He was talking about something that happened in April 2004 in Baghdad and how Gerald was the Man. And that the Man had taken twenty million. Then Gerald looked at him and this guy turned paper white. Gerald looked scary mad."

Harry knew what happened when men like Gerald Montez were enraged. Everyone turned to him.

"Harry," Nicole said, blinking. "Did you just *growl?*"

He shook his head sharply, getting rid of some bad thoughts. He picked up Ellen's hand and brought it to his mouth. "Remember you're safe now."

Sam and Mike looked at each other again. Harry didn't give a shit. This was his woman. One thing for sure—Sam understood. He'd tear the throat out of anyone who threatened Nicole.

"Can you try and remember more about exactly what this man, this Arlen, said?"

Ellen sighed. "I've tried over and over, but he was so drunk. Half of what he was saying didn't make sense. Arlen mentioned another name, but I haven't been able to find any mention of him in any database. Malowski. Or Makorski. Something like that. Arlen was really, really stewed." She wrinkled her nose. "And he had a sort of speech defect, like a lisp. He sprayed spittle—*ew.* I was too busy trying to stay away from his breath and the spray."

"Nicole," Sam said.

"On it," she answered, going to Harry's laptop.

She switched it on and disappeared. To all intents and purposes, Nicole was no longer in the same room with them.

Harry was really, really good with computers, but Nicole was better at research. That hurt. She ran a translation agency and was used to carrying out major research for her translations. Her agency had a list of expert collaborators that spanned the globe, men and women who did online terminology research for a living, and they communicated daily. She also had low-level clearance to check government databases. As a result, Nicole could find anything.

"So you ran when this guy showed up dead?" Sam looked at Ellen.

"Yeah," she answered softly. "I spent three months on the road, and I ended up in Seattle."

Three months on the road. Harry didn't have to ask what that had been like. Three months from anonymous motel to flea-bitten boardinghouse, because those were the kinds of places that didn't require ID. Sleeping lightly, looking over her shoulder.

Sam leaned forward. "So Montez got to your agent. How'd he know where to look? You kept Eve under cover."

Ellen shook her head. "I honestly have no idea. I was really careful. The records were produced by a shell company that I set up very carefully. Registered in the Caymans and with no connection to me. Paying my taxes took real creative accounting, let me tell you."

"Were you this big draw at the bar where you worked?" Sam asked.

"No. The bar's clientele is . . . well, let's say *messed up.* Most of them don't pay too much attention to anything. I can't imagine anyone there connecting the waitress who sang a few nights a week with Eve. Except, of course, for Kerry."

"Kerry?" Mike swiveled his head, frowning.

"Dove," Harry and Mike said at the same time.

Mike's frown deepened. "You guys met? Talked? What are the odds? That's not good."

No, it wasn't. Kerry was supposed to stay undercover forever. Never let her secret out.

Ellen turned to him. "I don't know, Mike. The Blue Moon is sort of tailor-made for . . . for women like us. The owner wants us off the books and he doesn't care at all what our background is. If we can do the work—and it's not rocket science—he pays on time and asks no questions at all. The customers are mainly sad men who don't even look at us. There aren't that many jobs you can get without showing up on any books. And Kerry was . . . she was lonely."

"If she's one of ours, she's not supposed to talk." Mike's deep rumble held disapproval.

For someone who slept around a lot, Mike didn't seem to have a good handle on women. They were hardwired to talk.

"She recognized I was like her." Ellen gave a sad smile. "She said if I was ever in danger to get to San Diego, and she gave me your card."

"Guys," Nicole interrupted. She lifted her fingers from the keyboard and looked triumphantly at them. "I think I've got something."

Seattle

It was raining. It seemed like it was always raining in Seattle. For a moment, Kerry Robinson missed San Diego. She thought with longing of the warm springs, hot summers, beautiful falls and mild winters. It rained rarely, and often the weather had the good taste to rain only at night, like in Camelot. She missed it so much.

On the other hand, if she were still in San Diego, she'd probably be dead. There was that.

She hopped from puddle to puddle trying to keep her shoes as dry as possible. Working an eight-hour shift in wet shoes was miserably uncomfortable, she knew from bitter experience. She had two pairs of shoes, neither of them rainworthy.

Once upon a time, she'd had three hundred pairs of shoes. She'd had an entire closet for her shoes. Those days were gone.

A drunk crashed into Kerry while she dashed from storefront to storefront, trying to keep dry. She barely managed to avoid falling into a huge puddle that had accumulated in a pothole in the sidewalk.

The drunk mumbled something and staggered off, uncaring of the rain dripping off his lank, greasy long hair and soaking his tattered green sweater. No raincoat, no boots, dank rotten smell. He looked homeless. No doubt he'd settle on some corner and panhandle until he got together the money for another beer. Or another whiskey. Or maybe even to score some drugs.

Kerry knew that there was a taxonomy to despair but hadn't quite gotten the classification system down pat yet. No doubt a cop could tell whether the smelly man staggering down the street was a drunk or a junkie or just plain crazy, but she couldn't. Not yet. It filled her with desperation that sooner or later she'd be able to distinguish all the stripes of horror down here at the bottom of society's ladder.

It was all so very far away from La Jolla. No homeless people in her old world. Everyone in it had been pampered and manicured to absolute perfection. No out-of-control drunks, no junkies, no crazies. No poor people at all, unless you counted the help. The ones who kept the gardens green and trimmed, the houses spotless, the streets pristine.

It had been a wonderful world and a wonderful life, if you didn't count being beaten up on a regular basis. That had sucked.

Her husband had loved her, so very much. So much that he couldn't stand for her to be imperfect. Any imperfection had to be punished. For her own good, of course.

For three years, Kerry had gone to a different hospital with a different story each time, but there were only so many hospitals in the area. When she found herself at the same hospital for the third time in a year, she mixed her story up. Most well-to-do matrons don't walk into doors that often.

A social worker had visited her in the hospital and had been questioning her when Tom walked in. Tom had, of course, turned on the charm. He had a special spigot, twenty-four-karat gold. He was tall, handsome and well dressed. He managed to be elegant without coming off as a dandy. He was almost dazzlingly handsome, well spoken, with charm in spades. The rich knew how to smooth over any kind of unpleasantness. He'd come into the hospital room, understood the situation in a glance and had taken over the conversation. Within five minutes he discovered that the social worker enjoyed rock music, promised her front-row seats for the upcoming Springsteen concert at Petco Park and escorted her to her car.

The look he'd given her as the hospital door closed behind her terrified her. His rages had been escalating as her errors multiplied. Now her mistakes included the way she spoke, dressed, ate and breathed. More or less everything she did was wrong now, and subject to punishment. She knew she wouldn't survive the next time.

Alice—the person she'd been before becoming Kerry—had shifted painfully on that hospital bed and had been surprised to hear a crackling sound. A card, which obviously the social worker had managed to slip onto the mattress as she was saying goodbye.

On it had been a beautiful bird in flight, a number and the words CALL NOW in big block print. The number didn't have any of the San Diego area codes. Alice didn't know where the number was, who the person was who the social worker thought could help her. She didn't know anything, except for one thing: If she stayed, she'd be dead within the week.

So, with a broken wrist, a damaged liver and a slight concussion, with an IV line with glucose and a powerful antibiotic running into a needle on the back of her hand, she'd escaped. She'd pulled the IV line out, pulled her clothes out of the little closet that had been provided and ran. If Tom had had any idea that she'd have the nerve to run away, he'd have taken her clothes away, no question.

But she'd never run away. That was the quickest way to a fatal beating she knew of.

When she emerged from the basement of the hospital and walked four blocks to hail a cab, she knew that she was running for her life. If Tom ever found her, her life would be over.

With shaking hands, she called the number and set in motion the events that led her to Seattle, to the life of a waitress in a dive, barely making ends meet, with no future to speak of. It wasn't much, but it was still definitely better than being six feet underground, food for worms.

Sam Reston had saved her life, and she wondered if someone had saved Irene's. Of course, she knew Irene wasn't her real name. Whoever she was, she was a good kid and had somehow stumbled onto the same awful planet of dangerous men Kerry had.

God, she'd had no idea that place had even existed until she'd married Tom. And Irene still seemed a little shell-shocked herself.

Kerry knew Irene was in trouble when she told her a man had been asking for her. Irene had turned icy white and just like that, Kerry knew. Turned out the guy was harmless, just wanted to go out with Irene. That was normal; Irene was a pretty woman. But the guy she was hiding from wouldn't want to go out with her. He'd want her dead. Irene had landed on Kerry's planet. That was when she gave Irene Sam Reston's number. Just in case.

Where was Irene? They'd gotten into the habit of taking tea at Kerry's a couple of times a week. Kerry was good at decorating. She'd turned Tom's home into a showcase. And even on a nothing budget, she'd managed to turn her hole in the wall into something inviting.

Both of them avoided public places. Kerry's little cubbyhole had been a safe haven for them both. Kerry never told her story, and neither did Irene tell hers. They didn't need to. They both knew.

Once Irene accepted the number, the last refuge of a desperate woman, they both knew she'd someday call it.

In the meantime, in their little time outs over the expensive teas Kerry splurged on, they talked of quiet, gentle things. Never anything personal. No information that could be used against them. Just books and movies and music. Kerry hadn't even known that Irene was a world-class singing talent until that evening when she'd stepped in for old Honorius. She'd nearly fainted, Irene had been that good. And she hadn't hinted, not once, that she sang or played.

Kerry didn't mind. She didn't need to know Irene's secrets. God knew she had enough of her own. The whole point of a secret was that it stay hidden. Her secrets could kill. She suspected Irene's could, too.

Where was Irene? She'd been gone for a week now, without communicating in any way. They had a secret online message board, set up by the two of them, as casually as if every person on earth needed a secret means of communication. Neither of them talked about it, but they used it often. To set up appointments, to exchange a few words.

For both of them, Kerry suspected, this was their only form of human connection—the odd cup of tea in her cozy, cheap little apartment. They never spoke at work. They had different shifts anyway. There was an unspoken imperative: Don't let anyone know we're friends. They both respected it.

Kerry was just starting to get worried. Whoever was after Irene—had he caught up with her?

What kind of man was after Irene? Was he like Tom—a pillar of the community? The kind of man people instinctively looked up to? The kind of man no one would ever believe was capable of cruelty?

Where was Tom? Had he moved on to some other woman-victim? God, she hoped so, though she pitied any woman under his harsh rule. But if there was another woman, maybe his obsession with her was abating. Maybe she was hiding out here in cold, rainy Seattle, doing a maid's job for a pittance, for no discernible reason. Maybe she could go back to her first love—interior decoration.

Oh God. For the first time in a long while she allowed herself to think of the future. Or at least *a* future. Something more than merely staying alive.

The rain was pelting now, drops splashing down so hard they bounced almost a foot high. She chanced a glance at the sky. It was pewter-dark, without a break at all in the clouds. She knew by now what that meant—rain for at least the next couple of hours. Holing up in a storefront wasn't going to help.

She was going to have to run down the street to the Blue Moon.

She dashed down the street, glancing for a startled second at a man who was coming toward her fast. He was an idiot without an umbrella. You got drenched with an umbrella; without one . . . well.

He was tall and thin and blond. For a horrified instant she thought he looked like Tom, only without that pampered spa look, and dressed in casual clothes.

He wasn't Tom, though. That thought made her so happy she nodded at him as he walked by, the nod two strangers caught in a downpour would make.

Lousy weather, isn't it?

You can say that again!

Suddenly, Kerry felt a strong hand grip her arm from behind, almost lifting her off her feet. A sharp prick in her biceps. The rainy world turned entirely to water, long, streaming silver stripes that were fast turning black.

She had time for one panicked thought.

Tom found me.

Chapter 12

San Diego

They crowded round Nicole. Ellen noticed that Sam kept a hand on his wife's shoulder, in encouragement, support. That must feel . . . nice, she thought. To have someone always on your side.

Then a heavy, warm hand landed on her own shoulder and she looked up, startled, into Harry's sharp, golden eyes. He wasn't looking at Nicole's monitor, he was looking at her, face somber.

Suddenly, he smiled. Straight at her, looking her right in the eyes. Harry had a face that didn't smile often; the lines and muscles of his face told her so.

This smile lit his face up, made him look younger, approachable. For the first time Ellen realized that he couldn't be that much older than her. Maybe six or seven years. He'd seemed lifetimes' older, with his detailed knowledge of the inner workings of violence and with hidden tragedies she could sense.

The smile did something else. It lit her up inside, as well.

Crazily, with all that had happened, even with the fact she had a dangerous man after her, a man who'd tortured and killed her agent, a man who'd probably killed Arlen—when he smiled at her, it all disappeared.

Her head knew that there were monsters outside, monsters with sharp teeth and claws, but for this instant in time, it all felt far away, happening to someone else. Another Ellen Palmer, not this one. This one had made love all night with the big golden man who was now standing so close to her she could feel his body heat. That huge hand, elegant and long-fingered, had touched her everywhere. At the end, it had seemed as if he'd known her body better than she did. He had a Reality Distortion Field around him, and when she was inside it, danger and fear were far away. They didn't have anything like the hold on her that sex with him did.

Sex.

God, why hadn't anyone told her about the sheer *power* of sex? That it felt like plugging in to some primordial power source? Who knew?

Sex had been sometimes fun, sometimes boring, sometimes a little painful, but that was usually her fault because often she wasn't turned on very much.

Sex was always lopsided. One always cared more than the other, and when it finished, someone always left someone else. At times, Ellen had felt as if she made love in some kind of invisible carapace that stopped her from feeling much of anything.

Well, with Harry that had flown out the window. Her entire body had become a giant touch screen, where she felt everything he did to her. Her skin had become so sensitive she'd felt every aspect of his scarred body: the long, striated muscles, so clearly delineated he could have served as an anatomy plate, the textures of the hair on his body, starting from the hair on his head, silky and warm, the crisp dark-gold hairs on his chest, the golden fur on his legs.

She remembered every second of his kisses, the sharp, biting ones, the deep, tender ones. Each one with a flavor of its own.

The feel of him inside her . . . oh God. Heat and strength, mind-blowing pleasure even when he stayed still inside her. And when he moved . . .

He knew what she was thinking. She must be a bright shade of red by now. She had a redhead's pale complexion, the kind that showed everything she was feeling. His smile widened.

He'd smiled just like that last night, on top of her, nose an inch from hers, his member deep inside her. She'd smiled back and he'd surged inside her, becoming somehow longer and thicker. At the memory, her vagina tightened, hard, pulling stomach and groin muscles.

"Okay," Nicole said, and Ellen thought *okay*. Clearly, they had to go back to the bedroom together and—

She froze, pulled her gaze away from Harry's. It was incredibly hard to do. *Stop that,* she told herself sternly.

They weren't alone. They were with his two best friends and Nicole. All of them were doing their best to keep her safe, even Nicole, who was four months pregnant. They were working hard for *her* and she was thinking about going to bed with Harry, just as soon as physically possible.

She was still red, only this time with shame.

Nicole had been looking up at her, cobalt-blue eyes narrowed, head tilted so that her shiny, blue-black hair brushed her shoulders, full lips pursed. She was such an incredibly beautiful woman. No wonder her husband was crazy about her. She was more than just gorgeous, though. She was smart and kind. And she was looking at Ellen as if . . . as if she understood what had been going through her head. And, crazily enough, as if she didn't disapprove.

"What?" Ellen shook herself. She needed to find out as much as possible right now, while she still had people—smart, good and brave people—on her side, because soon enough, she'd be on her own again.

She wouldn't even be able to go back to Seattle, to her tenuous friendship with Kerry, so full of unspoken secrets. No Seattle, no Kerry, no music.

Nothing.

"I checked a couple of government sites I often use for research. They have a low-level degree of confidentiality and I use them ever since I got clearance. There's nothing terribly secret in these databases, but they are mines of information and you can't access them through Google. There are also the armed forces news sites, which are not always rendered public. And look what I found for May 2004."

Nicole shifted her head so everyone could see what was on the monitor.

It was a PDF copy of what must have been a printed article. It was written up newspaper style, in four columns. The article was below the fold and continued on page four of the publication. Nicole had split her screen into two so that the entire article could be read.

Baghdad, Green Zone, May 28, 2004,
byline Sgt. Katina Petrescu

Investigators from Washington landed yesterday to investigate the loss of $20 million from the Green Zone. The loss was discovered by accountants the week before. Investigators believe the losses might date to last month.

"The CPA was barely in control," Harry explained. "Bremer said he needed money and it came. In C-130 transport planes, filled with pallets. The pallets contained forty boxes and each box had twenty bricks of one hundred thousand dollars each. The pallets were stored in a warehouse and just kept there. CIA agents would stroll in and stroll out with bricks in their arms. Sometimes they'd use wheelbarrows. It was like the Wild West out there. For a while, it rained money. They just kept it on hand in a storeroom, couple guys had the key. More than a billion dollars was lost, unaccounted for."

"Gerald was stationed in Baghdad in 2004," Ellen said. How he'd played that up. Tough-guy talk, together with coy references to how he couldn't say exactly what had gone on. National security concerns, of course. Whereas the truth was, he'd stolen twenty million dollars. "His tour ended in June. He didn't re-up. He came home and founded Bearclaw in July 2004."

"Which immediately landed incredibly lucrative contracts from the U.S. government. Nice work. And look." Nicole tapped a pink-tipped fingernail at the screen. "Look at the lead investigator's name."

"Frank Mikowski. That must have been the guy Arlen was referring to. Do you think he was bought off by Gerald?"

"No." Nicole shook her head, her glossy hair rippling around her shoulders. "Not at all. I think the problem was, he wasn't bought off." She clicked to a new page and scrolled down. "Here. Looks like Mikowski investigated the wrong guy."

This time it was a State Department cable, declassified on June 17, 2010, referring to events six years before.

Frank Mikowski had been found floating facedown in the Tigris River on June 3, 2004. Forensics established he'd died of a bullet wound to the head and had been dead for at least two days. Sunni insurgents were blamed.

Sam bent to kiss his wife's cheek. "Nice work, honey."

"Yes," she smiled. It was so dazzling a smile her husband blinked. "It was."

"Sunni insurgents, my ass," Harry growled. "That wasn't a terrorist takedown. He was executed to stop the investigation. And it worked, damn it." Harry was glaring narrow-eyed at the screen as if it were personally responsible for the theft of twenty million dollars, the death of the investigator and the danger to Ellen. "I mean, people know Montez and know his operation is corrupt, but I don't think anyone knows about this."

"So we've tied him possibly to two murders—Mikowski's and Arlen's," Sam said. Like Harry's and Mike's, his face had gone hard, eyes cold. At that moment, Ellen was really glad that they were her friends, not her enemies.

"And my agent, Roddy," Ellen added. "Don't forget him."

Her heart gave a lurch. Roddy—dear, sweet, harmless Roddy. He was a sweetheart, dedicated to music, with a good ear and a good heart. Snuffed out like an irritating bug. As if he didn't mean anything at all. It made her so *angry*. He'd merely been an obstacle for Gerald, who'd probably ticked him off a list of things to do to get his hands on her.

"Three murders. Definitely something he'd kill to keep quiet," Mike said, jaws clenching. "Not to mention the theft of a fortune in cash."

Ellen shivered, and the room went quiet.

Nicole checked her wristwatch and started. "Oh my gosh! I've got an eleven o'clock telephone appointment with a client. A New Yorker. They're always so terribly punctual. I must run."

"Thanks, Nicole." Ellen smiled at her as she rose. Nicole was dressed in a beautifully tailored turquoise silk dress and pearls, her pregnancy just visible. She looked cool and professional and gorgeous, and she'd provided invaluable information. At that moment, Ellen loved Nicole. Nicole winked at her as she closed down her computer.

Ellen liked her so much. She was going to miss her. "See you this evening, then."

The three men froze and turned to her as if she'd opened her mouth and toads had hopped out. Ellen looked from one hard face to another. "What? What did I say?"

"No way are you staying here alone." It was a miracle he could talk at all, Harry's jaws were clenched so tightly. He was looking at her with a *don't even think of arguing* look. Harry was clearly not to be reasoned with, so Ellen turned to Sam, but he looked exactly the same as Harry, and then to Mike, who looked like he'd just chewed nails. "What? I thought it was safe here."

"It is." Harry looked like he'd just swallowed the nails Mike had chewed. "But—"

Nicole touched Ellen's arm. "They do have very good security here, sweetie, but I think Harry would feel better if you would just come in to the office, where he could see you. Otherwise I don't think he'd get any work done at all." She shot a glance at her husband. "I know if I were in danger, Sam would want me by his side."

"Absolutely." He put his thick, muscled arm around his wife's shoulders at the thought.

Ellen didn't think Harry could possibly care for her as much as Sam cared for his wife, but Nicole was right. Harry was clearly a man who took his duty seriously, and right now, she was under his protection. If he wanted her where he could see her, he had every right. And if the thought of just sitting around while others worked wasn't appealing, that was her problem, not theirs.

Unless . . .

"Sure, I'll come in with you, but—I'd love to make myself useful. I don't have Nicole's investigative skills, but I'm a really good accountant. Tax time is coming up. Would any of you like me to check your returns, or prepare them if they aren't ready?"

Four blank looks, which quickly turned into excitement, eyes wide, like kids just promised chocolate ice cream.

"Oh, man," Nicole moaned. "Me me me! I hate bookkeeping!"

"Me, too!" the three men echoed in chorus.

Okay. So she had some work to do. It made her feel better.

Seattle

At first she thought she was in her apartment, in bed, after a particularly nasty nightmare. Nightmares often accompanied her sleep. The one she had most often was running from terrible danger, only her legs wouldn't move and she couldn't scream. She'd wake up with a pounding heart, gasping and shivering and sweaty.

Kerry's brows came together in puzzlement. How could this be? She was awake, she knew she was, but somehow still in the nightmare. She couldn't see, couldn't move, couldn't talk, she found, as she made a sound deep in her throat that came out soft and muffled.

She snapped her head back, tried to look at the ceiling, but her eyes wouldn't open. All she could see was blackness.

"—out of it," a man's voice said.

"Yeah." Pronounced *Yiah*. "She's coming round." Another man's voice, not American. Australian?

Her senses returned, all at once, in a painful rush. She was blindfolded, gagged, tied up. To a chair, she found as she tried to kick her feet. They were bound at the ankles, and as she swung her bound ankles side to side they encountered spindly wooden columns. Chair legs.

Her heart nearly stopped. *Tom,* she thought, terror welling up, cold and icy. *He's found me.*

He was going to kill her, beat her to death, and her hands were tied. She had an escape, but she needed her hands for it and her hands were tied.

How could she not have imagined he'd tie her hands?

Because he wouldn't.

Kerry remembered how Tom had laughed when she tried to hit back once. It had amused him. She remembered his disdainful laugh, the half-smile as she tried to defend herself. He'd studied martial arts since he was a boy. There was nothing she could do to him with her hands that would hurt. He'd never tie her hands. It was an ego thing.

She was puzzling over that when she heard quiet steps, much quieter than the thundering of her heart. The steps approached and she braced herself, but the steps walked past her, behind her. Hands at the back of her head, and the blindfold was pulled off.

At first she couldn't see anything. There was a blinding light in her eyes. They hurt as they tried to accommodate.

There was the sound of something being scraped across the floor, and a figure came slowly into focus. Black shoes, black pants, black sweater, dragging a chair. Everything about him was elegant, expensive. Another scrape and she saw a face.

Hard, dark, triangular. High cheekbones, the kind of beard that grew dark after five p.m. Dark eyes, dark hair. A face she'd never seen before, a face she'd never forget.

But not Tom.

"Who—who are you?" she said, but the words were muffled by the gag.

The man flicked his forefinger and the man behind her

untied the gag. Kerry dropped her head, coughed. Her mouth was completely dry.

The man had somehow understood. "Who am I?" He edged even closer and looked her straight in the eyes. "It doesn't matter who I am. What's important is what I want. I'm looking for the woman who sings under the name Eve. Her real name is Ellen Palmer, but she's not using that name."

So. Kerry stared into the man's blank black eyes. This was Irene's Tom, worse than her own Tom. And apparently Irene wasn't Irene. She wasn't Eve, either. She was Ellen.

Kerry looked into those eyes and flinched. No wonder Irene—Ellen—had been on the run. Those black eyes were utterly dead, like the eyes of a crocodile or a corpse. His eyes didn't even reflect the light. They were like two dark pools of stagnant water.

Impossible as it seemed, there was something worse than Tom.

Tom was crazy, no question. But no matter that his emotions made no sense, he felt them, and keenly. All he wanted, he said, was for her to be *his* and to be perfect. Even when he was hitting her, there was emotion there. Rage, a perverted and twisted kind of love, a need to dominate. His eyes had glowed with what he was feeling; it was almost visible on his skin.

This man felt nothing, nothing at all, which she now realized was scarier than rage.

Often she'd been able to talk Tom down, get him down from the ledge of crazy despair and wrongheaded love he'd felt. Reason with him, at least a little. Because somewhere in there was a man who was suffering, who couldn't get a handle on his feelings. She'd stayed with him way too long, but part of it had been out of a misplaced sense of pity.

This man didn't need pity. And he didn't feel pity. He felt nothing.

It was there, in his eyes, in his face.

And at that moment, Kerry knew that she was dead. There was nothing in this man she could in any way appeal to. No common humanity, no mercy. There was none in him.

She needed her hands. They were duct-taped together. She needed them *now*.

"Where's Ellen?" The question was quiet, factual. But she knew it was the first salvo of a coming firestorm.

She said the only thing she could say. "I don't know."

Those dead eyes watched her, watched her face. Could he tell she was speaking the truth? Was she? She knew where Ellen had gone, but she had no idea if she was still there.

Something of her ambiguity trickled through.

"You know," he said flatly. "You're just not talking."

He gave a short nod of his head and Kerry felt a large, male hand land on her shoulder from behind. His hand moved and suddenly two fingers pinched a certain spot and pain exploded in her body. Hot, crackling pain, unlike anything she'd ever felt before. Pain so intense she couldn't even pull in the breath to scream. Pain so intense she thought her heart would stop.

Only gurgling sounds were making it past her throat, then a strangled keening. The man in front of her nodded again, the hand was lifted and Kerry sagged against the duct tape, gasping and shaking.

The man sighed. "We can do this all day and all night, you

know. Just this and you'll be reduced to a screaming mass of protoplasm at the end. My friend here touched a special plexus of nerves that is extremely painful in humans. He exerted minimal effort. He's very strong and tireless. He can do this forever."

The chair scraped even closer, and through her own sweat and terror, Kerry could smell him now. He actually smelled good—of clean linens and expensive leather and some costly male cologne. She knew that if she ever smelled that smell again she'd throw up.

The man behind her smelled of nothing at all. She hadn't seen him yet, but already he seemed larger than life, inhuman as an insect or an alien.

"Now, the reason my friend here found that particular spot so very easily is that he's an expert at extracting information." The man in front of her was watching her carefully, gauging the effect of his words on her. He didn't need to assess the effect, though. He terrified her and she didn't know how to hide that. "He knows exactly what he's doing, and he's broken hundreds of men. Men who were very strong, highly trained to resist torture. And he broke them down into parts. He'd have them whimpering, begging for him to stop. He never stops until he gets what he wants. And he sure won't stop with you because you're a woman."

She needed her *hands*!

Another scrape and a small table was brought forward into the circle of light. On it a leather case, much like a traveling case for jewelry. The man slowly opened it up, like opening up a flower for someone's delight. First the left-hand flap then the right-hand one. The upper one, the lower one.

Kerry flinched and closed her eyes against the glare of the gleaming steel instruments.

"Now, these are not carpentry tools," the man said casually. "They're tools for extracting the truth out of living flesh."

Kerry's breath was caught in her chest like hot rocks; she couldn't breathe in or out. Sweat dripped down her face, fell between her breasts, between her shoulder blades. It dripped down into her eyes, big salty drops, stinging her.

She couldn't clear her eyes.

She needed her hands.

The instruments gleamed brightly, as if brand new or recently polished to a high sheen. You couldn't even pretend they weren't for hurting. Every surface came to a point or a sharp edge. The handles were made to augment the strength of a hand. These two men's hands were plenty strong. The instruments would only allow them to hurt her more.

The man across from her, Mr. Elegant, simply waited, one leg thrown over the other, one expensively shod foot flexing every now and again, his only concession to nerves.

Kerry had no doubt that her nerves would snap first. Her nerves, her bones. She could be reduced to a mockery of a human being and he wouldn't break a sweat.

Quiet. Utter and complete silence.

For the first time since coming to, Kerry wondered where they were. Someplace where no one would come galloping to the rescue, that was for sure. Rescues were for novels and movies. No one was going to rescue her.

There was no one to come. The deep silence could only be that of a place that was utterly deserted. Where? No clues at all. Bare concrete floor. Small Formica-topped table, inexpensive wooden kitchen chairs. That was it. She couldn't even see the walls beyond the pool of light thrown by the spotlight.

This place could have been a basement, a storage space, a warehouse. It could be anywhere.

"So," Mr. Elegant said finally. There was no impatience in his voice. No impatience, no anxiety, not even curiosity. Nothing. "Are we ready to talk, or do we have to use these?" He flicked at the table holding the instruments. "It makes no difference to me, because the end result will be the same."

She needed her *hands*. In her worst nightmares, she'd always had the use of her hands.

As if he'd heard her, Mr. Elegant picked up what looked like needle-nose pliers, only of a superior steel, coming to a sharp point. He weighed it in his hand, turned it this way and that in the bright spotlight, as if admiring its workmanship.

"Perfect for pulling out fingernails," he murmured. "Designed for it, in fact." When he lifted his head to look at her, there was no menace. He wasn't making an idle threat. He was stating a simple fact.

She shivered.

"Now." Mr. Elegant put his open palm over the instruments and looked at her. "Are we ready to talk?"

The shivering took her whole body, as if she'd been suddenly plunged in ice. She opened her mouth to speak, but nothing came out.

He waited.

"Y—yes," Kerry choked out. "I—I'm ready."

"Excellent. Where is Ellen now?"

"I don't know."

His hand fisted over the pliers.

Kerry wheezed to get air into her chest. "I don't! I don't know! I haven't seen her in days! Last time I saw her I was coming off the day shift and she was coming on the evening shift. More than a week ago. She hasn't come in for work since then. Our boss is worried. It's not like her. She's always been very reliable."

He drummed his fingers once on the edge of the table, processing this.

"Where do you think she is?"

Running away from you. "I don't know."

His eyes slid sideways and the man behind her pinched that point on her shoulder. The pain shocked her so much she jumped in her chair, lifting it off the ground. This time he kept his fingers there, on and on and on.

She was rendered down to rock bottom by the time he lifted his hand away from her. Her head hung down, curly hair forming a dark curtain around her face. Tears spurted out of her eyes, mucus ran out of her nose, both dripping down onto her knees.

She could barely stand stage one. Stages two, three, four and beyond were right here in this room.

The shivering was beyond her control. She looked down at her knees, knocking together, though the movements were hampered by the duct tape around her ankles. Her breathing was loud in the room, sharp intakes of breath and sobbing.

No way out.

Except one.

"I need to go to the bathroom," she mumbled. She could barely get the words out.

"The *bathroom*?" Mr. Elegant asked, black eyebrows raised, as if the very concept were foreign.

"Please."

She couldn't stand another session of pain. And they'd only just begun. Kerry didn't have much information on Irene. Irene had been very closemouthed about her story and now Kerry understood exactly why.

But the fact that she knew so little would just enrage the man sitting across from her. She could feel it. Years with Tom had taught her a lot about male rage. This type's rage wasn't explosive like Tom's. This type had rage hidden under the skin, cruel to the bones. Even after she'd told everything she knew, he'd punish her for knowing so little.

Kerry couldn't do it.

She had two things to give. She'd give one, then beg to go to the bathroom.

Her hands, she needed her hands.

"Bathroom," she mumbled again, trying to dry her eyes on her shoulder. "Please."

"How did you two communicate?" the man asked abruptly.

It was a question she was expecting. Still . . . *Don't make it easy.* She let her head hang for a minute, then raised her eyes. She tried to look shaken, disoriented. It wasn't hard. Her muscles held the memory of the red-hot pain and a pounding pulse had set up in her head.

She opened her mouth.

His voice dropped, became ice cold. "And don't tell me by cell phone, because you didn't."

Actually, they had. Kerry should have realized the type of

man who was after Irene by the precautions she took. Irene had three cell phones, prepaid, untraceable. One to communicate with her, one to communicate with her agent and one for their boss, Mario.

These men didn't know that. Oh God, every piece of information she could withhold—if only she could get to the bathroom!—was something that might help Irene survive.

Her own life was lost, she understood that. Given a choice, she'd have chosen to save her own life instead of Irene's, but the choice wasn't hers.

Life, fate, destiny. Whatever you wanted to call it, it was operating here. She was already gone. A ghost. Her thirty-two-year journey from Denver to Vassar to marriage in San Diego to life on the run was over. She'd never know the love of a child, of a good man. Never feel the rain on her face, never rock to Aerosmith again. Never eat ice cream, never finish *War and Peace*.

Her life ended here. Her only choice was between betraying a friend who could fall into this man's hands, after hours and hours of unspeakable pain, or controlling the situation in the only way she knew how.

"How did you communicate?" he asked again. He wouldn't be a man to ask three times.

"Computer." Kerry coughed the word out. It tasted bitter, like betrayal. But of the two, this was better than giving a cell phone number. Or—God!—forcing Irene out in the open to save her. "Message board." She gave the access data and password.

Mr. Elegant nodded to the man behind her. The man whose

hands held such pain in them. An electric whir, a faint bluish light reflecting off the concrete walls. The trill of Windows firing up. The tapping of keys.

"Got it. Yeah." The way he spoke was weird. Clipped, the vowels all wrong. *Yiah.* "Scrolling through. Mostly messages about meeting up. Nothing interesting."

No, there wouldn't be anything interesting there. Both she and Irene would never have committed anything potentially dangerous to writing. So no, these two dangerous men wouldn't find what they needed in the message board. Which meant they'd probe, hard, for the next thing.

Pain, much more pain, was coming. With death at the end of it.

Kerry suddenly bucked, the back legs of the chair coming up off the floor. She opened her mouth, tightening her stomach muscles, retching with forced dry heaves.

"Please," she whispered. "I'm going to throw up. Please let me go to the bathroom."

They exchanged glances. They were going to kill her. But disposing of a vomit-drenched body was going to be marginally more unpleasant than disposing of a body that had been allowed to throw up into the toilet.

With a disgusted sound Mr. Elegant waved his hand. "Take her to the bathroom." He pinned her with his black, crocodile gaze. "Try anything and you'll wish you'd never been born."

Forcing herself to retch had brought up bile, made worse by his words and the images they conjured up. She nodded her head. The man behind her came around, bent, pulled out a long, sharp knife, as gleaming as the instruments on the table.

With a smooth movement, he sliced through the duct tape holding her ankles together and the tape around her breasts anchoring her to the chair.

With a strong hand he lifted her up out of the chair. If he hadn't kept a grip on her arm, she'd have fallen straight to the floor.

For the first time, she got a good look at him. He was the man on her rainy street. The man she'd thought was Tom for a horrified moment.

Turned out he was worse than Tom.

"Hurry it up," Mr. Elegant said sourly.

Tears pricked at her eyes. Yes, she should hurry up and die.

"Okay," she whispered.

The blond man holding her arm in a tight, unbreakable grip, Kerry shuffled more than walked to a door in a corridor she hadn't seen before. Her legs were extremely weak, from being bound, from the terror she felt.

The man with the funny accent almost carried her. When her knees buckled, he just picked her up with one arm around her waist and hustled her to the bathroom door. Inside was a malodorous cubicle, stained and filthy.

Kerry stopped at the door, shuddering deep inside herself, long deep tremors. Oh God, this was it. Her life, stopping now. However awful the past year had been, on the run from Tom, once or twice she'd thought that somehow some day it would all stop.

She could start her life up again. He'd forget about her and she could move on, into the sunlight, into a regular life, instead of huddling in the shadows. Maybe even start an interior decorating business. Maybe find a nice man to marry. Maybe—maybe even have kids.

And even in the fear and terror of this past year, there'd been good moments. Tea with Irene, the odd funny client. She'd read a lot from the local library, listened to a lot of music on the radio. Solitary pleasures, but pleasures nonetheless.

All ending, right now.

A thump on her back, hard. The door of the bathroom yawned before her. "Get going. We don't have all day here." *Hiah*.

Kerry turned, licking her dry lips. "I'm—I'm going to need my hands." She looked at him, at his light-blue eyes, like colored marbles, just as devoid of any humanity as Mr. Elegant's. "To . . . um." Her mind whirred uselessly. "Need my hands," she repeated in a whisper.

He'd either cut the tape or not. She couldn't do anything about it.

He whipped out that sharp blade again, the steel whispering against its scabbard, and with one deft move cut through the duct tape. An amazing feat. He sliced through without touching skin, though her wrists were tightly bound together.

So he was handy with a knife. Real handy. She shuddered even more deeply.

He nodded sharply at the bathroom, not even bothering to waste words with her.

"Can—" Kerry was shaking so hard her mouth could barely form words. She flexed her hands, trying to get some circulation going again. It would be too horrible if she botched this. "Can I close the door?"

He shook his head.

Oh God.

"Can you—can you turn your back?"

Without a word, he turned on his heel, presented his broad back to her. Kerry suspected it was more because he didn't want to see her vomiting than to provide her with some privacy.

This was her chance, right now. She stepped into the filthy, stained cubicle. It was dark, with only a small window way up high. There was no question of her being able to escape from it, and she knew the two men realized it as well. Even if she were athletic enough to leap up onto the toilet seat, smash the filthy glass pane and try to haul herself up and out, this man would catch her in less than a second.

No, there was no way out.

So she looked around, heart pumping with dread, tears bleeding from her heart. This was where she'd end her life, in this fetid abandoned bathroom, with only two heartless strangers to witness her passing.

Such a miserably lonely and squalid place to die.

"Hurry it up," the man with the funny accent said. *Come on, get going, do what you have to do so we can torture you to death for information that's not in your head.*

Suddenly, a hot flush of rage ripped through her system and she welcomed it. It chased away the icy chill of fear, and even the sadness, because she was going to do what these two men thought was impossible.

She was going to beat them.

"Okay." Kerry put soft humility in her voice, just as he'd

expect. She understood very well that they *liked* degrading her, humiliating her. Just as they would *like* hurting her.

Fuck them.

She put up the toilet cover, a sound the man would be expecting. Only instead of bending over that filth, she held up her right hand and examined the ring on it. It was a sleek, modern design, pure titanium. *Will resist a conflagration,* the online brochure had said.

Of course the subtext was, *If they burn your body, something will remain.*

The company was as mysterious as its owner—a legendary beauty who hid from the world. Whoever she was, she was brilliant—a designer of jewelry that doubled as weaponry, only for women. Necklaces that broke apart to become small, razor-sharp scythes or hid garrotes, bracelets that held a small amount of C-4 and a detonator that came with detailed instructions and was just enough to blow someone up. The solutions were endless and fascinating.

Kerry had opted for a ring, very simple and unobtrusive, but beautiful nonetheless. It was disguised as the kind of ring that at first glance looked like something you could pick up at a crafts fair or on any costume jewelry stand.

Perfectly ordinary ring except for one thing: Press a tiny hidden button on one side and out shot a spring-loaded mini hypodermic syringe preloaded with enough neurotoxin to fell a bull. The syringe could also be preloaded with a powerful tranquillizer, but Kerry knew that if she ever became desperate enough to use it, she'd need to kill. So it had been option A, neurotoxin.

There was a second option to the ring, which Kerry had barely paid attention to. Twist that tiny button instead of pressing it, and the syringe would pop out on the underside, penetrate the skin of your hand and kill you instantly.

If the man who stood with his back to her had been alone, she'd have stabbed him in a heartbeat. Reached over and jabbed him in the neck, hard. He wouldn't be expecting it at all. He'd die at her feet and she'd rejoice.

But the syringe was preloaded with just one dose. Kerry hadn't thought it through but she realized how incredibly clever the designer was. If you needed two doses, you were better off killing yourself because you'd never prevail.

"That's enough," the man muttered and turned around, giving her a quick, impersonal up and down look. She hadn't gone to the bathroom, she hadn't vomited. "What the fuck—"

Staring him straight into his dead eyes, Kerry wrenched the button, felt the white-hot prick of the needle, welcomed it, and dropped where she stood, dead before she hit the ground.

Chapter 13

San Diego

They drove up out of the condo's garage in single file. One, two, three. Mike first, then Sam and Nicole, then Harry and Ellen. They turned right and followed the ocean for a couple of miles, then turned inland over a beautiful bridge.

They all drove at exactly forty miles an hour and kept the exact same distance from each other.

It took Ellen a while to realize what this was: a convoy.

She turned her head and looked blindly out at the passing scenery. This was an unusually beautiful part of San Diego, but she barely noticed what she was seeing.

This, then, was the life of Harry, of Sam and Nicole and of Mike. Reduced to moving in a convoy as if through Baghdad, through incredibly hostile terrain.

Because of her.

Roddy, dear, sweet Roddy, was dead.

Because of her.

"Hey." Harry's deep voice broke the silence. He picked up her hand and brought it to his mouth. He kissed the back and returned her hand to her lap, all the while staring at the road up ahead. "It's not your fault."

"Are you a mind reader now?" Ellen's voice was froggy and she cleared it.

"Don't have to be a mind reader to know what you were thinking. It was all over your face."

She huffed out a little laugh. He hadn't looked at her once since they'd come up out of the garage, so clearly he had 360-degree vision. It wouldn't surprise her; he seemed to be Superman. He'd prevailed over three of Gerald's men.

He continued staring straight ahead. "There was nothing you could do for your agent. And it had nothing to do with you. Montez is a bad guy and your agent was caught right in the middle of his machinations. Just bad luck, like being run over by a truck. You can't beat yourself up over it. It won't do you any good, and above all, it won't do him any good. The only person to profit would be that fu—would be Gerald, because you'll be a little less alert."

He was right, of course he was right.

"Besides, you've got other things to think about. Like my tax return. We're all going to dump tons of pieces of paper on you, and man, you're going to regret your offer."

No, she wouldn't. She was actually looking forward to it. "Nicole comes first."

He dipped his head briefly, and a touch of a smile crossed his face. "Of course. Ladies first."

"No, not because ladies come first but because she figured out what happened in Baghdad. That deserves a reward."

"Yeah." He frowned. "I can't believe she's better at some types of computer research than I am."

Ellen laughed. She *laughed*. When was the last time she laughed? Over a year ago, surely. It felt odd, and came out a little rusty, but it was definitely a laugh.

He slanted her a glance. "Sounds good, you laughing."

"Yeah," she whispered, surprised at herself. It felt good, too. With all her troubles, and she had a mountain of them, she felt her spirits rise.

Her situation in general sucked, and she had no future to speak of, but right this second, life was good. She was very safe right now, in a vehicle that she was sure was armored, with Harry at the wheel. Gentle, sexy Harry, who was good with violence. He wielded it like a surgeon wields a scalpel, *for* her, not *against* her.

In the vehicles in front of her were three people who were fast becoming her friends, two of them warriors.

Amazingly, all of them had gathered her into their little circle of protection and friendship. Crazily enough, though she was in terrible trouble, she'd never felt so safe. So safe, so warm, so protected.

Don't get used to it, she warned herself. Because it would be easy to just sink into it, like into a warm bath, and never get out. There would be a deadline to all of this, no doubt. Harry and Sam and Mike would be working to come up with a plan for her. A place to go, documents to fit into a new life that they'd conjure up out of thin air.

They'd do a better job of it than she could. Would she have a say in what life they chose for her? Music was out, of course. At the thought, a heavy lump of lead settled into her chest. No more music, no more singing, not even amateur singing in a choir. Her voice was too well known by now. Somehow Gerald must have traced her back through her music, so music was out.

Accountancy, too, of course. Even she knew, you don't take up your old profession when on the run.

She didn't want to waitress any more. It had been fun for a while but it was hard drudgery, and for better or worse, she had lots of money stashed away, so she didn't have to do it.

Maybe a job in a bookstore? She liked reading. Or, or . . . her mind turned blank when Harry took her hand again, raised it to his mouth. This time the kiss wasn't reassuring, it was pure sex. She felt his warm lips, the slight bite of beard even though he'd shaved. His mouth lingered, a touch of tongue, and she suddenly flashed on last night. How his beard had scraped her shoulder as he kissed and lightly bit his way down to her breast.

He'd stopped moving in her, hot and hard and heavy inside her, while he kissed his way to her breast. Then he'd lifted his head, fierce golden gaze locked to her eyes. Sliding his hips forward to be more deeply into her.

Oh God, just remembering made heat blossom all through her body.

Harry chuckled. "I know what you're thinking."

"I'm red, aren't I?" Her voice was resigned.

"Like a stoplight, honey." The little convoy took a corner and she looked blindly out the window, trying to cool off a little. His voice roughened.

"I don't blush, but—" He took her hand and put it over his groin. Right over the hot steel column in his pants. It was a shocking thing to do. Probably she should protest, but there wasn't any blood in her head to think, and all the air had left her lungs. "I'm thinking of the same thing you are."

He pressed his hand down hard over hers and she gasped as she felt his penis jump, lengthening a little. It had done exactly the same thing last night when she'd nipped him under his ear. It hadn't been planned; she hadn't thought it out. It had been instinct, an urgent curiosity to find out what he tasted like, and whether he liked being lightly bit as much as she did.

The answer had been yes. Hell yes.

She'd felt the pulse of new blood flooding into his penis buried deep inside her and her vagina had clenched tightly. Thinking of it, remembering it, her hand instinctively tightened around him and the breath exploded out of his body.

"God." The word came out rough. His jaws were clenched, muscles rippling up to his temples. She'd have said he was in pain if it weren't for the fact that his hand tightened over hers to keep it right where it was.

His eyes quartered the street. "We're going to be at the Morrison Building in about four minutes. Where am I going to go with *this*?" His hand clenched around hers and his penis surged again against the palm of her hand.

Blood suffused her face; her hands trembled. The little convoy was slowing down. Soon they'd be parking and the two of them would have to emerge from this SUV with her burning face and his erection.

"We have to think of something that will cool us down," she gasped. Something as big and as cold as Antarctica, the way she was feeling.

Harry lifted his hand from hers and she released him.

They drove down into the gloom of the building's underground garage, the bright sunlight abruptly gone, as if a switch had been thrown.

"Not hard," Harry said, parking neatly beside Sam and Nicole's vehicle. "Just think of Gerald Montez. That's enough."

Turned out that Nicole's office was just across the corridor from her husband's. Pretty convenient.

She had elaborate security, involving a palm print and a keypad code. The only thing missing was the retina scan. When her door clicked open, like that of a bank vault, Nicole put her hand to Ellen's back and urged her inside. Nicole turned back to the three men.

"Ellen's spending the day with me." Harry opened his mouth and she shook her finger at him. "With *me*. And I don't want to hear any discussion about it."

Harry looked at Sam, who made a strangled noise in his throat. It was clear who called the shots in that family. Mike just looked amused.

Nicole leaned forward a little. "Harry, you know perfectly well that Sam made sure my office is as secure as yours, and he watches who comes in and out of my office on his monitor anyway, don't you, Sam?"

Sam looked at the floor and had the grace to look a little bit abashed. It was hard to tell, though, on that rough face. He was even worse than Harry at showing emotion.

"Ellen is going to be much more comfortable spending the day with me, aren't you, dear?" Nicole turned to her.

Walking around in an office of men she barely knew, except for one who turned her on so powerfully she'd have to avoid him as much as possible, or staying with Nicole, cool, calm, friendly Nicole. There was only one possible answer. "Ah. Yes."

"This is your way to make sure that she looks at your books before she looks at ours," Harry said sourly.

"Absolutely. So embrace the suck, as you military types say." Nicole smiled as she closed the door in their faces. She leaned her back against it and blew out a little breath. "Now. We've got rid of them, so we can relax."

She waved a graceful hand at the small office. "Welcome to my little lair. You work on that laptop over there and I'll work at the desktop. Around eleven one of Sam's men will go downstairs and get a skinny decaf latte for me and you'd like . . . what?"

"Cinnamon chai," Ellen smiled.

"Great." Nicole pressed a button on a fancy intercom system, murmured *Cinnamon chai* and hung her jacket up on a brass clothes tree.

Nicole went to a beautiful antique console under the window, brought out two big cardboard boxes and placed them on the table next to the laptop. She opened the flaps, looked inside and winced.

"Oh, man. This is what denial looks like. I've been putting this off for way too long. I started Wordsmith while my father was very ill, and it took all my energy to do the work and take care of Dad. So bookkeeping came a very distant third." She tilted the boxes so Ellen could see inside. There was a wild tangle of bills and check stubs and invoices. It looked like weasels had nested in there. Nicole peered again into the box and back at Ellen. "This is really bad. Sorry."

Ellen looked around at the tiny little office. Small as it was, it was gorgeous, decorated with a few antiques and lovely watercolors and pretty knickknacks, and it smelled of potpourri. It was like being inside a little jewel box. Just being here made her feel good.

"I can't imagine anything I'll like more than repaying your kindness by doing something I enjoy doing. So no thanks necessary."

Nicole's beautiful cobalt-blue eyes widened. "You *like* keeping accounts?" she asked, in the same tone as you'd say, *You* like *genital herpes?*

"I do, yes. Strange as that sounds. So, Nicole, you've made me a very happy woman. Tell me how your system works."

"System." Nicole thought while tapping on the lid of one of the boxes with a manicured pink-tipped nail. "Um, I don't really have much of a system besides Throw the Piece of Paper into the Box. On that laptop you'll find chronological files of work as it came in and the quotes I put out. Then you'll have to match those to the bills. I do translations myself and bill those directly, but a much bigger part of my business is matching clients with translators, and I take a ten percent commission for that. So there are two different sets of accounts." She looked worried. "It's really complicated. Maybe I should—"

Ellen put her arm around Nicole's shoulders and squeezed gently. "I'll be fine. Don't worry about it. This is what I do, so let me do it."

"I thought you sang."

"Yeah, and keep books." Nicole just looked at her, shrugged, and sat down at her desk. She slid in a portable hard drive into the processor and fired up her desktop. Within a minute, she was lost to the world, tapping away at the keyboard, totally absorbed in whatever it was she was translating.

Ellen understood completely. Numbers did for her what languages did for Nicole. She loved them, trusted them. They loved her back and had never, ever let her down. Numbers just—they just always made *sense.* When the people around her had never made sense, numbers had.

When she had math homework she could forget about her mom's latest loser boyfriend, about the rent her mom hadn't paid that month, the cigarette cough that wouldn't quit. Her mom getting thinner and thinner . . .

It all went away, thanks to the beauty of math.

Her love for numbers naturally flowed into accounting. She wasn't a genius mathematician. She was just good with numbers, and accounting was great for that. Money in, money out. When more money came in than went out, you were doing fine. When more money went out than came in, you were in trouble.

So simple. So easy.

She dove right into Nicole's messy files, and inside a minute, she was gone, too.

Nicole had a . . . creative filing system, which was code for no filing system at all. So the first thing Ellen did was put things in piles—invoices, rent payments, utilities, deductible bills. After that, she started to get a handle on Nicole's business.

Nicole was doing well, so she must be good at what she did. There had been a period in which the company hadn't been doing so well and it coincided with when Harry said her father had been dying. So that was understandable. Now it was thriving. No doubt, once the baby was born, it would be put a little on the back burner.

This was exactly as it should be.

Work is important. Family is more important. Not that she'd know that firsthand. Her own family had been highly dysfunctional, the next best thing to not being there. But Ellen had eyes and she could see. Family was something she'd never had, and now, considering what was awaiting her, possibly never would have, but she could see its power in others.

Sam's love and concern every time he looked at his wife, every time he touched her, was clear. And Nicole's love just shone in her eyes when she looked at Sam. There was no doubt that the little girl Nicole was expecting was very much wanted.

At eleven the office doorbell rang. Nicole opened the door to a giant of a man with a slab for a face and basketballs for biceps, holding a big cardboard box with the luscious smell of coffee and cinnamon tea wafting from it. Every line of his huge, muscled body spelled trouble. Ellen tensed for a second until she saw how untroubled Nicole was.

"Thanks so much, Barney." She took the box, placed it on her desk and gave him a blinding smile. Ellen was standing to the side and *she* was nearly blown over by the force of the smile. "That's really sweet of you. How's Zip? The vet figure out what was wrong?"

Slab—evidently called Barney, and if ever a man was misnamed, it was this man—blushed red all over his rough face. He'd have tugged a forelock if he'd had hair instead of a shaved, tattooed skull.

"Doc says Zip's gonna be okay, thanks for asking, ma'am. Kidney trouble. Gave me medicine." He wound down and just stood there, a huge hunk of a man, standing in the doorjamb, almost as big as the door frame.

"That's great," Nicole said gently. "Thanks again for the coffee and tea—we appreciate it." She smiled as she slowly closed the door in his face.

"Wow. Your own personal gorilla." Ellen lifted up her cup, pried open the lid and sniffed deeply, appreciatively. Was there anything better than cinnamon chai? "Who's Zip?"

"His pet iguana. Three feet long. He loves that animal more than his motorcycle, and that's saying a lot." She laughed. "Sam employs some colorful characters, but they seem to get the job done." She took a sip of her decaf. "Gets great coffee, too."

They both dove back in their work, Nicole tapping away at the keyboard, Ellen finishing up classifying Nicole's paperwork.

At noon, Nicole's cell phone rang. Distracted, she picked it up, saw who was the caller, and sighed. She spoke quickly, all in one long sentence. "Hello, darling, no, I'm not working, I'm lying down on the couch with my feet up, just like you told me to, as a matter of fact I was taking a nap, no, that's okay, I needed to wake up anyway, I don't feel tired, I feel just great, so don't worry, see you soon."

Ellen looked, startled, at the little couch where Nicole definitely was not resting. She was at her desk, working hard.

"I love you too," Nicole said, blew a kiss into the receiver, folded her cell closed and sighed. "If I don't tell him I'm resting, he comes over and stands there with his arms crossed looking like Neptune on steroids on a bad day. Lying to him is easier."

"He loves you," Ellen said.

"Yes," Nicole sighed. "And I love him. But he needs to back off a little. He was bad enough before, but he's gone overboard ever since I told him about the baby." She smiled and rubbed her belly.

"Must be nice," Ellen said without thinking. "To be loved like that."

Nicole turned her deep blue gaze on Ellen and looked at her thoughtfully. It was like being hit by blue spotlights. She simply looked at Ellen for a while, assessing her.

"What?" Ellen gave a half laugh. "Did the foam leave a mustache? Do I have lettuce in my teeth or hay in my hair?"

"*You're* loved like that. By Harry. You can't see it because you don't know Harry that well. Like Sam and like Mike, he doesn't express his emotions well. But to someone who knows him, what he feels for you is right there."

"I—ah. Um." Ellen's tongue flapped uselessly in her mouth. "He, um, he doesn't love me. He can't. We've only known each other—what? Five days? Six? And I was unconscious a lot of the time."

"Sam asked me to marry him the fifth day after we met." A memory that made Nicole smile crossed her beautiful face. "It was a terrible proposal, very badly botched, but I accepted anyway. I've never regretted it."

No, Ellen could see that she didn't.

Whoa. All of a sudden, Ellen realized that she could pump Nicole for information on Harry. He was so damned closemouthed. They were lovers, yes, but she knew so little about him. Now that she thought about it, he always deflected personal questions. Often with a kiss, which always worked. He could kiss her through a nuclear detonation and she wouldn't even notice.

"You say all three men have problems expressing their emotions. Is there a reason?"

"You mean besides having a Y chromosome?" Nicole rolled her eyes. Then her face turned serious. "Yes, there's definitely a reason they're more closemouthed than most men. All three of them had a terrible childhood and adolescence. They became friends—more like brothers, actually, and they think of themselves as brothers—in a brutal foster home. Sam says that they would have died if they hadn't had each other's backs."

Ellen shivered. "How awful," she breathed.

Nicole nodded. "Yes, I think it truly was awful. Sam rarely speaks of it, but you can see the effects of it. The tight bond he has with Harry and Mike and their dedication to helping women in trouble. All three of them have seen a lot of cruelty to women and children." She caught Ellen's eyes. "Harry in particular. He's never actually told me the story—Sam has. He told me that when Harry was twelve years old, he was living with his mother and baby sister in a hovel in the Barrio. His mom was a junkie and had men coming in and out of the house, sometimes violent men. Sam says Harry throws up if he gets too close to the house where it happened."

"What?" Ellen swallowed. "Where what happened?"

Nicole took a deep breath and let it out slowly. "Okay. Looks like I'm going to have to be the one to tell you, though rightly it should be Harry himself. But Sam says Harry never talks about it, ever. And that's not fair to you, because you should know."

"Whatever it is, I'm already feeling dread." Ellen leaned forward on her elbows. "So . . . something happened when Harry was twelve. Something awful."

"Yes. The three of them were living with Harry's mom's boyfriend du jour, who was a meth addict. A very violent one."

"Oh no," Ellen whispered, knowing where this was going.

Nicole nodded and closed her eyes briefly. "On Christmas day, the methhead got it into his crazy head that Harry was hiding money from him. He took a baseball bat to Harry's mom and staved in her skull, then he broke . . ."

Nicole's voice wobbled as her eyes grew wet. She stroked her belly, where her little daughter was growing. Her voice was hoarse as she continued. "He broke Harry's sister's arm. Her name was Crissy. Christine. She was five years old, and she loved Harry. Sam said that Harry said that she was the sweetest little girl on earth." Nicole wiped a slender, elegant finger under her eyes and checked the finger for mascara. "I can hardly think about it. That madman broke Crissy's arm, then picked her up by the broken arm and smashed her against the wall. She died instantly. Harry did everything he could to save his mother and his sister, but this monster took a bat to his legs and shattered both femurs. Even with two shattered legs, Harry managed to kill the man, but it was too late. His mother and sister were gone. When he was able to walk on crutches, he was sent to the most brutal foster home in the system."

Ellen could actually feel her heart swelling with pain. "Oh God."

"But Sam and then Mike were there and they had his back. They couldn't look out for him in Afghanistan, though. He came back in pretty bad shape. Was blown up by something called an RPG—I guess sort of like a flying bomb. When I first met him, Harry could barely stand. He's done miracles since then, mostly because Sam and Mike forced a physical therapist on him he called the Norwegian Nazi."

"He told me about the Norwegian Nazi." The Norwegian Nazi was very, very good at his job because Ellen could remember the steely muscles under her hands, lean and hard. The grace with which he moved. You'd never have known he'd been grievously wounded, twice.

"Of course, you helped, too."

She'd been thinking of Harry's muscles. How hard he was all over. Intense heat had crept into her thoughts. "Um, yes, he said he listened to my music quite a lot."

Nicole wasn't smiling. "They say Harry listened to your two CDs obsessively, over and over and over again. He couldn't sleep at night, so he listened to you, and somehow your voice pulled him through. Sam and Mike were really worried about Harry, about his will to live. I think thanks to you, he found the will to put himself back together."

Oh God. Ellen blinked the tears back. "I don't know what to say to that."

"I do." Nicole leaned forward, incredibly serious. "Last year, some bad guys came after me. It's a long story. I'll tell it to you some day. Even worse, these guys came after my father, who was very ill—dying, in fact. They kidnapped him, *hurt* him." Her blue eyes blazed with what Ellen recognized as hatred, so strange on her beautiful face. "Sam saved me with the help of Mike and Harry. Sam said that when he and Mike set off to rescue me and Dad, Harry'd have done anything, given anything to be able to come with them, even though he could barely stand. As it happens, he helped Sam and Mike find me even if he wasn't there at the showdown. He's one of the good guys, Ellen. A really good guy. He's had more than his share of tragedy. He loves you. I know he's completely on your side and he'll protect you with his life. I couldn't bear to see him hurt in any way. So think about this carefully. Because if you hurt him in any way, if you break his heart, you'll have me to answer to. And Sam and Mike. But trust me, I can be meaner than Sam and Mike. I'm the one you should be afraid of. Is that clear?"

In that instant, Ellen understood completely why Sam loved Nicole so much. Not for her beauty—though that was off the charts—but for her fiercely loving heart.

"Completely," she answered. "And for the record, I think it's more likely that Harry will break my heart instead of the other way round."

Nicole was still watching her intently. At Ellen's words she suddenly broke into a smile. "Okay." The smile broadened as she sat back. "Okay. That's settled, then. Well." She rubbed her hands briskly. "Now that that's taken care of, I say we all have takeout pizza tonight and a salad to make it officially healthy. And afterwards—you'll sing for us? For Harry?"

There was only one possible answer. "For you guys and for Harry? Sure."

Chapter 14

Seattle

"Fuck fuck fuck!"

Montez paced around the small rental storage unit muttering, walking in circles around the dead body of the woman, all but tearing his hair out.

Piet watched him emotionlessly. This was a real waste of time and energy, but the *fokken gek*—fucking moron—clearly had to get it out of his system. Some operator, wasting time on this shit.

But—he was the boss. Though really, he wasn't the boss of anything, least of all himself. Still, Piet always followed the client, even when the client was stupid.

It wasn't his problem. If it had been, he sure as hell wouldn't be walking around in circles with a dead girl at his feet. He'd have already taken care of the girl and moved on.

After a while he got tired of watching Montez. It was one thing for Montez to piss away his time in theatrics. But every second in which Piet was with that dead body was another second in which he could be caught.

Doing time in a U.S. prison for this asshole was not in the cards.

"Calm down," he said finally.

Montez whirled. "Calm down? Calm *down*? This—" His shaking index finger pointed at the girl lying on a tarp in the middle of the small space. "This is a disaster! Goddammit, this should never have happened! Now we're left with nothing but dead meat!"

Piet tuned him out and studied the girl's face. He'd laid her down on her back. Whatever poison she'd taken had acted incredibly quickly. The only poisons he knew that worked so fast were neurotoxins. Only an autopsy with a tox screen would tell exactly which one, but she sure wouldn't be getting an autopsy.

He studied the face carefully. A pretty woman, pretty even in death. Death had come for her so quickly her features weren't distorted. She looked like she was sleeping quietly, in a better place than she'd be right now, because he'd have inflicted a lot of pain and he'd have made her talk.

Montez had been getting hard looking at her, thinking of the pain to come. He hadn't realized it, but Piet had seen. Those guys were the worst, the ones who got wood during interrogation.

It amazed Piet that Montez had been in the army at all, though he knew the Yanks had become less selective about the boots they were putting on the ground. Back in the day, qualifying for South African Special Forces as a Recce, that kind of sick fuck had been weeded out right at the start. No place for them in a man's military. Violence was a tool, not an end in itself.

For just a second, Piet allowed himself a brief flash of regret, a short, intense wish that he could roll back the clock and be with his mates in the bush again. Good men, all. No sick fucks, just warriors.

While Montez was ranting, Piet continued observing the body. The girl's skin still held a faint flush, which was of course fading fast as the blood drained away from the skin. She'd dropped dead ten minutes ago. Right now, gravity was draining the blood in the capillaries from the front of her body to the back, which soon would turn dark red.

He'd made very, very sure that there was nothing underneath the tarp that could make an imprint on the skin. The pooled blood would show any object up as clearly as an image on a negative. Montez wasn't thinking straight, but Piet was.

The capillaries were draining the blood right now. They had a little window of opportunity . . .

He kneeled and started skinning her, making a sharp, straight surgical incision along the midbody line of the torso from base of neck to sternum and stripping away the skin on the left from her breast and shoulder. Like field-dressing a deer. No blood spurted, of course; the heart wasn't pumping anymore. But there was still enough blood in the arteries to pool sullenly around the body. Piet made sure none of it touched his shoes or trousers.

He had to get this done before rigor set in. Handling a body in the throes of rigor mortis was hard. Not to mention the fact that the internal organs had already begun decomposition. He'd seen bodies explode with the force of built-up internal gas in the intestines, though that took a while.

Montez was watching, slack-jawed. He'd stopped his ranting and stared. "What the fuck?"

Piet didn't sigh, though he wanted to. This guy was supposed to be *smart*. He headed up a multimillion-dollar company.

"We're going to do with her what we did with the agent, only this needs to be scarier. This has to be a real message to Palmer: *Look what we can do*. Do you have the tape?"

"Yeah." Montez held up a Flip camcorder the size of a USB key.

They'd filmed the first part of the interrogation.

The idea had been to film the entire session and send it to Palmer. But instead of an hour-long session, they'd had about ten minutes.

"Didn't last long, so we'll use stills," Piet said. He cut a fine incision on her forehead along the hairline and started pulling back the skin.

"Jesus!" Montez shouted. He held a hand to his mouth. "God, you're scalping her!"

No shit, Sherlock.

Montez wouldn't have been averse to torturing this woman to death, but scalping her after death made him retch.

Piet couldn't wait to finish the job and get away from this moron.

He finished scalping and stood back, assessing the effect. Should scare the shit out of this Ellen Palmer. He waited for her to bleed out then lifted the woman in his arms. He settled her back in the chair, wrapped the duct tape around her chest again. The woman slumped, head down, red skull gleaming, looking like she had on a patchwork red shirt. "Take a couple of stills of her. We'll add it to the still of her screaming and send it to that bulletin board."

Montez took out his cell, took several snapshots and downloaded them onto his laptop.

Piet put together the stills into a narrative anyone could understand. The woman bucking against his hand on her, mouth open in silent screams, then the stills of her now, after what Palmer would think was horrible torture. It worked. He switched on the laptop's mike and digitized his voice.

"Ellen Palmer. Look at your friend Kerry. She's still alive but won't be for long if you don't get in touch with us. Send us a message with your location right now or we'll keep on hurting her. Eventually she'll die, but it will take her a while. Get in touch with us and we'll take her to a hospital right now. If you don't get in touch, you're signing her death warrant. It'll be on your head." Piet sent the file with the stills and the digitized voiceover to the message board.

It was in the lap of the gods now. Palmer would open it when she opened it. But when she did . . . they'd have her.

Montez watched and didn't speak until Piet powered the laptop down. "Now what? We need to be close to where she is when she opens the laptop. Where is she?"

Piet thought about it.

He'd had Montez take him to Palmer's apartment and leave him alone in it for an hour. The human equivalent of giving a hunting dog the prey's shirt to sniff.

In an hour, he'd gotten her measure. No drugs, no alcohol

beyond a dusty bottle of whiskey in a cupboard with half a glass missing. No fancy clothes, no fancy jewelry, very little makeup. Basic cable. Lots of music CDs, bought and not pirated. Lots of books, paperbacks.

Montez said she hadn't missed a day's work in two years working for him.

The singing was a surprise because she had apparently kept her talent hidden, which was interesting. She'd only put her voice out there when she needed the money. Otherwise it looked like she'd been perfectly happy being a waitress, earning minimum wage.

She was a perfectly ordinary woman who'd been on the run for a year, who'd been flushed out of one safe haven, who'd found another in San Diego, and found a protector with it. She wasn't a warrior or an operator. Protection would be welcome.

She wouldn't leave where she'd found it.

"She's still in San Diego," Piet said. "I'd bet anything on it. Let's bury this"—he flicked a thumb at the redly gleaming corpse on the chair—"and get down to San Diego fast. I have an idea."

In flight, over Sacramento, California

A private jet is a good way to travel, Piet reflected. It beat military transport hands down. He'd been around very rich men for a long, long time now, but their luxuries still fascinated him.

He was a man who'd been flown halfway around the world on retrofitted C-130s for personnel transport, sitting on canvas seats, strapped to webbing for thirty-hour flights. No food, no water, and you pissed in a bottle. If you had to shit, tough shit.

The South African Armed Forces for a while had used beat-up Vietnam-era Hueys. The noise level penetrated even the cheap ear baffles. It had been like riding inside a huge, metal shaker with sharp edges designed to rip you to bits if you didn't hang on.

Miles and millions of dollars away from this Learjet 45. They'd flown in style and comfort from Georgia to Seattle and now were flying in style and comfort from Seattle to San Diego.

The cabin smelled of new leather and lemon polish. The captain and his copilot had welcomed them aboard like royalty and they'd taken off from the General Aviation section of Sea-Tac ten minutes after they'd boarded.

No waiting, no fuss, no inspections.

Piet would never be this rich, and even if he were, he wouldn't have a private plane. Keeping a plane like this meant leaving a huge footprint in the world. You had to hire pilots and maintenance crews, file flight plans, hire a hangar to keep the damned thing when you didn't need it. It was a giant fist in the face of society—*Look how fucking rich I am*. Montez clearly needed to wave that fist, make the point.

Piet didn't.

They sat across from each other in ergonomic seats covered in soft, butter-colored leather with a designer fiberglass table between them. Piet was peering into his computer monitor when Montez spoke.

"So why the fuck are we heading back to San Diego?" Montez's voice was sullen. He was still mad at having lost the girl before he could have his fun, the moron. "She could be anywhere by now."

"Mm." Piet finished what he was doing before answering. Montez, being Montez, would find it a sign of disrespect, but he didn't give a shit. "It's a question of psychology. She's been on the run for a year and she'll be tired of that. She went across the country and settled in the last city you can be in before falling into the ocean and stayed there until you flushed her out."

And lost her.

The words were unspoken, but a dull flush appeared under Montez's dark skin. "For some reason she goes straight to San Diego. And it turns out that the reason she's there is because she's got a protector of some kind. Girl's not ex military, doesn't have a martial arts background. Near as I can tell, she's just an accountant who sings. She's got someone—I think she'll keep him. As long as he's around, she'll stay."

"Even if you're right, San Diego's a big town. We're looking at three million people in an area that's almost four hundred square miles in size. And that's not counting Tijuana just across the border." Montez slapped the expensive leather of the seat. "Shit! We'd know where she was now if that bitch hadn't offed herself!"

Piet doubted that. But whatever. The woman was dead and indulging in theatrical outbursts wasn't going to bring her back to life, and more important, it wasn't going to help them find Ellen Palmer. Cool, calm logic would do that.

"Look at this." Piet turned the laptop so that both of them could see the monitor. It was a map of a section of Seattle. Red lines connected dots of different sizes. It was the same map with the same data points that had helped them find Kerry Robinson.

Montez's jaw muscles clenched. "Yeah, so? We found her friend and now she's dead. How's this going to help us?"

Piet didn't sigh, but he did want to punch that childish pout off Montez's face. "Look at these routes." Piet ran his finger from the Blue Moon to where Ellen Palmer had been living to Kerry Robinson's apartment. The lines made huge dog legs. "What do you see?"

Montez fixed him with a hard, black stare. "I don't like guessing games, Van der Boeke."

Geeste bul, Piet thought. Damned idiot.

"This," he indicated with his finger, following the dogleg routes, "is how she got to work and how she went to visit her friend Kerry."

Montez stared at the monitor, scowling.

"And this," Piet continued, pulling up another online map, "is a map of the bus routes in Seattle." He manipulated the images until he found the section of town on the first map. The bus routes followed the doglegs exactly.

Montez wasn't getting it, and that made him angry. "Get to the point," he growled.

"I think Palmer ditched her car before she arrived in Seattle or else ditched it in Seattle. I don't think she had access to a car. I think she took the bus everywhere she went. And look at this . . ."

He brought up another map, a tangle of streets. Montez leaned forward, staring at the map with narrowed eyes. "So? What am I looking at?"

"A map of San Diego." Piet tapped two points. "This is the hotel she booked and this is the Greyhound bus station." The two were a block apart. "I think she took the bus from Seattle to San Diego and checked in to the first hotel she found."

"Okay, okay." Montez sat back. "I get it. She's without a car. How does that help us?"

"When she came back to the hotel where your men were waiting for her, how did she get there?"

Montez was paying attention now. "The last word I had from my men was she was getting out of a cab."

"Exactly. I hacked into taxi company records. There are fifteen cab companies in San Diego, and in the fourth company, I found a record of a fare being dropped off at that hotel at 11:52 on the fourth of April. He picked the fare up on Birch Street, which has a lot of fancy high rises. It's in the heart of the business district. And the security cameras there worked just fine. Here she is. Coming out of the Morrison Building."

Piet clicked and brought up the file. No grainy photogram-per-second film for that street, no sir. Top-of-the-line cameras with high-definition digital film that showed everything clearly. And it clearly showed Ellen Palmer running, hailing a cab and taking off. A white script in the bottom right-hand corner showed the time in digital display: 11:34.

"Fuck," Montez breathed. "That's her."

"Yes." Piet realized that this was the first time Montez had seen Ellen Palmer in over a year, and it was taking him a minute to process her image on the screen. His eyes were wide with surprise.

Christ, how had this guy ever become a soldier? Real soldiers process new intel instantly, no matter how surprising;

otherwise they're dead. Green-haired Martians could appear in front of him, and he'd have his weapon up and firing in a second.

Montez blinked, coming back to the here and now. "So what's in there?"

"What's in the Morrison Building? It's a big complex. There are almost a hundred different companies in the building." Piet clicked on the print function and paper scrolled out of the small laser printer on a console built in to the bulkhead. He plucked the paper out of the printer and slid it across to Montez.

He hoped the guy wouldn't have the smarts to ask the obvious question—which office did she come out of—because the answer was, *I don't fucking know.*

It made him angry that he hadn't been able to crack the building's internal security cameras. Someone really good with computer security had made the building's system almost hackproof. But nothing was completely hackproof. When Piet got back home he was going to crack the system, on principle. In the meantime, though, he had fuck-all.

"There are fifteen private investigation services, eight security companies specializing in various areas, most international, and a shitload of lawyer's offices. Many of them specializing in criminal law."

There, that would take Montez's mind off wondering why Piet couldn't hack his way into the building's system.

Montez scrutinized the paper. His hand was firm, but he was sweating. A drop of sweat trickled down from his forehead, over his temple and dripped down onto his white linen shirt. He ignored it.

"We're going to get a ping when she accesses that bulletin board she set up with the dead bird. I'll triangulate from there. But she'll be in San Diego, and I'm willing to bet good money she'll get back to whoever she was dealing with in the Morrison Building on Monday morning."

The intercom came on and the pilot announced that they'd begun their descent into San Diego.

Piet sat and buckled his seatbelt. He tapped his laptop screen before powering it down. "That's our lead, right there. We're going to stake out the Morrison Building during the day, sleep in a hotel across the street during the night, taking turns keeping watch. Sooner or later she'll show up."

San Diego

Turned out nagging didn't work, but tears did.

She started by dropping gentle hints, which Harry totally ignored. She even batted her eyelashes, to no avail. Harry stood firm, like a man.

But when Ellen teared up a little, Harry broke. The tears weren't fake. She yearned to go for a walk in the sunshine so badly her heart ached. She drew the line at pouting, but the tears were real.

It took most of Sunday morning, but she did it.

"No," he said at first, and kept repeating it. No no no no.

Seducing him softened him up for the kill. They had brunch in bed, and she was lying on his hard chest, listening to the deep vibrations of his voice as he patiently listed the reasons why going for a walk on the beach was a bad idea.

Though he couldn't know specifically where she was, presumably Montez realized she might still be in San Diego. Never underestimate the power of coincidence. They might be walking along and one of Montez's thugs might be casing the beach at that exact moment. Montez wouldn't have access to NSA satellites, thank God, so they didn't have to worry about something Harry called Keyhole, some superspy satellite. But Montez could have a couple of ships at sea, men with binoculars lined up along the railing. And maybe one of those men might be looking through a scope of a rifle, on the lookout for her.

That stopped her for a second, then she shook the thought away.

"Harry. Listen to me." She reached up to kiss that strong, firm mouth, and it turned down.

He patted her behind. "I know you think you can get anything from me using sex, and it's true, you can get more or less anything you want, just not this. Diamonds and rubies, yes. This, no."

"I don't want diamonds or rubies." Ellen drew a circle in his chest hair until hair swirled around her fingertip, then pulled.

"Ouch." His voice was mild. "And torture won't work, either."

She'd been teasing, but now she sat up, covering her breasts.

"Oh man." Harry sighed in regret at seeing them disappear behind the sheet.

Ellen looked him straight in the eyes and spoke to him from the heart.

"I've been on the run for over a year now, and I've lived mostly in the dark all this time," she said quietly. "I crossed the country sleeping in motels during the day and driving by night.

When I waitressed I always chose the evening shift. In Seattle, too, I worked the evening shift and stayed inside during the day. And anyway, it rained most days. I haven't gone for a walk in the sunshine in over a year."

She'd got out of bed at dawn to draw back the curtains, and now she gestured to what she could see through the large French windows: a blindingly white beach and an achingly blue sea that met a slightly lighter sky way off on the horizon. Buttery sunshine from the sun that hadn't crossed the rooftops yet cast a gentle glow over everything. A soft, gentle breeze moved the curtains slightly. It was going to be a scorcher later, but right now the morning was fresh and cool. It felt like the first morning in the history of the world.

Ellen actually ached to be outside, to feel the sun on her skin, warm wind against her face.

She kissed his cheek, his mouth, pulled back and looked at him. "This past year, I've been indoors, alone and afraid. Gerald has taken everything from me—my job, my home, my life. My freedom."

She knew he'd spent the past year indoors, too, wounded and alone. Surely he'd understand.

"I'm not stupid. I understand there's a slight risk he could have tracked me down, though I can't see how." Now for the big guns. She reached out, lightly placed her hand on his chest, right over his heart. "Harry, if I have to spend the rest of my life in hiding, in the *dark*, it's not a life. Nicole told me a little about your past, and I think you understand what it's like to feel deep despair. To feel like you're condemned to the darkness forever."

Her eyes grew wet. She wasn't faking it, not much. Most of it was real.

Harry closed his eyes, swallowed convulsively, placed his big hand over hers. She could feel the strong, steady beat of his heart under her palm, and the strength and warmth of his hand over hers. Strong and steady, the two attributes of Harry.

He swallowed again.

"Honey . . . I can't stand the thought of you being hurt. And the thought of you falling into Montez's hands . . . it drives me a little crazy."

"Yes," she said. She could see that. "I know what I'm asking you. But I need to feel the sun on my face. Even for just half an hour."

His jaw muscles worked as he processed this. Ellen simply waited. She had no way to make him do something. If he wanted to keep her indoors, she certainly couldn't wrestle him to the ground and escape, or trick him. And she didn't have any more words to sway him with, because they stuck in her throat, tight with longing. She'd told him how she felt and now it was up to him.

Harry opened his eyes and looked down at her, his golden gaze fierce and penetrating. "You will never be more than a foot away from me at any time. You stick to my side like glue. Is that understood?"

Her heart took a delighted leap. "Yes, of course."

"I'm taking Sam and Mike with me, and we'll be armed. Is that clear?"

Oh God, she was going to wreck their Sunday. Was it worth it? She consulted her inner compass and decided yes, yes, it was worth it. She felt starved of fresh air. Inside she was already pumping her fist in victory.

"We stay out half an hour, tops."

Half an hour wasn't much, but it was better than nothing. His gaze never wavered from hers. There was only one possible answer.

"Yes, Harry."

He reached across to the bedside table, keeping his eyes on hers as he flipped opened his cell phone and dialed a number on speed dial.

"Harry, yeah. Listen, Ellen wants to walk on the beach. I'm against it, but the thing is, she hasn't had a walk in the sunshine for a year, and I know exactly what that feels like. I don't like it, but I can understand it. Half an hour. Can you and Mike—" He expelled a breath in relief as he listened. "Yeah, thanks. See you downstairs in fifteen minutes." He flipped the cell closed, turning to her with a half smile. "So what are you waiting for? Get dressed. We're going for a walk on the beach."

Yes!

Ellen was waiting at the door two minutes later, hopping from one foot to another with excitement, waiting for Harry to get ready.

Downstairs, to her dismay, Nicole was waiting with Sam and Mike.

Ellen turned to Sam to protest Nicole's presence, but before she could speak, Nicole smiled at her and winked. "Ellen, hi. What a great idea to go for a walk. It's such a beautiful day, isn't it, Sam? Come on, let's go." She gave her husband a sharp look that told Ellen that they'd argued over this. Sam grumbled something and Nicole ignored him, taking Ellen by the arm and walking out.

The men scrambled to create a security cordon around them. Ellen and Nicole strolled down the walkway to the beach like two Hollywood divas surrounded by bodyguards.

Ellen would have felt shame, but oh God, it felt so *good* to be outdoors! She lifted her face into the sunshine and inhaled deeply, eyes closed. So many scents, all of them good. The brine of the ocean, traces of the juniper that lined the walkway, the scent of pine.

The sun was so blinding that for a moment she felt like a bat, blinking against the bright light.

The men were walking grimly by their sides, narrowed gazes darting this way and that, on super-high alert. On a rotation, they even checked their backs, what Harry called his "six." He was holding her elbow with his left hand and his right hand was held free at his side, fingers flexing. Sam was so close to Nicole, her breezy dress floated against him. Mike wasn't holding on to anyone, both big hands down at his sides, fingers slightly curled.

She had no doubt that wherever their guns were hidden, they could access them fast.

Harry had told her a number of stories about Mike's prowess with guns. One of the best shots in the Marines, he'd said. And the way he said it was in exactly the same tone he'd use to say that Mike walked on water.

They headed down to the sand in a phalanx. Ellen forgot about the peculiarity of her little tribe and simply soaked in the sun and the sea, the smells, the feel of the terra-cotta walkway under her feet. She felt like a cocker spaniel that had slipped the leash. Sensations bombarded her skin, like little bomblets of delight. The silkiness of the wind, balmy and perfumed, the warmth of the air that heated up her muscles, relaxing her, the luscious deep blue of the ocean.

Oh God, she needed this so badly. A year hiding alone in the dark had broken something inside . . . walking in the open air and sunshine made her feel as if her very soul were unfurling.

Once they reached the beach, Ellen stooped and slipped off her shoes. Her toes sank into the fine, silky white sand and she shivered with delight. She chanced a glance up at Harry. True to his word, he stayed within a hand's span of her, and she didn't even try to move away from him. Being this close to him was part of the joy of this little outing.

Though he was glancing out to sea, checking the four boats that were way out on the ocean, she knew he was perfectly aware of everything she was doing. One side of his mouth was curled upward, which was Harryspeak for hysterical joy. He was happy that she was happy.

"Thanks," she said softly.

His eyes slanted down to her, then off to the right side of the beach, then the left. "My pleasure."

And though what she really would have liked to do was run down to the dappled water and dive in, she sedately moved down to the wet packed sand, her little retinue following. Ducklings following mother duck.

"Oh man," Nicole sighed. She'd taken her sandals off, too. They dangled from her hands as she walked into the water. They watched their feet as a tiny, gentle baby wave curled over their feet, then was sucked back into the ocean, taking sand with it. It was like a gentle foot massage. "Did I need this. Thanks for thinking of it."

"No problem." Ellen leaned into Nicole and lowered her

voice. "Frankly, I'm surprised Sam let you come, seeing as how he's so, ah, protective."

Ferocious would have been a good word, too, but Ellen didn't want to belabor the point.

Nicole smiled down at her feet. The breeze blew her light, loose linen shift against her body and the swell of her belly was evident. "Surprising what a little wheedling can get you."

Ellen knew precisely why Nicole had insisted on coming: So that this would have the flavor of an outing. So it wouldn't be a forced march along the beach with three armed men who couldn't wait to get her back under wraps.

"Thanks," Ellen said softly. "Can't have been easy to convince him."

"No, it wasn't." Nicole's foot dabbled in the clear water. "But I figured if you could convince Harry and you've only been together for a few days, I wouldn't be worthy of the name woman if I couldn't get my husband to let me go on this little walk, too."

Nicole's joining them put her at risk—okay, minimal risk, but Sam seemed like the type of man to whom even a slight risk to Nicole was too much to wrap his head around—simply to make Ellen more comfortable.

Ellen's eyes swept the horizon—only three boats now—and the beach. Families with kids and sun worshippers as far as the eye could see. "You up for a little stroll?"

"Oh yeah."

They moved off, shoes dangling from their fingers, at an easy pace. After a while, they stopped talking. The day was talking to them. A little siren song about enjoying life.

It was all so wonderful. The little bite of exercise, the glorious sun growing warmer and warmer, the heat mitigated by the cool, gentle breeze off the ocean. Wavelets curling like white lace on the surface of the ocean.

Kids farther up the beach were playing an impromptu game of volleyball, and Ellen smiled as she watched them. Strong young bodies, laughing, leaping, no cares other than having a good time.

She drew in a deep and delighted breath, almost heady with the fresh air. She could feel her blood circulating again, muscles warm and relaxed, the clean air reaching deep into her lungs.

The background noises—the soft plashing of the ocean, children's laughter, adult conversations heard in snatches, the wind—together formed a sort of soft lullaby. Ellen relaxed a little more with each step.

The men were more relaxed, too, she noted. They were still vigilant, but that tense grimness was gone. Their body language was softer, less rigid. Sam was teasing Nicole about the color of her toenail polish and Mike and Harry were in a heated argument about some ball game. She didn't even know which one. They were swapping insults that were funny and inventive, luridly profane and anatomically impossible.

It had turned into what she'd wanted with all of her heart. A little outing with friends.

And these *were* her friends, she could feel it. Sam and Mike and above all, Nicole. They cared for her and she cared for them.

And then, of course, there was Harry. She loved him. It

hadn't been a bright sudden flash of recognition. It was as if the knowledge had been there all along, even that first day in his office. So big and so still and so golden. Like a god. A benevolent god.

She hadn't told him yet, but she knew. She'd never felt anything like this before. Of all the terrifying things in her life, this was maybe the scariest, but there was nothing she could do about it. However long their relationship lasted, this was the man for her to the end of time.

They walked on, all of them smiling, even the men. It was a day made for smiling. For smiling and laughing and enjoying your friends. For feeling the hard-packed sand against your feet, cool and textured, for turning your face to the wind, letting it ruffle your hair, for having the warm sunbeams penetrate deep into the muscles with gentle fingers.

Ellen walked along, enjoying the banter of the men, the sun and the breeze and the low murmur of all the people on the beach, soaking up the unusually warm spring day.

The loneliness of the past year—and if she had to be honest, the loneliness she'd felt all her life—was starting to drift away, like dense, black smoke dissipated by a clean, strong wind. However improbably, it looked like she might actually have found a home here, with these good people. Good, kind, smart, capable people. Her people.

The knowledge wound its way into her heart, warm and gentle. She tucked it away. She'd done that as a child—tucked away a few good memories amid the chaos and craziness. Then she'd pull the memory out during the bleak, black times.

This memory, too, would be cherished. Except—well,

maybe, just maybe there would be more days just like this one, down the line. Harry, Mike, Sam and Nicole—they had stable lives and were stable people. They would be here for a long time.

Maybe she would, too.

Don't think that. She wanted it so much she instinctively shied away from the thought. You jinxed things if you wanted them too badly.

Live in the day, don't want too much, be grateful for what you have right this very minute—her mantra. It was a philosophy that had seen her through a lot of hard times.

Harry's big hand smoothed down the back of hers, then gently clasped it. His hand was warm and hard, callused, the grip firm but not tight.

She could do this forever. Just walk straight ahead until they ran out of beach then turn around and walk back. Everything felt so damned *good*.

Mike shifted his gaze from the boats at sea. "Hey guys, how about this evening I fire up that new barbecue I bought a few weeks ago? Gotta try it out sometime. I've got some inch-thick steaks in the freezer, throw some jacket potatoes on that sucker and voilà! Dinner."

"Not so fast, slick," Nicole said. "We're missing vegetables and fruit on that menu."

The men groaned. Sam rolled his eyes. "God, just as long as it's not that broccoli you made me choke down the other night. I'd rather eat rattlesnake balls."

"Wuss." Nicole smiled. "And rattlesnakes don't have balls. Maybe I could make some fresh coleslaw . . ."

There were several loud pops and that was the last thing Ellen heard. Half a second later a ton of man fell on her and her face was pushed deep into the sand.

Harry was on top of her, big black weapon out, tracking. Sam was on top of Nicole and his weapon was out, too. Mike had the biggest gun and was down on one knee holding it in two fists, moving in measured beats from sand to sea and back.

Ellen couldn't breathe, could hardly understand what was going on. Time stopped, stretched.

"Clear!" Mike shouted.

"Clear!" Sam and Harry's deep voices echoed. Harry lifted up a little and Ellen gasped in a breath, together with sand. He was a big man and he'd jumped her so hard the breath had whooshed out of her lungs. Her ribs hurt and the sand had abraded her knees and elbows.

Harry and Mike and Sam straightened up, guns still out.

She lifted her head and saw people in a circle around them, frozen at the sight of the dangerous-looking men with guns out. Two little girls hid behind their father's knees. The shock wore off. One of the little girls screamed. She was holding a fistful of balloons. Several had popped. That was the noise they'd heard.

"Sam," Nicole groaned and everyone turned to her. She was lying on her side, curled up in pain.

"Nicole!" Sam went ashen, fell on his knees next to her. "Oh my God, honey. Did I hurt you? Fuck, I hurt you. Oh fuck oh *fuck*! Where do you hurt, baby?" He was frantically touching her all over, trying to find out if she had any broken bones, yet almost afraid to touch her.

He was a big man, heavier even than Harry, and he was just

now realizing he'd thrown his entire weight on her. On his pregnant wife.

"Sam," Nicole whispered. "Sam. The baby."

They all looked down in horror at Nicole's hand protectively curled around her belly and at the blood seeping through her dress.

Harry put the phone down and went over to where Ellen was huddled in the corner of his sofa. She had her legs drawn up with her arms around them, one pretty bare foot curled over the other, shivering, though the day was still warm.

She looked up at him and Harry winced at the pain in those beautiful green eyes. She looked like she'd been whipped.

"That was Mike." Sam couldn't be trusted behind the wheel. Mike had driven Nicole and a stricken Sam to Sharp Coronado Hospital and had apparently broken a couple of land speed records to do it. He could do it because he was the Man. He was ex–San Diego PD. A ticket would never stick.

"And?" She could barely get the word out, her voice shook so much.

He gently unlocked one of her hands from its fierce grip around her legs, as if her arms were the only thing holding her together, and clasped it. It was icy cold. He sat down on the hassock in front of her, just looking at her, trying to warm her hand up.

Even pale and shocked, shaking and terrified, she was so beautiful it hurt his heart. She was much more shocked at the idea of harm to Nicole and the baby than she'd been at the danger to herself.

God, he hated to see her like this. And he hated it that

Nicole had been harmed, even slightly. But Mike had given him good news, the best.

"It's okay," he said gently. "Nicole's okay and the baby's doing just fine. Mike said even Sam was reassured. The doctors were really clear that the baby was in no danger. Sam calmed down when they had him listen to the baby's heartbeat. The bleeding stopped right away. They didn't even call it bleeding, they called it spotting."

Harry had no idea what the difference was, but as Mike called in the doctor's report it was clear that there was a difference and that Nicole was on the right side of that difference.

Ellen's breath left her body in a long, pent-up stream, as if she'd been holding her breath. Actually, both of them had been holding their breath for the past couple of hours. Harry loved Sam and Sam loved Nicole, so Harry loved Nicole, too. For herself, because she was a good woman with a loving heart, and because she was so good for Sam.

Waiting for news, when he'd mouthed a few platitudes to Ellen about everything being all right, he hadn't even believed it himself.

It was only now, with the baby in possible danger, that he realized how much he was looking forward to having a little niece to pamper. They didn't really talk about it, but he knew Mike felt the same way. And Sam—well, Sam was already crazy about the little girl.

Having a little girl around, watching her grow up safely in a loving family, being uncles in heart if not in blood . . . well, the idea felt good. Really good. Something new and fresh and clean in their lives.

"They're both okay, mother and child," he repeated softly.

She was still staring up at him, stricken, trying to read his face. Trying to figure out if he was telling the truth. "As a matter of fact, Nicole's agitating to come home, but I don't know if she'll manage it. Mike says that Sam is still pretty freaked."

He felt it first in her hand as it shook and then wildly trembled in his. The tremors went up her arm until her whole torso shook. She bit her lips. The words came pouring out in a flurry of agitation. "It's all my fault. This wouldn't have happened if I hadn't been there. If I hadn't taken my problems with me. I can't even think about it. Nicole could have lost her baby and it would have been *my fault*."

She hadn't cried waiting for the news, she'd simply huddled in on herself in misery, but now the tears started flowing.

Harry couldn't stand it. He simply couldn't stand seeing her like this. He lifted her up and sat down with her on his lap.

Ellen didn't even try to pretend she wasn't crying. She turned her face into his neck, let out a high keening sound of misery that raised the hairs on the back of his neck, and let go.

God.

It lasted forever.

She cried so hard he thought she might choke, so hard she had to gulp twice to pull in air. Harry didn't even try to stop her. As her chest heaved and she wet his shirt, he simply held her, as tightly and completely as possible, one arm around her waist, one hand covering the back of her head, trying to touch as much of her with as much of him as possible. The comfort of his body is what she needed right now, and he was more than willing to provide it.

She was curled up on his lap, arms around his neck, holding on for dear life, weeping her heart out. Crying for Nicole and the baby she almost lost, yes, but also for the year of her life that was stolen. For having a world-class talent she was terrified to show in public. For the death of her agent, which deep down she also considered her fault. For being forced to live a life always ducking, always checking her back, always fearful.

Harry would have loved to have reassured her that her troubles were over, that he was here now. But no matter how much he wanted to protect her, no matter how close he stayed by her side, a bullet could find her at any second. A silenced sniper rifle from a mile out was something no one could protect against. The president of the United States was protected at all times by something like two hundred highly trained men and women, and look how that turned out. Every once in a while a president got popped.

So though he could promise he'd protect her, he couldn't promise he could keep her alive. She knew that.

She'd spent the past year on red alert, adrenaline coursing through her body, probably checking her six every five minutes, jumping at unusual noises, being suspicious of strangers, allowing herself only the most shallow of slumbers because the nighttime was when the terrors were worst.

She'd essentially spent a year in war, under fire.

Soldiers had access to shrinks, had understanding buddies if they lost it, and at least they were trained to fight back.

Fuck with a U.S. soldier and a world of hurt came raining down on your head. She'd been alone and vulnerable, every second of every fucking day.

This was a beautiful woman with an unparalleled talent the world should be celebrating, and instead that fucker Montez made her scuttle around in the darkness like a cockroach.

She had every right to weep.

The crying jag was winding down, more because it had exhausted her than anything else. She finally heaved a huge sigh and settled more fully against him.

Thank God she was curled up on his lap and not over his groin, so she couldn't feel his boner. Though it would be a miracle if she didn't feel the heat from it. Shit, it was burning him up alive, like a hot poker some joker had stuck down the front of his pants.

If there was one trick he'd learned having nearly died twice and having twice made that long, long trek back to life, it was the ability to shut off signals from parts of his body.

Last year, he'd shut out the pain of the surgeries and the shattered hip. He'd just blanked out all sensation from his waist down. He tried that now, because at the time it had been a neat trick to cut off the pain. Helped along with a little alcohol and some Eve in his iPod. So now that he wasn't feeling any pain at all, you'd think he'd be able to pull that no-feeling-below-the-waist thing.

But no.

His dick was actually screaming at him to get going. To get inside Ellen as fast as he could, now that the crying jag was over and she might be a little amenable to some belly bumping.

No. Harry didn't do this.

He knew men who equated sex with pain. Who loved fucking women in distress, even better if they were the ones to make them hurt. Women's pain was like an aphrodisiac to them. He'd seen that a lot—his mom had fucked a lot of men like that.

Harry was better than that. He'd spent his whole fucking life proving that he was better than that.

Sex between consenting adults was one of the great pleasures of life. Mutually satisfying fun. Making love with someone you cared about, loved—that was holy.

And Harry loved Ellen. Maybe he'd loved her before he even met her. The instant he'd seen her—a beautiful, frightened woman in his office—it was as if something in the universe slotted into place. Something real, something necessary.

So getting a boner while she wept desperately in his arms shamed him, disgusted him. It made him no better than fuckhead Rod. It made him a monster.

He'd get Ellen a cup of tea and go and take a cold shower and see if he could jerk off, get the boner back down. Or if that didn't work, put ice on it, hammer it down, do *something.*

He shifted on the couch, preparing to lift her off him when she sat up, swiveled her head and looked him in the eyes.

And—fuck—her hip landed straight on his cock. Oh, shit.

"I'm sorry, honey," he said miserably. "I just—"

She made a shushing sound, placing the palms of her hands against his cheeks, forcing him to look into her eyes.

Oh God, how could she be so beautiful after weeping for half an hour? Most women looked like shit after crying. Eyes and face red and swollen. Ellen simply looked rosier than the icy white she'd been before, her eyes lustrous with tears, a sadness on her face that cut bone deep.

Hell, even seeing her like this, why wouldn't his fucking boner *go down*?

"Harry?" she whispered.

"Yeah?" he whispered back.

"Will you do something for me?"

"Anything you want, honey. Anything."

She leaned forward, her lower belly right against his cock, lips touching his. Against his mouth she whispered, "Take me to bed and make love to me."

She needed this like she'd needed the sunshine this morning. A celebration of life. A celebration of the fact that Nicole and her baby were okay and so was she, for the moment.

And moments were all you were guaranteed in life, weren't they? No one could promise her that she or Harry might not die today, tomorrow. It came down to celebrating each and every moment of joy.

And being with Harry was pure joy. The more she knew him, the more she could see past that incredible tough-guy exterior. He was, yeah, really tough. He was strong and brave and could outshoot three bad guys.

But inside, inside that tough exterior, was a tender heart. The kind of man who still mourned his murdered mother and little sister, who'd fought almost to the death for them. The kind of man who, together with his brothers, unquestioningly put himself on the line for women and children in need of protectors.

This man made the perfect protector. And he did it with such a light touch, without smothering. If you weren't on the lookout, you wouldn't even know you were being protected. He was just . . . there.

It was a quality she'd never met in a man before. Men

took—sex, love, your money—everything, if you weren't careful. It was so strange to have a man who gave instead of taking.

Maybe she could give him something back.

"Come on." She stood up and tugged at his hands until he stood up, too.

It was a beautiful evening. The apartment was suffused with evening light, turning everything golden, including the man following her into the bedroom. The other times they'd made love, he'd initiated it, but this time he seemed content to follow her lead. And she liked it, she discovered.

She'd never taken the lead before and now realized it was because she hadn't cared enough. She cared now. Oh yeah, she cared.

She turned to him in the bedroom, white cotton curtains fluttering in the evening breeze, bringing in the smell of the ocean. They were standing a few inches apart and Ellen had to crane her neck to look Harry in the eyes. Those calm, golden eyes. Patient and steady, taking his cue from her.

Well, okay then. First order of business, clothes off. Easier said than done, she discovered, as she pulled his black T-shirt out of his jeans and tried to slip it over his head. There was no way she could reach up that far, not even when she stood on tiptoe. She dropped down on her heels, kissed his bare chest and said, "You'll have to take it from here."

"Okay," he whispered, his eyes never leaving hers. In an instant the tee sailed to the floor.

He had somehow understood that she wanted to stay in control, so he didn't move, just stood there, feet slightly apart, big hands hanging by his side. Ellen unbuckled his belt, unsnapped and unzipped, smiling a little as he winced. He was massively aroused, and the zipper had to hurt a little. Ah well, he was a tough guy, he could take it.

She pulled the jeans down those long, muscled legs, scratching the inside of his thigh to see what he'd do. He didn't do anything but looked pained, but his penis . . . ah, that jumped inside his white briefs. Just as a muscle jumped in his jaw.

Mmm.

Within a minute, T-shirt, jeans, briefs were neatly folded on a chair, shoes and socks off, and he stood there in front of her, in all his golden glory.

Ellen studied him greedily, committing everything to memory. The long, lean muscles, the straight soldier's stance, the gold-tinged hair on his chest narrowing down over his lean stomach, the hair on his groin thicker and darker and framing . . . oh my.

His penis was so thick and long, nearly reaching his navel, blood coursing through it in small ripples every time she looked at it. It was so enormous it was a miracle her body could accommodate him, but it did.

It was readying itself for him even now, just looking at him. The flesh between her thighs grew warm and moist, and she could feel something unfurling deep inside, her sex and her heart, both.

She made no move to touch him; right now just looking at him was enough.

"You're so beautiful," she whispered. She'd surprised him. His head jerked back a little. One side of his mouth curled up, Harry's version of a full smile.

"That's my line."

"Is it?" Yes, he'd told her often enough he found her beautiful. "I mean it, though. You're so beautiful. You're—you're perfect."

This time there was a full-fledged smile, one of the few she'd ever seen on his face. "Ask my brothers about that. I think they'd beg to differ."

"They love you," she said.

"Yes, they do." His chest expanded on a deep breath. "And why are we talking about them at a moment like this?"

Because they are such an important part of you, she wanted to say, but didn't. There were a lot of things she wanted to say to him, but there was no time. So she reached out and touched him, finally, placing her open palm over his heart.

Oh, how she loved doing that. Feeling the crisp hairs, the lean hard muscle below that and underlying it all, the strong beat of his heart. She stepped closer and felt that heart rate speed up.

She had that power. The power to make this warrior's heart race.

"Come with me," she murmured. They were alone in the house; there was no reason to keep her voice low, but the moment called for it. The whole world was hushed, as if waiting for something, and any noise would just be a distraction.

He stepped forward as she backed up to the bed. Ellen put her knee on the bed, rolled over, held her hands up. There was no need for words at all. As naturally as breathing, Harry covered her body with his, slowly entering her as he kissed her. Everything slow and gentle, because the moment called for it. He slid into her fully, kissing her deeply, and soon his breathing speeded up and she could feel his stomach muscles tensing to start moving in her.

She held him with her hands on his hips. "Not yet," she whispered, and he stilled. Content with being inside her and kissing her.

Ellen arched as she opened her legs wider so he could seat himself fully in her. She didn't want him to move, because that would speed things up and she wanted to freeze time, hang on to this one moment forever, she thought, as she memorized every inch of him she could with her fingertips. This moment was so very precious.

Because this time tomorrow she'd be gone and would never see him again.

Chapter 15

Monday morning, they drove into the city center in the little convoy again, all three driving down into the underground garage. When they got out of the vehicles, the men surrounded the women in a tight tense knot of security.

Women because Nicole insisted on coming in to work, too. She said she'd go crazy staying home in bed, as Sam insisted. She was fine, just *fine*.

They went up in the elevator in a tight cordon of men, no one talking and no one smiling. At the ninth floor, the doors opened onto a creative type, standing there with carefully tousled, gelled hair, a tight sharkskin suit and with a tasteful stud piercing a very cute, surgically sculpted nose.

He took one look at the three huge men glowering at him and scampered away to another elevator.

As the men walked them down the hall, their collective body language was a Dirty Harryesque *Come on punk, make my day.*

When the door of Nicole's office closed behind them, Ellen opened her mouth and Nicole held up a finger. "If you apologize one more time, I swear I will scream. And then Sam and Harry and Mike will come running and we'll never get anything done at all."

Ellen felt so miserable. Nicole looked tired. The spotting had stopped almost immediately yesterday, but she'd spent the day in the hospital undergoing tests before coming home and she clearly hadn't slept well. There were slight bruises under her eyes.

Of course, that was nothing compared to what was under *her* own eyes, because she hadn't slept at all last night. She hadn't even been able to close her eyes, staring wide-eyed at the black ceiling, listening to Harry's heartbeat, savoring his solid warmth by her side, waiting for the dawn.

Thinking awful thoughts. Knowing what she had to do and dreading it.

"All right." Nicole hung her jacket up neatly on a perfumed hanger and hung that on the brass clothes tree. "I've got an urgent translation for a Luxembourg bank to finish, and you've got to save me some more money. So let's get to work." She sat down to her desktop and slid in her portable hard disk.

Her tone was brisk, but her movements were slow. She was battling through this in a way Ellen recognized and respected.

Nicole could use a thousand excuses and no one would think less of her. If she had wanted to stay home today—and all next week or even all next year—her husband would be more than happy. But she had a company to run and people who depended on her for their livelihood and clients who expected her to deliver a good product in a timely fashion, so here she was, tired and shaken, but ready to start her working day.

The least Ellen could do was offer her a little something. Nicole had been ridiculously behind with her accounts. Ellen had made her a simple, rational system that would be easy to keep up, and she was working hard on finding ways to save on taxes.

Ellen settled down at the desk, reaching down to the case at her feet. She was using Harry's laptop instead of Nicole's because she'd worked on Nicole's files over the weekend and her spreadsheets were there. "I nailed another couple of thousand in tax deferrals and with a little luck I think I can set up a slightly different corporate structure for you so that you can deduct more stuff. That'll save you at least ten thousand in taxes over the next five years."

"Wow." Nicole tipped her head to the left of the monitor and gave her a dazzling smile. "That's great. Thank you so much. And"—she held up an elegant pink-tipped finger—"don't apologize again. If you apologize I'll do you bodily harm. Don't forget, I can be meaner than Sam or Harry or Mike. I don't think any of them could hurt a woman, but I can. Don't make me hurt you."

Ellen had opened her mouth to thank her, and to apologize once more, but she closed it. The idea of Nicole wrestling her to the ground was so ridiculous, she just had to smile.

"Hold that thought." Nicole's processor beeped and she bent over the keyboard. "Go save me some more money. Lunch is at twelve thirty. Goat cheese salad, grilled vegetable sandwich with focaccia bread, sliced apples for dessert, everything washed down with green tea. I ordered the same lunch for the men. It's a good thing these walls are fairly soundproofed, because you'd hear the groaning from here. Now let's concentrate." And she disappeared into her monitor.

Ellen opened Harry's laptop and plugged in his Bose headset. The laptop he'd given her was loaded with fabulous music. She loved isolating herself from the world with music when concentrating on work. In a second, she had a spreadsheet program open and Billie Holiday purring in her ears.

Okay.

Ellen was going to do extra-good work for Nicole today. She was going to set her up with a specially designed program that would automatically calculate the best billing method and Nicole's commission, weighted for urgency of the translation, technical difficulty and rarity of the language combination, together with a streamlined tax statement structure. It was going to be her good-bye gift to Nicole.

Before disappearing.

She'd struggled with this decision all night, staring dry-eyed into the darkness, held close to Harry's heart.

There was no way around this except for straight ahead on the hard rocky road of necessity. Montez would be after her forever. Year after year of fear and hiding. Of being afraid to be out in the open, of forcing her new friends to live under a shadow.

It was very likely that what Nicole had found out was the extent of what a civilian could discover. The next steps had to be taken by law enforcement officers, preferably the FBI.

There was a moral issue here, too. The longer Ellen waited to tip this tangled mess into the FBI's capable hands, the longer Gerald had to mess with any evidence that might be left.

It might even be too late. Maybe she'd been wrong to spend this past year afraid and in hiding. Maybe she should have been bolder, gone to the FBI before. She'd been so scared, so terrified of sticking her head above the ground, that she might have ensured that Gerald got away with murder, twice. Three times, actually, including Frank Mikowski. If Gerald got away with it, it would be her fault.

Gerald would spend the rest of his life getting richer and richer, becoming ever more powerful, never paying for his crimes, while Ellen stayed hidden in the dark, worried every single second of the day that she was endangering people she'd grown to care for. And in the case of Harry, to love.

Unthinkable.

Yesterday had been a false alarm—a couple of balloons popping. But Harry was right, it could have been Gerald or one of his guys. At any moment, she could be in the crosshairs of some sniper employed by Gerald.

In five months, Nicole would have her baby and Ellen would be in a permanent sweat of anxiety that Gerald could kill her and Nicole and the *baby*. He wouldn't hesitate. If he found out where she was, he'd kill everyone with her, on the off chance that she'd talked.

It was too late to keep Nicole from becoming a friend. Everything she knew about Nicole told her that she cared for Ellen and that she was intensely loyal to the people she cared about. She wouldn't stay away from Ellen just because there was a vague possibility that Gerald would catch up with her.

It was more than just a vague possibility, though. He'd caught up with her in Seattle; he knew she'd been in San Diego. Gerald was smart and rich and had huge resources.

He'd know how to track her down somehow. He'd done it before.

Ellen had been careful when having the records produced. The musicians, puzzled, had been in the next room and had never seen her, nothing had been signed in her name, not even in the name of Irene Ball, but in the name of a small company she'd set up where no one's name actually appeared except that of a lawyer who worked online just for companies like hers.

But Gerald had found Roddy, had tortured him. Who knew what he'd been forced to say? Who knew if Roddy had said something that would help Gerald find her? Who knew if she'd covered her tracks enough?

It was a very lucky thing that she had kept her friendship with Kerry a secret. Without ever talking about it, they had never shown each other warmth in public, rarely called each other and never went out together. They had a message board accessible only to themselves, and that's where they made plans to meet. Mostly at Kerry's place.

Not even Mario, the owner of the Blue Moon, realized how close they were. So Kerry shouldn't be in any danger. But there were other ways to find people.

The streets of San Diego were covered in security cameras. Could she go through life here wearing huge sunglasses, shapeless dresses and wide-brimmed hats? Every single day? Without making a mistake once?

She'd go crazy. Most of all, she'd drive Harry crazy, too, and ruin his life. And since he was embedded in a tight group of people who loved him and were starting to love her, she'd ruin their lives, too.

And Nicole's baby . . .

Ellen's mind kept circling back to that terrifying thought. Harm to the baby. What it would mean to Harry. Harry had lost his baby sister. He'd never survive Nicole and Sam's child being killed. She'd never survive it, either.

The longer she stayed, the worse it would be. The longer she stayed, the more she'd care for them, the more embedded in their lives she'd be. And after the baby was born, she'd love the baby, too. One more hostage to Gerald's craziness and cruelty.

Oh God.

She had to go. She had to go now before one of these wonderful people got hurt.

She wanted to stay, but she had to go.

Billie's sad, beautiful voice came over her headset, begging for a dream or two.

The dreams were all gone.

The screen in front of her blurred, grew refracted as tears filled her eyes, but she willed them back, dashing the back of her hand angrily over her eyes.

Tears were a dangerous weakness.

What she was going to do—had to do—in the next half hour was tricky, because she was going to have to sneak past Nicole, who was no fool, and past three men who were very alert. No tears, no second thoughts, no hesitation. She had to be brave and decisive, take it step by step.

First, dropping the whole mess into the lap of the FBI.

The San Diego FBI Field Office website was very informative. The person in charge of the office—the official title was Special Agent in Charge—was a woman, Karen Sands. There was even a photo of her, a handsome woman with straight, light-blond hair, looking boldly into the camera. She was reassurance itself and looked capable and fearless. Just what Ellen needed.

Between songs, she lifted an earphone and heard the reassuring sound of Nicole deeply immersed in her translation, keying the words in a steady patter. Nicole wasn't paying her any attention. Good.

There was a CONTACT US button for reporting crime. Ellen hesitated for just a moment, fingers curled over the keys.

This was it. After alerting the FBI, there would be no going back. She would be cutting Harry and his friends out of her life and she would break Harry's heart.

But better to break his heart than be the cause of any more death.

After a moment's hesitation, Ellen filled out the data page with her real name, without giving an address. Presumably they'd be able to track down her location using the IP address, but by that time, she'd be at the office itself.

In the message field she stated that she had reason to believe that a government contractor, Gerald Montez, CEO of Bearclaw, had stolen money from the U.S. government in Baghdad and had killed three people.

Should she ask for an appointment? No, she decided. Better not to wait for a response. Better just to show up at their offices.

The address given was Aero Drive, in the northern part of the city. The site gave a photo of the façade of the building, a distinctive combination of white marble and dark glass shaped into a big dark Y. She'd recognize it when the cab pulled up.

The door opened and closed. Good. Nicole had gone to the bathroom down the hall. She complained about practically living in the bathroom now that she was pregnant. She'd be a while. When she came back, Ellen would slip out. Only instead of going to the bathroom, she'd keep on walking down the hall, into the elevator, into a cab, into the FBI office and into a new life.

A barren life, an empty life, but a life where everyone she cared for would be safe.

It would take a while for them to discover she was gone. By the time Nicole realized that Ellen was taking too much time in the bathroom, she'd be on her way to Aero Drive in a taxi.

She'd finished the spreadsheet program and she'd straightened out Nicole's accounts, happy that she could leave her a little something, a little thank-you for her friendship.

What could she leave Harry?

Her heart.

My dearest Harry,

This is for the best and you know it. It's a waiting game and time is on Gerald's side. The more I wait, the more time he has to find me, the more we'll all be worn down with worry, you included. Nothing happened to Nicole, but it could have. I could never live with myself if she'd been hurt or lost the baby, and I think the same holds true for you.

I'm going to the FBI and ask for protection, so don't worry about me. I should have done this a year ago, but instead I took the coward's way out and ran. Yet maybe, as a New Age friend of mine would say, the universe wanted me to be a coward because I got to meet you.

I love you, Harry. I love you so much I have to leave you, because I can't stand the thought of you being hurt.

I don't know what else to say.

Ellen

She sent him the e-mail quickly before she lost her nerve and before she could break down. When she pressed the send button it was like pressing the button that detonated her heart.

Still, maybe there was some room for hope. Just a little. The FBI had huge resources. Maybe they could make a case against Gerald quickly. Put him away forever, dust their hands and tell her, *You're free to go.* It was possible, wasn't it?

It was wishful thinking, but oh, how appealing that thought was. A couple of months to make the case, Gerald tried and convicted fast. Ellen coming back to San Diego, stepping into Harry's arms, able to live in the light once more, with him. She'd share her life with Harry and sing and keep everyone's books.

Oh God. She shook with longing.

It wasn't going to happen, but it *could*. That thought was going to have to sustain her in the dark months and maybe years ahead.

Harry would be furious, maybe never forgive her. Though

she knew he cared for her, they'd had only a few days together. She knew she'd love him forever, but maybe if it took a long time to put the case together and she came back in a year or two or three, he'd have moved on. He'd be crazy not to move on.

So that was another horrible scenario to conjure up. Coming back in a year or two, excited and hopeful. Harry going, *Don't I know you?* With a child in his arms and a pregnant wife by his side.

That thought actually *hurt*.

There was one other person she needed to contact. Kerry.

Would she be allowed a laptop while in the FBI's care? Would they spy on her? Maybe they would.

She needed to contact Kerry beforehand, tell her she was all right, tell her not to worry. With all that had happened, she hadn't checked their message board. Kerry would be frantic. Ellen had disappeared without a word and hadn't been in touch since.

Right now Kerry didn't know if Ellen was in enemy hands, sick or dying or dead.

A pang of shame shot through her. Kerry deserved better.

She checked the message board, opened the video attachment, saw something terrible come up and simply froze. She'd been holding a pen and it clattered to the floor. The breath stopped in her lungs.

It was almost impossible even to process what she was seeing—a person with a red shoulder, with a red . . . cap?

Kerry. Oh my God. That was *Kerry*, slumped in a chair. She'd been—oh God—she'd been *scalped*. And part of her torso skinned.

Bile rose in her throat and she leaned over the wastepaper

basket and vomited the coffee and yogurt she'd had for breakfast.

A deep, digitized voice came online through her headset. "Ellen Palmer, this is your friend Kerry."

She sat, shaking, keening, rocking back and forth in shock.

She didn't want to hear any more, couldn't. This had escalated to a level of horror she couldn't deal with. That alien insect voice was saying something but she couldn't understand, didn't want to understand, so she cut off the audio.

All she understood was that her friend Kerry, gentle, kind Kerry, had fallen into the hands of monsters. *Her* monsters. Her monsters had come roaring up out of the deep looking for her and had found Kerry.

Out of sheer instinct, trembling so badly she could barely key the words in, Ellen forwarded the file to the FBI, picked up her purse and fled the room, stumbling. There was no one in the corridor, thank God, because she would have rammed through anyone who tried to stop her.

Her heart was pounding, legs barely able to hold her.

Kerry, sweet Kerry, who liked music and books and had been running from something, too. Kerry'd been skinned like an animal. That horrible digitized voice, like something echoing up from the bowels of hell, said that Kerry was alive, but how could she be? And maybe being dead was better than being skinned alive.

Ellen bent over in the elevator, stomach clenching, but all that came up was bile. Her eyes were tearing up so badly she could barely see. When the elevator doors pinged open, she was able to make her way to the exit only because it was straight ahead and the big windows let in light.

She followed the light because it was the only thing she could think of to do and because she instinctively wanted light after the dark horror of what she'd seen. In any other place, she'd have lost her bearings and banged into the walls.

Aero Drive. The words lit up in her head and she longed to be there, longed to be among FBI agents who would take one look at that monstrous video and arrest Gerald. Arrest him and put him into the deepest, blackest hole possible, forever.

Aero Drive. She had to get there.

Go go go! A voice in her head pounded. Because what she'd seen hadn't been human. No human being could do that to another. These were creatures from some other planet. The FBI had to deal with this, because she couldn't, not in any way.

Out on the street, she stopped, blinking in the bright light. Her throat burned from the bile she'd vomited, her stomach hurt, her legs hurt. Her heart hurt.

Oh, Kerry.

She glanced back to see if a taxi was coming but all she saw was a tall blond man, almost running toward her. If he wanted to ask directions, he was plain out of luck. She couldn't talk to anyone in any rational way. She felt barely capable of telling the cab driver where she wanted to go.

The tall blond man moved fast. She was starting to step out of his way when she felt a sting in her arm, a car drove up beside her, and the edges of the world turned black.

They were parked a block south of the Morrison Building, Piet riding shotgun, Montez at the wheel.

Piet had his ruggedized laptop open, carefully researching

the websites of all the businesses in the Morrison Building and its annex. There were more than a hundred, but he was patient, and besides, what else was there to do? Talk to Gerald Montez, who had a huge vein throbbing in his forehead, looking like a stroke in waiting?

He'd rather shoot himself.

He'd just opened the site of a group of lawyers and was perusing it—the rates these bastards charged per hour, and they called *him* a criminal?—when his laptop beeped softly.

Montez jumped. "What? What was that?"

"Easy, mate," Piet murmured, but his own heart had speeded up a little, the predator catching scent of the prey. It was the end game, now. "She's logged on to the site."

He tapped furiously at the keyboard. A three-dimensional map came up, rotated, the floor plan of a tall building. A green dot flicked on the ninth floor. "And she's . . . yeah, she's in the Morrison Building. Right fucking now." He manipulated the image, input some data. "And she's on the ninth floor. Hang about . . ." He pulled up the building's space allocation specs he'd preloaded during the flight. "Right. So she's on the ninth floor in an office called Wordsmith." He brought up the site. "A translation agency." He shot a glance at Montez. "She know languages?"

Montez shook his head, confused. "Not that I know of."

"You have any incriminating material you shouldn't have in other languages, like Arabic?"

That made Montez pause. "No," he said finally.

"Then what the fuck's she doing in a translation agency?"

"Hell if I know."

"Christ," Piet began in disgust, lifting his head to automatically check the street. His eyes widened. "There she is!"

"What? Where?" Montez shouted frantically, but Piet was already out of the car and running after a slender figure about fifty feet ahead of him.

Palmer looked behind her, but she wasn't focusing on him. She had no idea who he was. Maybe she was looking for a taxi.

Well, he'd give her a ride, all right.

In a few strides he had caught up with her. She was prettier than in her pictures, with rich, red-brown hair that shone in the sunlight, fine features, green eyes. Though right now she was crying.

Of course.

She'd just seen the video of her friend.

Well, good, she was off balance.

The whole op was embarrassingly easy. Didn't take more than thirty seconds. Smooth, textbook.

Piet reached out and put his hand around her upper arm. That was the thing with civilians—they never reacted. Touch him unexpectedly and he'd break your arm before you knew it. Fuck with him in any way and you'd find yourself staring at the haft of a knife that was buried between your third and fourth ribs, the blade slicing deep into your heart.

But not Ellen Palmer, oh no. Even in a state of shock, she was clearly going to speak civilly to him. Whatever she was going to say was lost, though, because the syringe he had hidden in his palm sank deep into her biceps and her eyes rolled up in her head.

The Mercedes had rolled up behind him, stopping with the

back door not a foot from him. At least Montez did this right.

Ellen Palmer's knees buckled.

He caught her before she fell.

Harry was putting together a quote for a client, but his mind wasn't on it. His mind was in the small, pretty office across the hallway from RBK Security, where his woman was. He had to really focus on what he was doing, because Ellen's beautiful face kept floating across his field of vision.

She'd been so solemn this morning, so sad. Distant and reflective, staring out the window at the scenery without really taking it in as they drove across the bridge and into the business district.

The incident yesterday had really spooked her. Well, hell, it had spooked him. But he was a soldier. You dodge the bullet and forget about it. There will be another bullet, but not today. Nicole was okay, the baby was okay, move on.

Ellen found it hard to move on. She had a tender heart, which made him even more determined to shield her. Crissy had had a tender heart, too, and she'd been mowed down by the creatures of the night. No one was going to touch Ellen, ever again. He'd move heaven and earth to prevent it.

There was an e-mail, from Ellen.

Before he could read it, Nicole stuck her head into his office, Sam hovering behind her.

"Harry?" Nicole looked worried, and for a second Harry was terrified that she was bleeding again.

Man, she'd scared the shit out of him yesterday.

He'd hidden it from Ellen because she was out of her mind

with worry and guilt, but deep down the thought of losing that little girl they were all looking forward to so much was horrifying.

But it turned out that Nicole was concerned about the only thing worse than losing the baby.

"Harry," she said softly, "it's Ellen."

"What?" Harry rose on legs that felt suddenly hollow. What could possibly be wrong with Ellen? He'd left her in Nicole's office, which was as safe as modern technology and three determined and savvy men could make it. "What about Ellen?"

In the field, Harry was known for keeping his cool. That emotional detachment that had defined him his whole life came in real handy on ops, and in firefights. It was easy for him—just disengage the gear that drove his emotions and he was firing on all cylinders. Fast and cool and deadly.

That deserted him now while cold terror roiled his guts.

"She's gone, Harry." Sam stepped forward, face somber. "Nicole was in the bathroom and when she came back, Ellen wasn't there. She'd thrown up in a wastepaper basket. She just ran out, the chair was thrown back from the desk. I clicked on her computer monitor and, shit man, I saw why she ran."

Oh God. "What? What was there?"

Sam hesitated. "Not good." He turned to Nicole, said gently, "Wait outside, honey," and kissed her cheek.

Looking sad, Sam placed the laptop on Harry's desk while Nicole closed the door behind her. Harry clicked on the space bar to turn the screen on and felt a rush of rage at the image. He processed it immediately.

A dark-haired young woman, pretty underneath the tears and terror, duct-taped to a chair. He quickly scanned the background, but there was absolutely nothing there. Not even a digital image specialist could pick up anything, he was sure. A bare gray space, no reflections, no objects.

Just stills of a poor, terrified woman, straining against the restraints, bucking with pain, a big hand pinching the brachial plexus.

It was excruciating, the kind of pain that could reduce a person to shuddering bedrock, down to something barely human.

"Wait," Sam said. His face was dark and grim. "There's more."

Another still. Something torn and broken appeared. Red and savaged. Barely human.

"Christ," Harry breathed.

"Yeah," Sam grunted. "That's Dove."

"Fuck," Mike chimed in. Harry hadn't heard the door open and close. Mike had extrasensory perception when it came to trouble. "That's serious shit."

"There's audio." Sam clicked on the icon and put a hand on Harry's shoulder. "It's real bad, Harry."

A surreal, digitized voice that sounded like it came from the lowest reaches of hell buzzed. "Ellen Palmer, this is your friend Kerry . . ."

He listened to the message through to the end, fury rising.

Bullshit. That woman was dead. They were fucking with Ellen's head, trying to get her to show.

Harry was sweating. He looked up at his two friends, his brothers. "She saw that. That's why she vomited." He clicked on his e-mail and read with growing horror the message she'd sent him. "And Christ, that's why she's gone. She went to the FBI."

"Well, fuck." Sam looked puzzled. "She wants to go to the FBI, why didn't she wait for you to take her?"

"I think she wants to ask for protection while they put together a case." Harry met his brothers' eyes. "She blamed herself for what happened to Nicole. She kept saying it was her fault. She'd be totally freaked if this was a friend of hers."

"Wasn't anybody's fault except for that fucker Montez," Sam responded heatedly.

"Yeah, I know. Try to convince her of that. I'll talk to Welles, see what I can do." Aaron Welles, former Ranger, now FBI. A good friend. Harry would explain the situation, they'd debrief Ellen and he'd convince her to come home. Actually, going to the FBI was a good move and one he'd have gotten to eventually.

"Shit!" Harry and Sam turned to Mike, who was pointing to the monitor that showed the building's security cams. "She didn't make it to the FBI. Look at that!"

The three men watched in horror at the scene unfolding. Mike had rewound. The white letters in the lower right-hand corner said 12:05 P.M. Ten minutes ago.

Ellen running out of the building, stumbling. The quality of the digital tape was so good Harry could see the silver tracks of tears on her face, the trembling of her hands. She turned right and walked quickly on the wide sidewalk, glancing back often, hoping for a passing cab.

Across the street a tall blond man stepped out of a Mercedes and ran toward her.

Harry's blood froze. Adrenaline flooded his system, making the scene appear as if it were in slow motion, though he knew it was in real time. He was in combat time as he watched the takedown.

Ellen turning her head around once more, soft, curly hair swinging over her shoulders, wiping at the tears on her face. Hurrying, but slightly unsteady on her feet. Eyes, mouth blurred with shock. He could tell the exact moment she saw the tall blond man running toward her, the slight hesitation. The instinctive attempt to help. As she slowed to see what he wanted, the black Mercedes left the curb, slowly made its way down the street.

"Oh hell. Haven't seen him in years." Mike's deep voice. Harry nodded without taking his eyes off the screen.

"Who?" Sam asked. "Who is he?"

"Piet van der Boeke." Mike's deep voice was clipped. "South African merc. Go-to guy for a lot of people. Really good at tracking. He'll kill if the price is right."

That shut Sam up.

All three men leaned forward as the screen showed Van der Boeke reaching Ellen, clasping her arm . . . Ellen buckling, Van der Boeke scooping her up, throwing her in the backseat of the Mercedes, which had caught up with them, jumping in the passenger seat, the Mercedes accelerating out of the frame.

The takedown had lasted less than a minute, smooth and slick. Anyone watching would assume Ellen hadn't felt well and friends bundled her into a car to take her to the hospital. No one would think that a woman had been seized in the light of day by two monsters who were capable of skinning and scalping a woman.

All three men exploded into action. "Mike!" Harry barked.

"Tell Henry to get the Sprinter. Have him bring it up to the Birch entrance. Stat!"

The Sprinter was one of the company vehicles, armored and loaded for bear. You could start a small war with the firepower stashed inside the vehicle. And with the gear in neat foam casings, you could climb a mountain, field dress wounds, capture signals off a satellite, beam messages to a satellite, swim fifty miles underwater or blow up a building.

He captured a still of the license plate, blew it up . . . "Shit!" he screamed. The license plate was unreadable. Someone had covered it in mud.

But there was another way.

He consulted his smartphone, saw that the Mercedes was traveling at seventy miles per hour, heading west.

Mike was strapping himself into his extra-wide body armor and held Harry's out to him. Harry talked fast as he suited up.

"I've got a bug on her. We can follow it via GPS on my handheld. They've got a ten-minute lead, but we can make that up." Plans, orders, action. The familiar rush of an op, to keep the panic at bay.

"As long as they're traveling, she'll be okay. If he wanted her dead right away, she'd be meat back on that sidewalk." Mike had finished suiting up and was already cradling his beloved Remington 850 with a mile of scope.

Harry met Mike's sober eyes. If they didn't want Ellen dead it was for one reason only. They wanted something in her beautiful head, and they'd shown what they were willing to do to get it.

Harry's stomach clenched as he thought of that young woman slumped in the chair. The insectoid digitized voice had said she was alive, but she wasn't. No one could survive injuries like that, but he'd said it to scare Ellen. To flush her out of hiding.

Prickles ran under his skin at the thought of Ellen—beautiful, gentle, talented Ellen—in these men's hands.

Both men took the time to check their weapons thoroughly. An extra minute wouldn't necessarily cost Ellen her life, but a weapon that misfired could get her and them killed pretty damned fast.

Sam was suiting up too.

"Sam, stop it." Harry put his hand over Sam's holster. "This isn't your fight. You stay here with Nicole."

"Goddammit, Harry—"

"It *is* his fight, Harry." The three men whirled to see Nicole at the door. "He couldn't live with himself if he didn't help you bring Ellen home." She fixed him with her intensely blue eyes. "So you make sure you bring my husband home together with Ellen, or you'll answer to me. Do I make myself clear?"

Harry didn't need to see Sam to know what he was feeling, but he heard a short sigh of relief behind him. Sam wanted to come with every fiber of his being. Nicole knew that Sam would hate being left behind. Her words released them.

"Let's go!" Harry shouted and they ran out the door.

At first, Ellen couldn't figure out what was going on, where she was.

She came back to consciousness slowly, a heartbeat at a time. Hands restrained in front of her, soft background hum. The smell of leather and dust and feet and some acrid chemical, a bitter taste in her mouth.

Her eyes flickered open for just a second, then closed again. It was too much of an effort to keep them open, and there was nothing to see. Her nose was ground against something soft and gray.

Her eyes opened again, stayed open a second or two. She struggled to make sense of what she was seeing. It was hard to focus, to concentrate while she was swaying back and forth with the movements of . . . the car. Of course!

She was in a car, had fallen off the backseat, and her face was grinding into the footwell. She couldn't use her hands because they were tied in front of her and the movements of the car prevented her from getting back up onto the seat.

How did she get here? Where was she?

"—about twenty minutes from the airfield. The pilots are waiting," a raspy male voice said, and shock jolted through her system.

Gerald! That was Gerald's voice!

Oh god, oh God, she was in Gerald's hands. How had this happened? She tried to concentrate, but her head hurt so badly. She felt so dull, so out of it, as if she were at the bottom of some impossibly deep well.

The car went fast around a corner and Ellen rocked forward then backward, scraping her arm against the seatbacks. Her right arm hurt more than the rest of her, hurt in a specific place, as if she'd been stung by a giant insect.

She looked down and saw a puncture wound on her right biceps, frowning. A scene flared in her head. She was running . . . running somewhere. Somewhere important. It was essential that she get there. And . . . and someone behind her, running toward her. Tall man. Blond. Running, grabbing her arm, blacking out . . .

She'd been stung by an injection of some kind of narcotic, and it still clouded her mind. Worse, much worse, she was a prisoner, in a car with Gerald Montez and another man.

She could remember the blond man, unfamiliar but a type. Hard face, hard, lean body, very fit. A soldier, she'd bet anything on it. A soldier hired by Gerald to find her. And he had.

It was her worst nightmare, come to terrifying life.

Helpless. Gerald's prisoner.

Heading for a plane in which they'd take her to where he could hurt her as long as he wanted and where Harry could never find her.

Chapter 16

Sam drove. Harry wasn't in any condition to. He said he needed to follow the GPS signal, but all three of them knew it wasn't that. He'd drive them into a tree or off a cliff if he was behind the wheel.

He called out directions to Sam because tracking a monitor and talking seemed to be the extent of his motor skills right now. He had to get his head out of his ass, fast. They were heading toward a showdown and he couldn't afford nerves, couldn't afford not to have his head in the game. Even if he was shit scared.

Not for himself. He'd been trained by the best. Delta operators were the finest elite troops on the face of the planet, SEALs be damned. It had taken an RPG traveling more than eight thousand meters a second to take him down. But two men? With Mike and Sam by his side? No motherfucker on earth could withstand them.

Except that Ellen was caught right in the middle. Lovely, gentle Ellen, who had no tactics in her, who wouldn't know how to move, how to find shelter, how to defend herself . . . She was a gorgeous sitting duck and it was all too easy to imagine her taking a bullet to the head, caught in a crossfire.

All too easy to imagine her head exploding into a pink mist, imagine her doubled over, gut-shot, insides spilling out, imagine her shot in the back, unable to move.

God, he couldn't think straight. It drove him crazy. He couldn't even sit still in the same space with the images zinging around his brain.

"Easy." Mike's big, strong hand reached out from the backseat and settled heavily on his shoulders. He'd seen Harry twist and turn with the horror of his thoughts.

He had to stop this.

He was dragging his buddies, his brothers, the men he loved most in the world, into a firefight where he could get them killed if he couldn't focus.

And he couldn't. Not even clamping down hard on his thoughts the way he'd done in rehab, concentrating so furiously sweat broke out. It didn't work. His mind kept sliding to Ellen strapped to a chair, glorious hair gone, in its place a red cap . . .

His stomach wrenched hard; bile came up. He clamped his jaws shut.

"Don't puke now," Sam said, not taking his eyes off the

road. Where traffic allowed, he shot over the hundred-mile-per-hour mark. If Sam weren't such a goddamned good driver, they'd have killed someone by now. "Puking's not going to do her any good, trust me on this one."

Sam had barfed right into their fancy designer wastepaper basket when Nicole had been kidnapped almost a year ago. "I know what you're going through, buddy, believe me. But you've gotta keep your head, otherwise . . ." His own jaws clamped shut before he could say anything more.

They'd all seen that video. They could all imagine Ellen being skinned alive. Maybe . . . right . . . now.

Harry was sweating so hard he stank like a goat. He wiped his hands carefully on his jeans, because whatever was going down, he needed his hands dry.

"We all set up back there, Mike?"

"Yeah, got everything handy." While Harry was negotiating Sam through the streets on the tail of that fucker Montez, Mike had been lining his ducks up in a row. Harry knew that right now Mike could lay his hands in a second on whatever they could possibly need. "We'll be ready whenever we get a clear shot."

Harry glanced down at his handheld, watching the screen.

Mike looked down over his shoulder. "What'd you bug? Are they going to be able to find it?"

Harry knew what he was thinking. If there was a bug in Ellen's purse or in a pocket, they could scan her and throw it out the window when they found it.

But he'd been smarter than that. Ellen had stepped out three times on smart men, including himself—just slipped away.

"They can't find anything, because it's wrapped up in a special porcelain casing that gives off a signal on a very high frequency. They won't pick up on it."

"And if they throw her purse out the window or make her strip?"

"Be hard to find it. It's embedded in her shoulder."

There was silence in the van.

"Jesus," Sam finally said. "You cut her open and placed a chip in her flesh? Man, you're braver than I am. The only thing I managed to do was seed Nicole's hard drive."

A year ago Nicole had stumbled onto a terrorist plot and had been kidnapped together with her sick father. They'd been able to follow Nicole because out of paranoia Sam had put a tiny tracking device in the portable hard disk she kept in her purse.

Otherwise Nicole's bones would be at the bottom of the bay, still anchored by chains.

"I didn't cut her open. She had a wound I stitched shut, remember? I just slipped the tracker in. It's tiny and tissue neutral and it's thanks to that we're able to track her, so shut the fuck up. I was planning on removing it later, anyhow."

When that fucker Montez was six feet underground or in a federal prison.

Harry's jaw muscles clenched. With Nicole it had come down to a two-second margin, when Sam and Mike had been able to pull the trigger first.

Please, Harry prayed. Let me pull that trigger first.

"Mike." He kept his eyes glued to the display. The Mercedes was tracking steadily west. Montez and Van der Boeke had a clear goal. So what the fuck was it?

"Yo." God, it felt good to hear Mike's steady bass. He knew that Harry was shaken. Mike didn't have a woman he loved on the line and could be counted on to stay cool.

Harry didn't dare take his eyes off the display and the road ahead. "Call the FBI SD Field Office. Number's 858-565-1255. Ask for Special Agent Aaron Welles by name. Give him a sitrep. I want him where we end up, fast as possible, with the whole cavalry. SWAT, Hostage Rescue, the works."

"On it." Mike's phone bleeped softly as he keyed in the numbers. "Special Agent Aaron Welles, please. It's urgent."

While Mike gave a concise report, Harry frowned at the moving dot. Where the fuck were they going? He scrolled up the map, extrapolating a few miles ahead of the Mercedes, and saw something he vaguely recognized. Where—?

"Fuck!" he shouted.

Mike stopped talking into his cell. "What?"

"They're heading for an airfield! Tracy Municipal Airfield. *Fuck!*" Harry slammed the armrest between the two seats.

"Shit," Mike breathed.

Sam didn't say anything, but the van leaped forward.

"If she gets up in the air, she's lost. We'll never find her. They can push her body out of the plane at any point they want. They'll fly over desert and forest. She'll be lost." He turned around and looked Mike in the eyes. "Tell Aaron to call it in to the airfield. To block every outgoing flight. Tell him to do what it takes, there's a kidnapping across state lines by a man who's killed three times."

Mike simply said, "Hear that? Roger." He closed his cell. "They're coming in force, Harry. As fast as they can make it."

"But we're the front line," Harry gritted.

"Yeah." Mike's eyes met his in the rearview mirror. "We're the front line. Tip of the spear. If we don't stop them, that girl is gone."

They seemed to go off the main roads, over a few bumps in the road, then were off again, racing over unpaved roads.

Lying down in the footwell, all Ellen could see was empty sky. No telephone poles, no street signs, no buildings, nothing. They drove for maybe a quarter of an hour over roads so rough she could hear and even feel rocks pelting against the underside of the car, and could see plumes of the dust they raised outside the window. Finally, they slid back onto asphalt.

The two men up front weren't talking. She had no idea what their plans were, except that she would never survive them.

Oh God. How could she have made this mistake? And how could Gerald have been just *waiting* for her? She'd barely stepped outside Harry's building, hadn't even had time to flag a taxi, and that blond guy had come running after her. A second later, the big black Mercedes rolled up to where they were.

They must have been waiting in the car right outside the building. But how? How did they know?

However they knew, it was too late to worry about it. Actually, it was way too late to worry about anything. She'd reached a dead end, a place where nothing she could do would influence the outcome. She was in the hands of two clever men, strong men. For just the few seconds in which the blond man had gripped her arm, hard, and pulled her against him, she'd felt tough, hard muscles, the kind Harry had.

There was no way she could overpower one of these men, let alone two.

She didn't even have her wits about her. Her thought processes were slow, sluggish. Making any kind of plan required clear thinking, and that was beyond her. Whatever they'd given her made it almost impossible to think straight.

Gerald was driving really fast now. Too fast. What kind of road could he be on that would allow him to race like this?

Though the car had that exceptional soundproofing of expensive vehicles, the occasional dull roar filtered its way into the cabin, a sound that started low and increased in pitch. And a sharp smell penetrated, a smell both chemical and familiar.

With a wrench of the wheels, the car drove in to some kind of shelter. The sun cut out immediately. As the car slowed down, it passed under something. Something long and metallic . . . a wing. An airplane wing. The car came to a stop, rocking her painfully forward then backward. She looked up out the window and saw the curved metal and rounded portholes of an airplane hull.

Even her dulled, hurting head was able to put it together. They'd reached an airport. Somehow they'd bypassed security and gone directly into a hangar and, oh God, a plane was right there.

Ellen shook. Somewhere in the back of her mind was the idea that somehow, she didn't know how, but somehow Harry would find her. Would just come galloping to her rescue and prevail, because he was a good guy and the good guys always won, right? Super-Harry to the rescue, swooping down and saving the day.

Wasn't going to happen. *Couldn't* happen.

Gerald and his—what? minion? henchman?—whatever he was, they were going to bundle her into a plane and she'd be lost forever. This wasn't a scheduled flight on a plane belonging to an airline.

Ellen knew that Gerald operated two planes, one for executives in his company and one he reserved for his own personal use. A Learjet. She knew how much it had cost, secondhand, how much it cost to operate, how much of that cost he deducted from his taxes.

This was probably his plane. He could fly out whenever he wanted, without asking anyone's permission. He could fly anywhere he wanted.

Bearclaw had a small airfield of its own. Gerald's pilots could land after dark and no one would ever know she'd been on the plane. If he did to her what he'd done to Arlen and that Mikowski and Roddy and poor Kerry—whatever that devil's voice from hell said, Kerry was dead—well, Gerald owned more than seven thousand acres of land, much of it swamp.

He could bury her where no one would ever find her. Not all the police officers and all the dogs in the world would find her.

She was lost and had no cards left to play.

Both front car doors opened as the men got out. Ellen squeezed her eyes shut. The only tiny advantage she had was the fact that they couldn't know she'd regained consciousness. Drugs affected different people in different ways.

If she could just pretend she was still unconscious, she could . . . she could what?

Live.

Live just a few moments more. Feel her body, racked with pain though it was. Breathe, even if it was dust and diesel fuel fumes. Think. Think of Harry and what, maybe, they might have had together.

Tears seeped from her eyes, though she didn't have the use of her hands to wipe them.

Harry.

Would what they'd found be true, lasting? Oh God. Images, dense, full of the color and the weight of truth, flashed through her mind. Harry laughing, sipping wine while she cooked. She wasn't much of a cook, but he loved her—he'd choke it down. Sitting with a half smile on his face while she sang for him. Unearthly joy on his face as he held their newborn child.

Hours, days, weeks, years spent together. Loving each other, loving their family. Their children would grow up together with Sam and Nicole's children in a tight and loving circle, utterly protected and safe. So unlike her childhood and Harry's. Mike would be a doting uncle.

Watching them grow up, day by day, year by year. She'd record songs, maybe play a few gigs in the San Diego area. Harry's company would expand because he and Sam and Mike were so good at what they did. She'd keep their books because she was good at it.

At the end of the working day, a happy family to come home to. Christmases, Easters, birthdays, anniversaries. All celebrated with love.

The mess and fuss of kids. Fights, laughter, triumphs, the dramas of the young. They wouldn't have to keep the tight rein on themselves she'd had to, because there'd be solid earth beneath their feet.

Strong, happy kids. Kids who grew up to follow their dreams. She and Harry would grow older, weaker, happier. Grandkids . . .

It was all something that would happen to another Ellen and Harry, in an alternate universe. In this one, she'd disappear, and he'd mourn another Lost One he couldn't save.

She'd die, lose all that love and laughter, and for what? So Gerald could keep his empire built on larceny and murder and greed. So he could kill with impunity. Just snuff out people's lives because it suited him.

It was monstrous. He was a monster.

Thank God she'd e-mailed the FBI and thank God Harry and Mike and Sam had the information Nicole had uncovered. They'd make sure it got into the FBI's hands.

Maybe Gerald would go down after all. The FBI was good, thorough, uncorrupted. They wouldn't be like Gerald's tame officers back home. They'd dig and dig and dig.

Utter hatred for Gerald pulsed in her. Hatred for all of them—for the man who'd battered Harry's little sister to death, for the man Kerry had been so afraid of, but above all, hatred for Gerald and all his men—prickled through her veins like some kind of drug.

She was going to die, but by God before she did, she was going to hurt Gerald, somehow.

The back door opened, and the engine noises and sharp

diesel fuel fumes assaulted her senses. She stayed completely still, eyes closed and unmoving. She'd be deadweight. Good. Make them work at getting her out of the car.

"You get her." Gerald's cold voice. She'd recognize it anywhere.

"Yeah. I'll take her up into the plane." The second man had an odd accent. The accent everyone spoke in a Clint Eastwood film, *Invictus*. South African.

"You do that. I'll talk with the pilots. They'll be ready for takeoff. Let's get in the air."

Ellen tried to will herself to be unwieldy, but the blond man was really strong. He didn't try to carry her across his front. He pulled her up and over his shoulder in a fireman's lift, steps loud on the concrete floor, moving swiftly up the plane's stairs, holding her legs with one arm around her knees.

She felt the South African dip and they passed into the cabin. The quality of the air changed immediately. Fresher, cleaner. The outside noise abated then disappeared when she heard a door thump close.

They were in the airplane.

She was unceremoniously dumped in a leather chair. She lolled, making her whole body limp, arms dangling.

Everything hurt, but she was alive.

Maybe they would stay here for a while, in the airplane. Maybe they were waiting for someone. Maybe the plane needed refueling.

Would there be a way for the FBI to find Gerald? Would a flight plan have been filed?

When she disappeared, Harry would read her e-mail and

contact the FBI immediately. As her head slowly cleared of the drug and she was able to put two thoughts together, hope surged through her.

Harry'd be pushing the FBI to find them, they'd be on the lookout, canvasing all roads, trains, buses, planes.

Maybe all she needed was for Gerald and this South African guy to stay in the plane while the FBI and Harry did their thing.

Stay here, she ordered the plane.

As if in answer, there was an incomprehensible announcement from the pilot's cabin over the speakers and the engines fired up. A minute later, the plane started slowly moving.

Ellen chanced cracking an eye open and saw that the plane was taxiing from the hangar out into the sunlight.

The place looked utterly deserted. Even if she sprang to her feet and pounded on the windows, there was no one to hear. No one to care.

The notes on the engines changed as the pilot engaged a higher gear. They were moving out.

This was it. She was as good as dead.

"How much farther?" Sam asked.

Harry made the calculations in his head, looking at the green dot, still now, looking at the overlying map. "Two miles. Couple of minutes." He lifted his head. "There!" He pointed straight ahead, where the airfield was slowly coming into focus. Several medium-sized hangars, a couple of small jets parked outside them. While he watched, a Boeing 707 lifted off.

Somewhere on that airfield was Ellen.

Hold on, honey. I'm coming.

"Where's the entrance?" Sam asked. He didn't even dare flick a glance Harry's way. He was pushing the vehicle to the max.

Harry ran his finger over the map, around, around . . .

"Shit! It's on the north side! If she's already on the plane, we don't have time to circle the perimeter."

"Hold on." Sam's face was grim as he gripped the wheel hard, wrenched it, brought the vehicle around forty-five degrees in a swirl of dust until they were facing the fence. He pressed the accelerator down to the floor and was doing at least a hundred miles an hour when they burst through the carbon-wire fencing, posts popping out on either side. "Which hangar?"

That was harder, and Harry had to get it right. He stared at the small monitor as if Ellen could post a message to him there. *Where are you, honey?*

There. His finger tightened on the green dot on the screen. She was there.

"Two o'clock. Green hangar. Mike—you got our gear set up?"

"Count on it," Mike's deep bass came from behind. And Harry did, because Mike was good with gear. "You got your head screwed on straight?"

Harry knew what Mike was asking. Was he going to be a member of the team or was he going to be an uncontrollable wildcard, capable of jeopardizing the mission, costing them their lives?

Harry looked ahead at the hangar, the size of a thumb on the horizon but growing fast. When they got there they would have one shot at saving Ellen. One. Any misstep and he could end up with a dead Ellen and dead brothers and his life in smoking ruins.

He was scared shitless he'd fuck up. He had to get his head out of that space, fast. He pressed his head against the head-rest, bracing himself, feeling every nerve and muscle in his body tense, heart pounding, the refrain *Ellen Ellen Ellen* beating fast in his head, hands curled, thick and clumsy, on his knees. His head felt light and for a second he just watched the hangar getting bigger and bigger on the horizon.

A sharp blow to his shoulder from behind. "Harry!" Mike said sharply. "Come back!"

And his head cleared, his hands felt normal again, and the palm-sized building on the horizon had Ellen in it, a hair's breadth from dying.

He hadn't been able to save Crissy, though God knows he'd tried. That fuckhead Rod had just picked her up and smashed her against a wall as if she'd been a doll instead of a delightful little girl.

They won. They always won, the fuckers. Always.

This stopped right here, right now. Ellen was the love of his life, light in darkness. She'd saved his life over those long painful months of rehab, that lovely voice in the darkness singing just for him. Understanding pain and turning it into magic. Magic. The woman was magic, the woman of a lifetime, and he was *not* going to lose her to Gerald Montez or to Piet van der Boeke.

His whole life came down to this, to this one moment. If he lost this, if he lost Ellen, and if his brothers got hurt or killed, his entire life was gone.

Wasn't going to happen.

He was back and he was going to win.

"Yeah," he said to Mike. "I'm okay. Get your weapon ready. We'll circle round—"

"Oh shit," Sam said.

All three of them stared in the distance, where a plane was rolling out. Harry checked the monitor, the green dot moving slowly. "It's her. We've got to stop that plane."

If that plane took off, Ellen was lost, and he was *not* going to lose her. Not an option.

A plan formed in his mind, fully blown, as if he'd had time to plan it over days. He mapped it out in his head, knowing that it would only work if he could trust Sam and Mike totally.

He could.

"Sam!" he rapped out. "Can you catch up with that plane? It'll taxi until it reaches the runway. Can you reach it and line up with it before the runway?"

"I'll have to, won't I," Sam replied calmly as the van took another leap and was now traveling at the outer limits of its capacity. Strong as the vehicle was, it started shuddering as if it were going to shake itself to pieces.

Sam kept his foot on the pedal as the shuddering grew louder, stronger. But the plane was now large in their windshield, gathering speed. With a swerve, Sam caught up with it, kept pace right behind the starboard wing.

He was probably in the blind spot, where the plane's radar couldn't see them, because the pilots showed no signs that they saw the vehicle. The plane was taxiing. The airfield wasn't full and they had the immediate area to themselves.

"Mike, take out their tires."

If anyone could do it, it was Mike, but even his abilities would be stretched to the limit. At this speed, it was hard for Sam to keep the vehicle steady.

"On it." He cracked open the back panel.

There was a small bench running around the perimeter of the spacious back section of the Sprinter, there for when they had to transport an entire team to an op. Mike placed one knee on the bench for stability, shouldered his rifle, a move smooth with years of practice.

"Sam . . ." he said.

"Steadying." Sam locked his arms on the wheel, providing as steady a platform as was humanly possible from a moving vehicle for Mike.

No one spoke. Mike needed to concentrate.

A loud blast followed instantly by another one as two of the four front wheels exploded. Immediately, sparks shot out from the wheels as the rims touched the tarmac.

Mike hadn't gone for sound suppression, which would have made the shot even more difficult. No one was going to hear a shot inside a plane with the engines revving.

The plane wobbled for a second, then Mike shot out the third and fourth tires of the front set. The plane was now trailing a bloom of sparks.

A beep in Harry's ear and Aaron's voice came over. "Harry, we're about seven minutes out. I viewed that video your lady sent. Whoever sent it, whoever did this, man, he's going down. I told the tower to stop all flights."

"Well, there's a plane going up, now, Aaron. She's on it. A

Learjet, and they're taxiing for takeoff. Mike's shot out the front tires but they're not stopping. What the fuck?"

"Maybe the pilot's under orders not to stop."

"But they can't land the other end without their goddamned tires!"

"They can crash land and hope to walk away. If he'd rather crash land than face you guys, either he's really crazy or really wants to hurt that woman. Either way, it's bad news. Stop him, Harry. We'll get there and help you take him down."

"Roger that."

Stopping Montez was easier said than done. The plane's speed was increasing, even with four missing tires. Harry didn't dare have Mike shoot out anything important from the fuselage. He had no idea if a bullet would hit the gas tanks and blow the whole fucking plane up, with Ellen inside. The plane veered left and got onto the runway. It was accelerating, though slowly. But if the pilot pushed it, or had a gun to his head, in another five minutes it would reach V1, take off speed, and they'd be gone.

"Mike!" he yelled. The engine noise was almost overpowering. They were right under one of the big Pratt and Whitney engines and it was like being inside a cement mixer. "Give me the grapple gun!"

Mike slid back from his station, still holding on to his Remington with his left hand, and opened up one of the gear boxes lining the back. The right box. Mike never got the gear wrong.

He handed it over, a brand-new toy that had only been tested in the lab, from a young company run by former soldiers who were also enthusiastic gearheads. A long, thick weapon that looked like a space ray gun, except that it shot a powerful grappling hook.

It was a one-shot deal. Miss, and you missed your chance. But even if there were two shots in it, it would be too late to try a second time. The plane was laboring and wobbling, but if Harry didn't stop it, it could take off. He'd watch Ellen climb into the sky taking his heart with her, knowing that nothing could ever save her.

So he just wasn't fucking going to miss.

Their van had had a sunroof carved out—not for sightseeing or sunbathing, but because sometimes that exit option was useful, like now. He rolled the roof back, stacked a couple of boxes and climbed on top. He lifted himself out onto the roof, a knee on either side of the opening.

He reached his hand down and Mike slapped the grapple gun in his hand. Their eyes met. If this didn't work they were fucked. Even if it worked, he had a one-in-a-thousand shot at getting Ellen back.

"Steady!" he yelled at Mike, knowing he would relay it back to Sam. Sam was keeping the vehicle straight and firm—not easy, because the plane created strong crosswinds and was wobbling a little. Sam had understood what Harry was trying to do and was trying to keep him as close to the wing as possible without being sideswiped by the almost-out-of-control plane.

Focus.

It all fell away—the danger to Ellen, the runaway plane, two killers inside. There were only two things in his world: him and the leading edge of the wing. Between them was going to stretch the grapple, with its wire cable made of carbon nanotube fiber, the strongest material on earth, so strong that if they ever built the space elevator, this cable would run it. It was a closely held Navy secret that Sam had gotten his hands on.

Mike reached up and handed him thin shooting gloves with Kevlar palms. It would interfere with his shooting aim a fraction, though since he was aiming at a span of sixty-one feet, he was hardly likely to miss. But he was going to climb his way up on the wing, hauling himself over a wire cable, and he needed gloves to protect his hands.

Mike looked up at him, waiting to relay instructions to Sam. It would be nice to wait for the exact right circumstances, but the situation was deteriorating by the second. Harry nodded, shot the grapple gun, dropped the gun so Mike could wrap the cable around a spar in the van, felt the bite of the grapple's engagement with the leading edge of the wing, heard Mike shout *brake!* to Sam, all in one second that seemed to last an eternity.

The noise of the van braking, Sam literally standing on the brakes, rose above the noise of the plane. The cable went taut, vibrations of tensile stress singing through it. Harry could feel the stress in his hands as the twenty-four-thousand-pound plane bucked against the fifteen thousand pounds of the armored vehicle.

To take off now, it would have to do so dragging fifteen thousand pounds behind it, because that cable was not going to break.

Harry took a deep breath and launched himself in the air, landing at the halfway zone between the Sprinter and the plane. The plane was wrenching around, wobbling heavily, shaking, the sound of sheet metal tearing so loud it overrode everything.

The instant his hands made contact with the wire he started hauling himself hand over hand along it until he reached the trailing edge of the wing. He held as tightly as he could with his left hand while he pulled himself up and over the wing. He rested for a second, feeling the airframe shuddering under his belly, panting, waiting just long enough so that he could breathe.

He lifted himself up on his hands and knees, looking down briefly to see Sam looking up at him. Sam lifted his fist, stuck his thumb in the air. *So far so good.*

The plane was slowing. One of the ailerons had sheared off, a section of the sheet metal of the leading edge had buckled.

The cockpit would have registered this. There would be alarms going off, visual and aural. No pilot on earth would ever try taking off under these conditions. The engines disengaged then throttled back.

The pilot was braking.

Harry scrambled over the wing, using every single handhold he could until he made it to the fuselage, crouching to avoid the rush of air intake of the huge engine not ten feet from him.

The overwing emergency exit had a manual opening mechanism. He engaged it as the plane finally came to a shuddering halt, skewed across the runway, smoke rising from the shot-out tires. The engines abruptly cut off and there was absolute silence except for the ticking sound of metal cooling.

The emergency exit door popped inward. For a moment, all

Harry could see was darkness through the doorway, into the cabin of the plane. It looked deserted. Harry clenched his jaw. He hadn't made a mistake. This was the plane and Ellen was somewhere on it. He'd stake his life on it. He'd already staked his heart.

Without even thinking about it, his Desert Eagle was in his hand.

He didn't dare take his eyes from the black, empty hole to look down at his brothers. He didn't need to. He trusted them to do what was necessary at the exact right time.

Time stretched. It felt like hours, lifetimes had gone by, but it had been only a few seconds since the plane had come to a screeching, grinding halt.

Shadows moved in the dark interior of the cabin and suddenly two figures appeared on the threshold, brightly lit figures on a stage against a black backdrop.

Harry's heart nearly blew.

Gerald Montez, holding a limp Ellen, an unconscious Ellen, but please, God, not a dead Ellen. A Glock 19 pressed against her head so hard a trickle of blood fell down her temple, down her cheek, dripped off her chin.

If she was bleeding, she was alive.

He knew who Montez was, but Montez didn't know who he was.

"You!" Montez screamed. "Whoever the fuck you are! Weapon down! Hands out to your sides and back away or I blow her head off!"

He had no choice. The heavy Desert Eagle bounced on the wing and slid off, the clatter as it hit the tarmac loud in the silence. He had two other backup weapons, but he couldn't go for either one as long as Montez was holding that gun to Ellen's head.

Montez was having trouble holding Ellen, who was so limp her feet rested awkwardly on the cabin floor, not holding her up. His left arm was doing that. He took one step forward and her legs bumped and dragged behind her.

Montez was strong, but holding the entire weight of an adult woman with one arm was straining him. Sweat dripped off his face.

Or maybe it was fear, because he didn't have too many options here, other than blowing Ellen's head off.

He knew that Harry had backup. The van with a driver was visible off the trailing edge of the wing. Mike was nowhere to be seen, but he was there. Oh yeah, he was there.

Montez screamed down to Sam. "And you! Driver! Get your fucking hands off the wheel!"

Through the windscreen, Sam lifted his hands off the wheel.

Montez turned to Harry. "Back away!"

Harry backed away, glad to give Mike a clear shot, but how could Mike take it? Oh God, Montez's gun was screwed tightly against Ellen's temple and his finger was white on the trigger. Mike couldn't even try the old trick of blowing his forearm off at the elbow, because it was tight in against his stomach.

Blowing a round into Montez's cerebral cortex, putting the bullet right at midpoint between the eyes, on the bridge of the nose, would be child's play for Mike. Hell, it would be child's play for Harry, if Harry's Desert Eagle—with almost too much stopping power for this distance—wasn't down there on the tarmac.

The thing was, if Mike caught him between the eyes, Montez would be blown backward, and even if he were already dead, the sheer physics of the situation would guarantee that his dead trigger finger would be pulled back, too, and Ellen's brains would spatter the elegant interior of the fancy jet.

Don't even think of that. He couldn't. It would make him weak.

He knew, like he knew that the sun would rise tomorrow in the east, that all he needed, all he and Mike and Sam needed, was the tiniest window of opportunity, the merest flicker of a chink, and Montez was history. It would come down to a fraction of a second and he had to be ready, because his whole life had come down to this exact moment.

He stood on the balls of his feet, muscles ready but not tense, mind empty of everything but the permutations of geometry necessary to wipe Gerald Montez off the face of the earth.

All he needed was a second. A microsecond. Just a tiny little something.

And then—a miracle occurred.

He hadn't even been watching Ellen because it hurt to see her and because every fiber of his being was caught up in Montez, in looking for the faintest hint of movement that would signal an opportunity.

Without moving a muscle, remaining a deadweight hanging from Montez's arm, Ellen opened her eyes. Her gorgeous sea-green eyes, alive and completely aware. Montez couldn't see her, but by God, Harry did. And Mike and Sam could see her, too.

The clock was up and running.

She was white-faced and terrified, with a gun pressed heavily against the skin of her temple by a maniac, but she attempted a smile, a slight movement of her lips.

And then she winked.

And Harry knew.

Everything that happened next happened in a second of blinding motion that somehow felt as if it were slow motion.

Ellen kicked Montez in the knee and threw herself forward, out onto the wing. There was no doubt that Montez would have aimed at her head and pulled the trigger, except that as Ellen was moving, in the fraction of a second in which her head cleared the muzzle, Montez's head blew apart, and Harry was leaping to catch Ellen, ripping a flashbang off his utility belt and tossing it into the cabin, grabbing Ellen, twisting in midair so she'd fall on him, pulling her head into his shoulders, because even at a distance the effects of a flashbang were devastating and highly painful. It went off inside the cabin and the windows glowed brightly with the flash, the 170-decibel grenade echoing loudly over the airfield.

Whoever was inside was going to be completely disoriented and would stay that way for long minutes.

Sam and Mike, cradling his rifle—which Harry wanted to kiss because it was directly responsible for his holding a live Ellen in his arms again—climbed up onto the wing from the roof of the SUV and dipped to enter the cabin, weapons out.

A few seconds later, another shot rang out, a pistol this

time. Mike appeared immediately in the doorway. "Van der Boeke," he said, and held up two fingers. Pilot and copilot. "Sam's taking care of them."

Van der Boeke was an experienced soldier and had recovered fast from the flashbang. But no one got the drop on Mike. Van der Boeke was history.

Harry ducked his head down, chin hairs catching in the flying strands of red-brown hair flowing over his chest. Ellen was trembling so hard he was afraid she'd hurt herself, and he tightened his arms around her.

"It's okay," he whispered to the top of her head. "It's okay, it's all over. You're safe. We're all safe."

His hand was on her back and he could feel her heart fluttering with the residue of terror. She shuddered once, violently, and gasped for air.

Four big, black vans came racing up, braking hard. "Go go go!" male voices chanted, and men spilled out of the backs of the vans. Armed men in full gear, four turning with their backs to them, setting up a security perimeter, the others down on one knee, rifles shouldered.

Ellen started shuddering again. "Who's that?" her voice was panicked and he rubbed her shoulder.

"The cavalry, darling. It's fine." He kissed her cheek, shifting her slightly so he could lift himself up on one elbow. "Aaron!" Harry yelled.

"Yo!"

"Up here! You're late to the party, but glad you could make it anyway. We've got two bad guys down. Two pilots, still breathing, probably bad guys, too. You sort it out."

"Harry?" Ellen raised her head, looking him in the eyes, dashing away a tear. "Is that the FBI?"

"Otherwise known as the cavalry, yeah."

"Gerald is dead?"

The words were music to his ears. "Oh yeah."

"There's another guy with him, tall, blond—"

"We know all about him, honey, and he is dead."

She just looked at him, wide eyes studying his. She needed to see the truth of that in him and he let her.

"So . . . it's over."

He laughed, for the first time in what felt like forever. "It's over."

She threw her arm around his neck, hugging him, and a small half laugh that sounded just a little hysterical came from deep in her throat. "Oh God, Harry, it's over." She pulled back to look him in the eyes again.

"Let's go home," she whispered.

"Oh yeah," he grinned.

San Diego
Christmas Eve

It was a small jazz club, the kind Ellen—or Eve—preferred. She didn't like stadiums or big concert halls; they weren't right for her voice. It was a Christmas concert she'd been practicing for since October. All Christmas carols, all in subtle jazz renderings that made them sound brand new.

Since the club was small, tickets were at a premium. Ellen

made everyone pay through the nose and donated half the proceeds to a women's shelter in San Diego, one few people knew about, one that worked.

Five minutes after tickets were available online, the club was sold out. There were fans hanging from the rafters.

Harry sat with Mike and Sam and Nicole and Meredith, who was on her best behavior. They'd gotten filthy looks when they settled at a table with a six-month-old baby. There were groans and comments from surrounding tables, which only died down a little when they saw how damned cute she was.

Merry was unfazed. She was a lady and a concert pro and better behaved than the drunk, fat guy to Harry's left. The instant she heard Aunt Ellen's voice, she stilled and listened. It was amazing.

But then Ellen had sung lullabies to her since she was born.

Harry thought that was amazing—to grow up with Ellen's voice in your head.

He still thought the whole thing was amazing—that this woman was his wife. That he got to live with her and listen to her sing anytime he wanted. And Christ, she even kept his *books*! No one was as happy as he was. Well, except for Sam, who was loony over Nicole and even loonier over Merry.

Ellen finished a long, slow, heartbreaking rendering of "Ave Maria" and there wasn't a dry eye in the house. There was a little hush. Even Merry, sitting on Daddy's lap, huge blue eyes fixed on her aunt, was quiet.

Then the house exploded and Merry laughed.

Ellen was Eve tonight. It was incredible how she could be these two entirely different people. Ellen was his beautiful wife, with the shiny hair tumbling over her shoulders, dressed casually in a white shirt and jeans, no makeup, who most evenings greeted him when he came home with a smile and a kiss and a new burnt dish, making his heart leap and his stomach groan.

Out of pity, Manuela, Sam and Nicole's housekeeper, sent down food a couple of times a week. Enough to feed an army of stevedores.

That woman was relaxed and happy and loving and man, he loved her back.

But Eve—oh God, *Eve*—she was this remote and mysterious beauty conjured up out of moonlight and stardust. As smooth as marble, elusive as a dream.

Just look at her, Harry thought. She was slender, even small, but she dominated the stage. One spotlight, the musicians behind her in shadow, standing before a microphone, holding the public completely in the palm of her hand.

Her voice filled the room, filled every single empty space. It would be impossible to think of anything but her, have anything but her in your head.

Harry looked around, transfixed by the expressions on the faces of the people in the room. Upscale professionals, mostly—the tickets were expensive, after all. The men elegantly dressed, the women in evening gowns and bright, shiny jewels.

An adult, sophisticated audience, and yet every face looked the same—transported to another place. A place of love and hope and loss and grief, where all those emotions were felt deeply, all at the same time. Unbearably moving, unspeakably beautiful, the carols everyone knew by heart, had heard in elevators and in malls and on TV and at drunken Christmas parties—each song took on a new meaning, as if being heard for the first time.

Christmas was joy and hope, a yearning for peace and goodwill. The old words took on a completely new and deeper meaning. Harry knew they'd never hear those songs again without thinking of tonight, a night when the most beautiful music in the world floated in the air.

And Eve herself—oh God, she just broke your heart up there. She looked like she'd been beamed down from another, better planet, in a shimmering green dress that matched her eyes, her auburn hair slicked back and swept up to showcase that long, pale neck and delicate jawline.

The makeup she never wore offstage painted her face with an old-fashioned glamour, mysteriously deep eyes, high cheekbones set off with the softest of blushes, that mouth . . .

Harry was sure there wasn't a man here who wasn't thinking about that mouth.

She was sex incarnate, but better sex than anyone had ever known, to a different beat. Her entire body was caught up in the jazzy rhythms, swaying gently, perfectly to the percussion. She carried every single nuance of every word, small gestures that somehow conveyed passion in peace, love in triumph.

The concert was coming to an end.

She finished "O Holy Night" and bowed her head at the applause, graceful as a queen accepting the homage of her adoring subjects.

Wait for it, Harry thought. The last song, her signature song, the song she sang at the end of every concert, whatever the type of music.

It had become her trademark.

She sang it a cappella, because just her voice was enough.

"Amazing Grace." It was their song, because she said it was only by amazing grace that she'd been able to find her way to him.

The song moved him, always. He'd heard her sing it hundreds of times, and it was always a dagger that pierced his heart, bloodless and painless and deep. The song made him feel keenly all the losses of his life. His mother, Crissy. Above all, Crissy.

He'd almost lost Ellen, and he thought of that, daily, hourly. It would be so easy to dwell on the losses, on the pain this life gave us all. To think of the darkness and sorrow, of loved ones gone forever, of the hatred and cruelty there was in the world.

All of that passed through his heart, every time. And every time he suffered.

And then every time, the song and Ellen's voice reminded him of the incredible grace in the world and he was pulled forward, through the pain and suffering and into peace.

At the end of the song, in the darkness of the room, Ellen shifted a little, unerringly moving her head to where he was. She met his eyes. Somehow she always knew exactly where he was, no matter how dark the room, no matter how many people.

She held his eyes and sang directly to him, straight to his heart, because this was for him.

Through many dangers, toils, and snares,
I have already come;
'Tis grace hath brought me safe thus far,
And grace will lead me home.

The last notes fell away like a dream, shimmering in the darkness, and Ellen bowed her head.

The spotlight dimmed, went out, and the crowd rose to its feet with a roar, clapping and shouting and whistling.

But Eve was gone. She never came out for an encore, because the song moved her too much. It was why it was always the last song. She could sing nothing after it.

The lights came on in the house, showcasing an empty stage and the musicians standing for their bows.

"Wow." Nicole wiped her eyes. "Seems hard to remember that that magical woman up there is our Ellen." She laughed. "Our accountant! It's like having Picasso mow your lawn."

Mike and Sam weren't listening. Mike was on his feet, two fingers in his mouth, whistling and stomping, and Sam was teaching the little girl on his lap to clap, laughing with her.

This part of his family was safe and happy. Harry slipped away to tend to the other part of his family.

She was backstage, her hair already down. Onstage, formal wear suited her. Her concert dresses were each one of a kind, created for her by an up-and-coming young designer who captured her innate elegance and class.

Eve loved the drama of the gowns, loved the shimmer of silk and satin, the flash of sequins, the glamorous makeup, the elegant upswept hair. But the instant Eve left the stage, Ellen wanted back into her casual clothes, her hair down, the makeup off.

The dressing room was so full of flowers you could hardly turn around, the scent going immediately to Harry's head. His two dozen pink roses were set on the small counter in front of the mirror, where she could see them.

All the flowers went the next day to the children's hospital, but Eve loved coming backstage and plunging into the riot of colors and scents.

She was standing, trying to reach behind for the zipper.

"Let me." Harry moved behind her, bent to kiss her shoulder. "A husband's privilege." He met her eyes in the mirror. "You were magnificent tonight, my love. And the last song . . . God."

"Amazing Grace." Ellen smiled at him in the mirror. "It's our song, isn't it? And it always will be." She turned and caught his hands in hers. Took a deep breath. "Okay. There will never be a better moment. Since 'Amazing Grace' is our song, I thought we'd call her Grace, because I just know it will be a girl. Grace Christine, for your sister." She stood on tiptoe and kissed him. "She'll be born just in time for your birthday. So Merry Christmas and happy birthday, my love."

And Harry's heart simply exploded with joy.

A year later

The woman who stopped in front of the Morrison Building was quietly beautiful, dressed with understated elegance and style. Light-blond hair moved in a shiny spill around her face. She had unusual light-brown, almost golden eyes and lovely, clear features.

There was nothing flashy about her, though, and it was a building made for flash. The men and women who worked in the building were busy conquering the world, making a lot of money at it, and it showed. Suits, haircuts, shoes, bags, briefcases—they were all the very latest, cutting-edge fashion.

Some of them were in advertising and design and wore styles that would be popular in five years. They looked edgy and interesting, like time travelers from the future.

And busy—they were all busy, rushing in and out of the big steel and glass doors, marching with long strides and determination on their faces, because they were all going places.

Was she going places? She didn't really know. Probably not. She had no compass, no direction, and a lot of her life had been empty, a yawning void she'd never been able to fill.

Everyone's busyness scared her, just a little, though it must be said that a lot of things scared her.

She shook off the thought. She'd come a long way, in very real and painful terms, to be here today. She couldn't be scared, wouldn't allow herself to be.

If it was a mistake, if she was wrong, well, then she'd be left exactly as she was before—empty-handed.

She looked down at the sheet of paper in her hand, which she'd printed out from her computer research. Nice big letters, all caps, laser print. Times New Roman, fourteen-point font. Nice and clear.

The paper trembled in her hand.

HARRY BOLT
MORRISON BUILDING
1147 BIRCH STREET

So few words, yet so very important. Words that could change her life. Or not. Because maybe he wasn't who she thought—hoped—he was. Or maybe, if he was, he wouldn't care.

The trembling in her hands had passed into her arms, until she had to impatiently fold the paper and tuck it into her purse.

She knew the words by heart, anyway. She also knew the rudiments of his life.

Harry Bolt. Partner in RBK Security, a highly successful security business. Former soldier. Married to a famous singer.

And maybe—just maybe—her long-lost brother.

Lisa Marie Rice

LISA MARIE RICE is eternally thirty years old and will never age. She is tall and willowy and beautiful. Men drop at her feet like ripe pears. She has won every major book prize in the world. She is a black belt with advanced degrees in archeology, nuclear physics, and Tibetan literature. She is a concert pianist. Did I mention the Nobel?

Of course, Lisa Marie Rice is a virtual woman and exists only at the keyboard when writing erotic romance. She disappears when the monitor winks off.

DANGEROUS LOVER

ISBN 978-0-06-120859-1 (paperback)

Caroline, in desperate financial straights, welcomes a tall stranger who wishes to rent a room in her mansion. Overwhelmed by the desire he sparks in her, she aches to experience his touch . . . and wonders who this mysterious man really is.

DANGEROUS PASSION

ISBN 978-0-06-120861-4 (paperback)

Head of a billion-dollar empire, Drake has survived numerous attempts on his life at the hands of greedy men everywhere. And when a gentle beauty turns his life upside down, he will stop at nothing to protect her and his newfound love.

DANGEROUS SECRETS

ISBN 978-0-06-120860-7 (paperback)

Charity never thought she'd fall in love with a man like Nicholas Ireland. Rich, witty, and sexy as hell, he takes her to new sensual heights. When he asks her to marry him, it's like a dream come true. And then the nightmare begins . . .

INTO THE CROSSFIRE

A Protectors Novel: Navy Seal

ISBN 978-0-06-180826-5 (paperback)

Struggling with a new company and a sick father, Nicole simply can't deal with the dangerous-looking stranger next door. But when evil men come after her, she must turn to the cold-eyed man who makes her heart pound—with fear and excitement.

HOTTER THAN WILDFIRE

A Protectors Novel: Delta Force

ISBN 978-0-06-180827-2 (paperback)

Harry owns a security company whose mission is to help abused woman escape violence. When a damaged beauty shows up on his doorstep with an army of thugs after her, Harry realizes that this is the woman of his dreams.

Visit www.HarperCollins.com/LisaMarieRice for more information.